TAIL OF HUMANITY

A NOVEL

ELIZABETH OLDHAM

DOPPIA
PRESS

Edited by Anna Bierhaus
Cover Design by César Gerardo Pardo Delgado

Library and Archives Canada Cataloguing in Publication

Oldham, Elizabeth, author
Tail of humanity : a novel / Elizabeth Oldham.

ISBN 978-1-7388226-0-7 (paperback)
ISBN 978-1-7388226-1-4 (ebook)

Published by Doppia Press
PO Box 143
Castlegar, BC V0G 1X0

In memory of my mother, Sue,
missed beyond words.

PROLOGUE

The beast turns up the driveway and heads into the yard as I'm trotting towards the valley, far from the cabin. The 'mans call them trucks or cars, tractors sometimes. So do I. But mostly I call them beasts. Terrifying, soul-sucking, vomit-inducing creatures that bugle and blare, swerve, steamroll and flatten. I've encountered a lot of beasts in my life. They're unavoidable except in the deepest mountains. And I can tell a lot about a 'man by the beast they show up in. This beast, large and loaded with hay, is a working beast with a slow rumble and a cough, driving slowly up the road, a lone figure holding onto the round collar inside the beast's head.

I lift my nose and sniff the air for a hint of what news the beast brings, but I am too far away to catch anything other than the stale scent of deer and a nearby pile of coyote scat inviting me to roll in it, which I do. I think about ignoring the beast, too far away to challenge it before it reaches Walter and the cabin. But as it rumbles into view, a monstrous green flatbed, I am compelled, both by my canine nature and by *Law #4: Protect the Pack*, to challenge it.

I lope back around the pond and scoot under the barbed wire that keeps the horses in the pasture. The old wound in my left flank flares as I lift myself up from under the fence, but I don't let it slow me.

Pain can be ignored. What I can't ignore are the Five Laws. For life with the 'mans. Humans, that is.

These laws didn't get passed down by my mama and can't be found anywhere else that I know of. They're mine, relevant to my life. Whether they're relevant to others, I don't know. Life's a solitary game, and we make up our own rules. Mine are basic, easy enough for any dog to follow, survival at the root of them all.

In fact, if not for *Law #3: Know Your Pack*, I wouldn't respond. Law #3 might sound silly on the surface, but packs are fluid. They can change with the throw of a punch or a fall down the stairs. It's important to know who's on your side. And who's not.

I've had several packs, each different, each led by 'mans. Which makes them temporary. If I've learned anything from my life with 'mans, it's that I'm expendable. Sure, the packs feel solid. They can last years. Until they're gone, and I'm on my own again.

'Mans make unreliable packs. No in between. They're either your pack or not.

Dogs are consistent, like Rose.

My heart sinks, and a familiar ache rises in my chest. I growl. *None of that.* I've been looking for years but can't find her. I shake my head and ignore the gut-wrenching ache of loss that never lessens.

I focus on Walter who's shading his eyes to watch the beast.

Walter's my pack. For now, I protect him and his things. It seems obvious, but there are hounds who will never be able to master this law. Chihuahuas, for one. Toy poodles, another. I'm sure they have other talents and abilities unseen to the naked eye. Tiny dog skills that help them fight rats or lizards or something. I've spent little time with small dogs. They have attitude, but I question their usefulness. I certainly haven't seen many of them in security roles.

Protecting my pack means Walter and his property. It should be easy. I am big. Strong. If I were born to do anything, it is this. But it's harder than it looks. Threats come from the most unexpected places, even other members of the pack.

I'm haunted by the times I've failed.

I scoot under the pasture gate and run through the chickens milling about in the yard. My lip curls. I detest chickens. They are loud, ugly, weak. I fight the urge to grab them one-by-one and shake them until they stop squawking. But Walter is very firm about NO CHICKEN PLAY, and I hold myself in check because of *Law #5: Learn and Obey, Unless the 'Man is Away.*

It's the only law with a qualifier. The 'mans expect you to know their rules, vague and different from one home to the next, but when they're not around, the rules typically don't apply. Most rules are basic – don't use the house as a toilet, always answer when called, announce all arrivals – but others aren't so clear until someone smacks your head with a broom. Or forces your jaws open to retrieve a favorite pair of glasses.

Or a chicken.

Maybe I engage in a small game of chase in the chicken yard when Walter goes to town. Perhaps I shred a blanket that's been spread out on the picnic table to dry. These things aren't always clear. Learning the rules and following them is hard because the 'mans are inconsistent. Many have a heavy hand when it comes to discipline. Knowing and following the rules can prevent a lot of pain.

The green truck has stopped, its mouth gapes open, and an unfamiliar 'man stands next to Walter. Her long dark hair is knotted and twisted, snake-like on her head. I move towards her, stiff-legged, barking, sniffing the air, growling.

"Shut it, King."

I barely hear him due to the barking. Mine.

Oops. I shut it and lean in to the new 'man. She lets me gather her scent – a deep earthiness, machine oil, hay and – *wait a second.*

Can it be? Is this for real? I push into the scent, nudging her leg and moving around to the back of her thigh.

"You're here early, Jules." Walter smiles broadly. He knows her.

I focus again on the scent. *Could it be?* It leads me to the open door of the truck. I place my front paws on the cab and sniff. It's faint, but it's real. *It's her.* I've found her.

"I'm heading to town early this morning, Walter. Got a few other loads to deliver before seeding. I've been using the after-noons to...."

"Hey! King! Outta there!"

I jump at Walter's voice and whack my head on the steering wheel. How had I gotten inside the truck?

I inhale and it comes back. *Rose.* The familiar scent of cedar, sap and earth lays heavy in the cab. I whine and sniff intently. The scent is strongest on a blanket lying on the bench seat.

"King, down! Outta the truck!"

I ignore him and my name. It's my fifth name, the one Walter gave me. The 'mans like to re-name us, a type of branding, though a lot less painful and permanent than those that I've seen cows go through. It's *Law #2: Know Your Name*, and it's not that I don't know it. I just can't respond.

Walter's hand grabs my collar, which surprises me, because he's normally a hands-off kind of guy. He pulls me out and away from the truck.

Away from Rose.

I flip and flop in a struggle against the collar, but Walter's grip only tightens. Frustrated, I whine and twist.

"What's gotten into you?"

"He's interested in my truck."

I whip my head back to the stranger. Deep brown eyes inspect me as I study her. She's sturdily built, browned by sun and covered with a layer of hay dust. Her scent appeals to me – sweat and earthiness and *Rose.*

She knows where Rose is.

Walter holds my collar tightly. "You got food in the cab? He'll find and devour anything that's edible."

My ears perk up at the mention of food. It's *Law #1: See Food, Eat Food.* Which shouldn't need explaining. It's a biological imper-

4

ative. Plenty of times I'd have gone hungry had I not followed the law.

"Nah, no food in there. My own dog's a food hound. She'll eat anything. Doesn't even have to be edible. Well, not by my standards." She steps back and looks at the truck laden with hay. "Walter, where do you want this?"

Still holding my collar, Walter points to the shed by the chicken coop with his free hand, and the 'man gets back into her truck and drives it slowly over there. He lets go of my collar, and I follow her. I've scented her now, my Rose, and I will leave with this new 'man to find her.

PART ONE
LUKE

CHAPTER 1
CHICKENS

L ife began in a cozy box with straw and a blue cotton blanket:
cardboard walls and floor, open ceiling. The warm bodies of
Mama and my sisters and brothers, the closeness of us all – a foot
in the jaw here, a nose in the gut there, hot breath in my ear – are
my first memories. We were six: my sisters, Lila and Molly, and the
boys, Scamp, Chucky, Melvyn and me (called Luke back then due
to *Law #2*). A mix of black and white with an odd patch of red or
gold here or there, short to medium fur, floppy ears and occasional
spots and patches, we were always tangled up with each other, a
mass of writhing furry, fuzzy bodies.

Mama stayed in the box with us day and night in the begin-
ning. A beautiful dog, Mama, with silken, black and white fur and
soft brown eyes. Her ears stood straight at their base, but the tips
flopped over, as mine do. Twice her size, the box had ample room
for us to snuggle, climb or wrestle in piles near her. I'd wake each
morning to the feel of her tongue gently cleaning my face.

We lived in the barn. When anyone entered, Mama's head
would lift, and her tail would start thumping. She'd push up to all
four paws and jump out of the box, leaving us yipping and circling
in panic at the chill of her absence.

Mama loved her 'man family, especially Roger and Sara, who

9

visited us regularly. They murmured, stroked our fur, held us up to their faces as we wriggled in their hands.

"Look at this, Roger," the woman said holding me aloft one morning. "One blue eye and one brown eye!" I sat still in her hands, inhaling her scent – lavender with a touch of sage – until she put her nose next to mine. Her face looked oddly flat at that angle, and her breath smelled sour. I growled. She laughed.

The man, who smelled largely of split wood, damp wool and iron, chuckled. "Well, Lady," he said, reaching down and scratching Mama between the ears. "Who's your baby's daddy?" Mama's tail wagged in the dirt where she sat.

"You think it's the Oakley's mongrel down at the junction?" he asked. "What is he, a husky mix? A wolfhound?"

Sara put me down and picked up Lila who yipped as she left the box's warmth. "I wouldn't be so sure about that. This one looks more like the Barker's lab."

He laughed and looked at the five of us still in the box. "Do you think our neighbors will want any of them? Could be a chore finding homes."

The woman returned Lila to the box and looked at Mama. "She's one of the best border collies in the valley," she said. "These dogs should be snatched up by anyone who wants a solid herder."

Two little 'mans – 'man pups – often came with Roger and Sara to play with us. The younger one appeared each afternoon with Sara. Not much taller than the sides of the box, she peered down, leaning on it, the sides sagging with her weight.

"Momma, can I hold this one?" She pointed to Molly one day. "She's the silkiest and softest."

Sara picked up Molly and set her outside the box on the barn's dirt floor. "Sure, honey. But keep her in the barn. She's too young to go outside yet."

Then Sara reached in and picked me up with Lila, placing us on the barn floor with Molly. "These two look like they want to explore a bit. Keep an eye on them while I run to the house to fix lunch and grab our boots. We'll stroll down to the lower pasture for a picnic after we're done visiting the puppies."

The girl nodded, and Sara left the barn for the house. Mama gave us a few nervous sniffs then trailed behind her.

Lila and I explored the area around the box in loops. There were familiar scents – Mama, the 'mans, the musk of sheep that covered everything – and scents that I'd only caught on the wind: leather saddles, fresh wood shavings, iron tools, hay. Molly sat frozen in the little girl's hands, whimpering, but we were already on our second lap. Head down, I caught a scent that both exhilarated and frightened me, a musty, tangy scent that made my fur stand on end. I followed it out the door.

The scent grew stronger as I entered the yard. Lila followed as I approached a small house surrounded by a thin wire fence where feathered creatures, colored brown, white and red and slightly larger than myself, milled around.

Walking stuffy toys! They looked like the soft, still creatures that the 'man pups carried. But they moved!

I ran straight into the heart of the noisy, feathered crowd. They clucked and scattered loudly, and I turned and barked as they fled in terror. Lila joined me as I chased them again. Amazing fun! I hadn't known such joys existed!

Suddenly the head of one of the birds, large, with bright colors and a long red growth below his beak, shot up. He crowed, beat his wings and ran at me full speed. My joy turn to confusion. Then fear.

I turned and ran in the opposite direction. A sharp blow hit me from behind. The force pushed my head to the ground; dirt filled my mouth and eyes. I somersaulted and rolled head over paws. Another blow landed on my shoulder, and I cried out with the sharp pain of it. I couldn't get away. He fluttered and pecked on top of me, behind me, in front of me. His wings flailed and claws raked at my fur.

Then Mama roared, and I felt the wind of her body as she hurtled over me. My attacker squawked then retreated. I huddled, trembling in the yard gagging on the dirt in my throat until Mama nosed my face and licked the dust from my eyes. My vision cleared, and I saw the birds grouped near the fence clucking loudly, disturbed. The large bird, a rooster, I learned, strutted around them, a full head higher than the rest, looking satisfied with his defense of the ladies. His eyes shone as he eyed Mama and I belligerently. I growled and barked at his cocky face.

Sara picked me up. Mama hovered near her elbow and Lila kept close to Mama. The little girl stood in the barn doorway crying.

"Did you forget about him?" Sara asked. The girl nodded and cried harder. Sara stroked her head. "These puppies don't know anything about the world, honey. They're too young to be out there alone."

She looked over me thoroughly, patting my head with her hands and feeling my legs and arms. I tried to lick her face.

"Lady shot out of the house like a bullet when she heard the pup yelping." Sara turned towards the girl. "Charlie could have hurt these pups, sweetie. Roosters protect their flock. It's what they do. Thankfully, Lady got there in time."

The little girl nodded, eyes red and weepy. Molly crouched on the barn floor near the box, forgotten and whimpering. Mama circled her and nosed her towards the box. Lila nipped at Mama's legs. Sara put me in the box, then Molly and Lila. Mama climbed in and circled around us all. I quivered and smarted from the rooster's blows, and my heart burned with a simmering anger at the ugly feathered creatures. Mama licked my fur until the trembling stopped, and I fell asleep.

CHAPTER 2
THE MOVING STICK

If Mama were the center of my universe, my sister Lila was a black hole, dragging me into her orbit, causing chaos for anything in her path. When I found an interesting smell, a knotted rag, or a piece of leather, Lila challenged me for it. If I were nosing my way around the far reaches of the pen and ran into a littermate, it would be Lila, growling and demanding her space. Like me, Lila did not like to sit still. Likeminded, we found ourselves together more often than not.

We graduated from the cardboard box and moved into a horse stall, a larger space with slat walls surrounding us. Except for my ill-fated chicken adventure, I still hadn't explored much of the barn. I got my chance one morning, after Mama had followed Sara into the house. Lila and I began roughhousing, and then Lila executed a sneak attack on Melvyn. She pounced on him, and he yipped, bolted forward and plowed head first into the stall door. It opened slightly, and Lila and I strode out of the pen and into the barn. Free to wander, the sights and scents excited me and my brothers and sisters. We scampered around, even Molly, noses to the ground, tails wagging and voices yipping.

But I soon tired of the barn, I strolled outside. Lila followed, and the world suddenly became much bigger. Across from the barn door lay an open yard of gravel with two cars parked on a flat cement pad. On the left side of the barn lay the chicken house. Memories of the recent and vicious rooster attack led me to turn right towards the green earth that led to the house. The soft green carpet bounced under my paws, and I scampered across it, head down, reveling in the earthy, fertile scents.

A small figure lay face down under a wooden stool. I approached and sniffed. It smelled sterile with a hint of the 'man pups from the house, definitely not alive. I wrinkled my nose and growled softly. Slightly smaller than me, it had long yellow hair and a hard, naked body. I barked at it and grabbed it by the back of the neck and shook. The head flew off and landed at Lila's feet. She grabbed it by the golden hair and held it in her mouth.

I dropped the body and stared at her. I wanted that head.

I charged her then grabbed the scruff of her neck and twisted my head side to side. Lila yelped and twirled, dropping the plastic head and turning on me. I let go of her and pounced on the head, snatching the golden hair and shaking hard. Lila grabbed hold of the hair, and, in a tug of war, I shook it then backed up. She jerked it backwards, and I stumbled. She jerked again. The head came out of my mouth.

Though smaller, Lila ran faster. She took off running, and I followed the golden hair across the grass. We tussled over the doll head, working our way across the yard until a strong scent brought me to a halt. I stood, head high, trying to determine the source and location of it – a wild, acrid smell that stung my nose and aggravated my throat. I felt angry, with no idea why. Lila dropped the head and growled softly beside me.

The scent came from the direction of the smaller car, and we tread towards it, golden head forgotten. It grew stronger as we neared, and beneath the car a small moving mound took shape under the corner farthest from our approach.

I slowed as I neared it, wary.

Lila didn't hesitate and padded around the car towards the front tire where the shape started to stretch out. A sudden loud hiss made me jump, then a rattling sound echoed under the metal. Lila shot away from the car, eyes wide and ears flat on her head as she raced towards me.

I growled and snarled in the direction of the hissing. Under the car, a stick shook and rattled behind the diamond-shaped head of a creature I'd never seen before. Its eyes were black and slanted into a malevolent stare above a tongue that flicked angrily at us. I barked and lunged, feinting.

I had no desire to actually go near the moving stick. It hissed louder and raised its head higher. The rattle intensified. I snarled and snapped. I pounced forward then back.

Lila joined me, and our frenzied barking electrified the creature. It turned quickly and slithered away from us. Emboldened, we circled as a team and pursued him as he began his retreat. Each time we neared, he'd coil himself up, raise his head and rattle his stick. We'd retreat and charge again when he turned away. He moved in a sideways kind of sliding manner, making it difficult to get behind him.

"The puppies are out!" A voice yelled. The front door opened and slammed shut quickly.

Lila moved forward to outflank the creature, but he swung his head wide and low off the ground and moved towards her. She stopped, bared her teeth and growled. The creature curled up again and raised its head, rattle flailing. Lila feinted one way then the other, barking while the diamond-shaped head followed her side to side. I joined her, bolstered by her bravado. We faced off and took turns lunging at it from different sides. Its head never retreated but watched us angrily. Then it suddenly sprang forward.

A large black shape – Mama! – hurtled into the space between us and the creature. They collided hip to head upon impact. She yelped then grabbed the creature and shook it violently, urgently, smashing its head repeatedly on the gravel in a matter of seconds.

She dropped it. The snake lay still.

Mama turned towards us, whimpered, and collapsed.

15

CHAPTER 3
SEPARATED

Lila and I ran to Mama's motionless body as an acrid smell from the creature drifted over us. Her eyes were open but unfocused. Her chest rose and fell slightly, and she stared blankly at the space behind us. I whined and nosed her ribs, heat rising in my chest. Lila yipped softly and nuzzled her nose. Anger flashed through me. I left Mama and stalked, growling, towards the creature lying behind her.

It lay still and bloodied. The rattle no longer moved; the diamond-shaped head lay battered, its rough scaly flesh shredded by the sharp rock of the driveway. Its mouth gaped open and two large fangs protruded below the nostrils.

What has it done? What has this evil creature done? I wanted to bite this creature hard and sink my teeth into it as Mama did, to shake it until she woke up. The ugly scent grew stronger as I moved towards its head. When I reached the glistening teeth, I snarled and snapped. Behind me, Roger hollered. Suddenly a rock bounced and hit my nose. I yelped and retreated then crouched low to the ground and began to inch towards the creature again.

"No!" Roger grabbed me by the neck and yanked me away from the creature's head. "Dammit!" He flung me to the far end of the driveway.

I yelped and tumbled hard, head first, pebbles and rock dust in my eyes and mouth. Lila came next, somersaulting in my direction and crashing into me, panting and stunned on top of my hips. I roared, shook her off and ran back in the direction of the creature. Sara suddenly blocked me and with a shovel hacked off the vile thing's head. She flung it into the back of the truck. I charged its body, but she shoveled it into the open truck bed as well.

Roger scooped Mama into his arms and ran with her to the truck. He opened the cab, set her inside then rounded the front end and climbed into the cab.

Sara ran to the house, returning quickly to hand Roger a jacket and keys.

He looked grim. "Call Dr. Montagne. Let her know I'm bringing in Lady."

Sara nodded. "Keep me posted."

Roger started the truck with a roar, backed it up and then lurched forward. The truck spit gravel and dust down the driveway, turned quickly and drove away, leaving Lila and I in a stunned silence.

With no sign of Mama other than the fading whine of the engine, I began to shake. My legs trembled, my shoulders shuddered, and a hole opened up in my chest. I watched the spot where the truck disappeared, lifted my head, and howled.

THE BARN STALL, so confining just hours before, felt cavernous and huge in the dark without Mama. The straw, which had always felt soft and warm, itched and pricked at my skin. Molly whined incessantly. Melvyn whimpered quietly. Chucky and Scamp chewed up the old cardboard box then shredded the cotton blanket. Lila and I paced and growled. I startled at sounds and movements in the shadows.

When Roger and Sara approached with food that evening, we mobbed them. I rushed to the dish as they set the food down and shouldered my siblings out of my space. All went quiet. The food warmed my belly and calmed some of the apprehension I'd felt since the morning.

Roger stroked my brother's back. "Andrew MacPherson will take Chucky. He wants a male, and Chucky looks most like a Border. And the Barkers might want Melvyn. Their lab's been moping since they put their old dog down. Melvyn gets along with everyone."

The bowl emptied in front of me. Lila, Scamp and I gobbled up every last crumb while our siblings licked the other bowl clean. I walked over to the second dish to inspect it and found the edges spotless. I cleaned it anyways. One could never be too sure.

Roger spoke, his voice firm. "We should keep one of the females."

He held up his hand as Sara started to protest. "Dr. Montagne thinks that Lady won't fully recover. She's still at risk of losing her leg, and even with a full recovery, it'll take months to get her back out into the pasture."

I continued to lick the food dish, though it now tasted of nothing but metal, and I growled at Scamp whose tongue moved into my territory. He laid his ears back, sunk his head, then leaned forward to sniff my teeth. I did the same, searching for food remnants. No luck, but soon we were tussling on the straw.

"I wanted to breed her." Sara spoke softly, tentatively.

Lila ran over and leapt on me. Scamp pounced on her. I clawed at Lila's belly and bit Scamp's foreleg.

"This might be our only chance to keep one of her puppies." Roger picked up Molly and handed her to Sara then grabbed Lila and held her up. She growled and attacked his knuckle.

"I think Lila's going to be the better herder. Molly's a bit timid. But with her looks, it should be easy to find her a home."

I tugged Roger's bootlace free and began to chew on the plastic tip. Scamp attacked the leather tongue flap. Roger set Lila down, and she jumped on Scamp.

"That leaves these clowns." He chuckled. "Scamp isn't the

sharpest tool in the shed. But his instincts seem really strong, and he doesn't mind being put in his place.

"Luke, though." Roger paused and studied me. "He's already a monster. With the size of those paws, I can only imagine how big he's going to get."

He picked me up and held me close to his face. I craned my head forward and stretched out my tongue, yearning to taste his nose. He held me just out of reach and smiled. The smile didn't reach his eyes.

"Luke, you keep causing trouble. And you'll keep finding it if you don't stop wandering." He set me down and stood up, rubbing his face.

They left the stall, latched the door and turned off the lights. Darkness swallowed us up.

THE NEXT SEVERAL days passed with no sign of Mama, but my siblings started to disappear. Roger entered the barn one morning accompanied by a round 'man with fur on his face and a large belly. Roger grabbed Chucky by the neck and pulled him out of the crowd. He dangled, immobilized, and stared helplessly at all of us until Roger handed him to the man.

I growled. Roger picked me up. I bit his finger. He grabbed my nose and held me tight against his chest while I yelped and struggled to get free.

The furry man held Chucky close to his face and inhaled. "Smells like a pup." He gave Chucky a treat, and I stopped struggling.

Hey! Over here!

The man threw a handful of treats into the pen. *Treats!* I struggled in Roger's arms until he set me down, then I scarfed up as many as I could. Lila snapped at every treat and sibling in her way. I muscled her out of the treat pile. She hurtled herself onto my back, and a struggle resulted.

When I lifted my head, Chucky and the two men were gone. So were the treats. I bit Lila's ear.

The next day, Sara entered the barn with an older couple trailed by a dog, a golden-white, short-haired, stocky dog with a round head. A male, I could tell from his scent. His ears hung rather than stood. *Trespasser!* I informed him loudly. He shot me a wary glance and sniffed around the far edges of the barn while the couple approached.

Sara opened the gate and reached down to pick up Melvyn. "Nothing seems to faze this guy, and he's friendly with all of the others."

She handed Melvyn to one of the 'mans. The 'man whistled then lowered my brother nose-to-nose with the older dog as he approached. Their dog crouched low on his front paws with hips in the air and tail wagging. Melvyn jumped onto the big paws and began to attack the bigger dog's foreleg.

The couple picked up Melvyn and left with Sara. The older dog pranced behind them, trying to sniff Melvyn in their arms. Lila and I barked at their departure.

Their car drove away, and I paced angrily around the pen. Molly whined and curled up in the straw. Scamp sniffed the last place where Melvyn had stood and whimpered.

What the heck? First Mama disappeared, now Chucky and Melvyn. I snapped at Scamp as he bumped into me. He retreated to gnaw on a piece of leather, and I chomped on a scrap of our cardboard box. Lila shredded what remained of the cotton blanket, and Molly shivered and whimpered. That night, the four of us curled up to sleep in an impenetrable, troubled, tangle of bodies.

A DAY LATER, Roger's truck drove into the yard and parked outside the barn. I peered through the stable as he got out, and Sara and the girls hurried to meet him. A sharp antiseptic scent floated out of the open passenger door, then Mama's scent – milk, moss and honey – drifted across the barn.

As her scent reached me, a fiery, prickly ball dropped from my chest to the bottom of my stomach. *Mama!* Then it flared into a howl, reaching the top rafters of the barn.

Wooowooo... Wooowooo... Wooowooo....

Lila joined me and howled. Molly and Scamp rushed the gate, and the four of us jumped and howled and scratched at the door in a frenzy. Mama yelped as Roger moved her out of the truck, and our voices rose frantically. I couldn't see her, but her scent flowed over us.

"How come Lady's not walking, Daddy?" The older girl followed Roger as he carried Mama into the barn. I stopped howling as she came into view. I whined softly.

Mama...

She panted, eyes large and dark. Roger set her on the barn floor, and she wavered on three legs. Her left hip hung limp and motionless.

"The snake's poison took all the strength away from her, honey." He put his hand on the girl's head as she wrapped her arms around his leg.

"Will she get better?"

Sara held the younger girl's hand and stroked Mama. "We don't know, sweetie. We're hoping, but we just don't know."

Mama wouldn't acknowledge any of us, her eyes locked on Roger. I burst into a staccato of frustrated yelping.

"Is she staying out here with the puppies?" Sara scratched Mama under the chin, and Mama closed her eyes and trembled. She braced her two shoulders wide and lowered her good hip to the barn floor, quaking. She collapsed into the dirt.

As her head sank, I barked.

Mama! It's me, Luke! Look, Lila's here, too. Even Molly is barking. Mama!

Why wouldn't she respond?

Mama panted and trembled. She refused to look at us. Roger squatted next to her, stroked her head, and sighed.

"She's not interested. I think she'll stay in the house with us."

ELIZABETH OLDHAM

I barked loudly, again, and again. *Look at me!*

"Can I touch her, Daddy?"

"Sure, honey, but be gentle. She's still hurt."

The little girl reached a tentative hand towards Mama's head and patted her softly. Mama's eyes were wide. She flinched at the girl's touch and panted rapidly, but her eyes never strayed from Roger.

I yelped in frustration. *Mama! I'm over here!*

Finally, she put her chin on the dirt and lay still, except for a slight spasmic shudder of her body.

Sara unlatched the gate. "Let's see how she reacts to the pups."

We burst past her and over to Mama. I ran up to her face and started licking her mouth. She lifted her head out of reach, curled her lips and growled. I jumped on her, paws scrambling on her neck. Molly and Lila sniffed her head and shoulders. Scamp climbed onto her back. Mama snapped at Lila and tried to rise to her feet. Sara pulled Scamp away. I clamped my teeth onto her ear and hung on.

When Sara picked me up, I bit her hand.

"Ow!" She slapped my nose. My eyes watered and my ears rang. I yelped and sunk my head. Sara stroked me softly.

"I'm sorry, Luke. No biting." Her voice was husky, and I licked her face. Her damp cheeks tasted faintly of salt. She grabbed Scamp and moved away from Mama. I struggled to get out of Sara's arms and back to her.

Roger picked up Lila and Molly. "Lady's got to focus on healing," Roger said. "She'll stay in the house with us."

They carried us back to the pen and latched the gate. Mama lay still and listless on the barn floor, eyes always on Roger. At his whistle she struggled to rise then got up and began a three-legged hop out of the barn. Sara and the girls left us, and we sat alone, stunned and forgotten.

Had I caused this? If I hadn't left the barn with Lila, would Mama still be with us? Would my missing brothers still be here? A

22

burning ball hovered angrily in my stomach. Mama didn't want us.

Lila approached me, and I snapped at her and chased her away. I retreated to a corner of the stall, tucked my tail beneath my legs, curled into a ball, and shuddered until I fell asleep.

CHAPTER 4
SOLD

Two days later, Sara entered the stall and picked up Lila. "Time to start job shadowing, Lila. Say good-bye to the others. They're going to find new homes today."

She turned Lila to face us, and our eyes met.

Not Lila! No!

I yelped and lunged at the gate as Sara latched it and set Lila down. I raised my voice to its highest pitch. Lila padded towards me until Sara whistled. Lila paused, gave me a puzzled glance, then turned and ran to Sara.

Lila!

I launched my body at the gate. Scamp and Molly began scratching, and we hurtled ourselves against the barrier. Useless. I sank to the ground. My bark became an unfamiliar, uncontrollable keening that stopped when Sara returned with a large box. She put the three of us inside, carried it a short ways then set it down in the car. The man pups got in the back.

I howled, and Scamp and Molly joined me. The car's rumbling silenced us, and the box began swaying and bouncing. My stomach churned. Scamp threw up. I retched. Molly vomited, then pretty soon all of us had lost our breakfast inside the box. Sara cursed in a quiet voice.

"Ewwwww!" The girls complained. I stumbled into Scamp's vomit and slipped. I whimpered and whined, miserable.

The car stilled, and the rumbling stopped. Sara opened the passenger door, backlit by a foreboding sky, and carried us to the sidewalk. Thick with humidity, dark gray clouds brooded over us. She used a wet towel to wipe the puke off of us and clean out the box. People streamed past in both directions.

"Oh, look, Mom! Puppies!" A young voice shouted.

A little girl christened Molly her "Princess" and took her away from us. I felt the familiar heartache and attacked Scamp in a corner of the box. He yelped and sank to the bottom, ears low and eyes beseeching. I bit his ear. He rose and attacked my right forepaw.

We wrestled a bit until the girls picked us up and played with us outside of the box. Eventually someone stopped again, and a set of hands reached for Scamp. The girls placed me back into the box, alone.

I put my nose into a corner of the box, laid down, and trembled until a soft voice spoke above me.

"Look, Aileen," it said. "He's all alone in here."

I looked up. A young woman peered down at me. Her face had thin dark eyebrows with colorful eyes and lips – like a doll's - not natural but kind. She reached into the box and stroked my head. Her hand, though soft, smelled of a sour smoke. I wrinkled my nose but licked her thumb anyways. *Not bad.* Thunder clapped. I trembled and shook as it rolled away.

"Lana, you ask Roy about getting a dog?" A raspy voice spoke behind the woman. "He's not a fan of dogs. He got rid of the last one before he hooked up with you."

The hand paused but then grabbed me by the scruff of the neck and hauled me out of the box. I froze, mid-air, face to face with a large-haired brunette who smiled broadly at me. She had friendly brown and green-flecked eyes that danced. She lifted my gums, touched my teeth, and felt my ribs. I smelled lilac and a mild scent of apples. She turned me around to face an older woman with a

25

round, sweaty face and tight curly, flaming red hair flecked with white.

"His eyes, Aileen! One brown and one blue! And his paws are so big – he's going to be a monster! He's perfect, seeing as how Roy's gone so much of the time...."

The other woman shook her head. "That's one ugly dog." She wore a loose pullover tunic with polka dots. She too smelled like smoke sticks with an overlaying scent of mildew and a nauseatingly sweet aroma like rotting fruit. I felt queasy. "I'm telling you, Lana. Roy don't like dogs much. You bring that home, you're asking for trouble."

"Oh, Aileen, he's adorable, and he's perfect!" The woman cuddled me next to her chest. I reached my tongue out to lick her chin and tasted sweat. *Not bad!* I licked it again and again.

Lana laughed and pulled her head away from me. I scrambled in her arms to reach her chin. "He's got energy!" She turned to Aileen. "Roy will love him."

Aileen shook her head. "You don't know my boy like I do. But you do what you want."

Lana smiled at Sara and the girls. "How much do you want for him?"

She spun back to Aileen without waiting for a reply. "Looks like he's got German Shepherd in him. Maybe wolf." She turned to Sara. "He got wolf in him?"

Sara shook her head. "His mom's a registered border collie, but we aren't sure about the dad." She studied both women. "He's $50."

Lana dug through her purse, balancing me on her shoulder as she took out a wallet.

"Here you go." She smiled and handed Sara the money. Then she turned and glared at Aileen. "It's lonely when Roy's away. He'll be happy that I've got company while he's on the road. A guard dog to keep away unwanted visitors. You know how sensitive he is about folks coming over when he's gone."

She snapped the purse shut and smiled at Sara. "Such a sweet puppy. Does he have a name yet?"

Sara told her my name, and Lana wrinkled her nose.

"Luke? Hmm, too biblical."

Aileen stared at her for a second. "Lana, Roy may let you keep him, but it's not going to turn out the way you think."

Lana's voice turned to ice.

"Roy doesn't control everything, Aileen. He wants me to be happy. Getting this dog will make me happy."

Lightning flashed as thunder cracked overhead. The skies opened up, and rain began pelting us. Lana's hand clutched me tightly, too tightly, as she turned and ran with me across the wet black pavement. She jumped into the passenger seat of a small, battered sedan. I couldn't breathe and gave her thumb a quick lick and then a nibble. She relaxed her grip, and I gasped for air then hiccupped. She laughed and nuzzled me, nose to nose, and I tried to clean her face. Aileen opened the door across from us and sat down hard on the saggy driver's seat. The car rocked slightly as she settled, and she looked at Lana stonily.

"He rides in the trunk," she said brusquely. "He'll puke all over."

Lana sighed, got out and moved to the trunk. She opened it. I glimpsed Sara and the girls one last time staring in my direction – Sara with the money in her hand – and I gave them a final bark before I left the last remnants of the only life I'd known. Another flash lit the sky before the box lid folded shut. The day blackened, the trunk door slammed, and a rumbling, thunderous noise grumbled beneath me.

My heart sank and my stomach roiled. I'd been sold.

PART TWO
DUKE

CHAPTER 5
AILEEN

I hunkered in the box, sliding side to side in the dark, struggling to stay on my feet. The beast turned one direction and the box slid until it banged to a stop on the other side. The other objects in the box – rubberized cables, a flashlight and heavy metal tools – rolled around me, and I scrambled to avoid them as the beast sped up. I slipped and crashed into the corner. My stomach twisted. The flashlight bounced up and crushed my toes. It knocked my head. Sharp bile rose, and my stomach heaved.

At one point the box flipped, dumping me onto a dank musty carpet littered with objects that made it difficult to stand. Finally, a few more turns, a long bumpy road, and the beast slowed and stopped. The rumbling died. I lay, panting, in my mess.

The beast's mouth opened. My eyes recoiled from the light, but I gulped in the fresh air. Lana's silhouette blocked the sunlight as she bent down to pick me up. Her face came close to mine, and her pencil-thin eyebrows rose in surprise, her mouth forming an "o."

"Out of the box! And icky." Her nose wrinkled as she held me out slightly from her body and carried me away from the open trunk.

The fresh air cleared my head. My stomach settled, somewhat. As we walked down the dirt driveway, I surveyed the property around me. We were heading towards a long narrow metal house lifted off the ground by concrete blocks. Nothing smelled familiar. No chickens, no sheep, no barn, no straw, no compost – I smelled the rot of garbage and food, rusty iron from engine blocks and neglected beasts, and motor oil.

The house sat with its back to a creek, running fast and wide. Across the creek lay a meadow, then a forest thick with trees that climbed up the mountain behind it. Between the house and the beast lay a garden of plastic soda bottles and aluminum cans, discarded lawn furniture, shredded fabric, assorted plastic bags and auto parts. At the end of the driveway, a large garage sat adjacent to a tilted, dilapidated shed with rusty lawn tools, broken appliances and an old mattress leaning into. It. The scent of decaying vegetation and garbage assaulted me, strange and exciting.

Lana set me down on a prickly rubber mat where I sniffed around the mat and squatted to pee. Before I caught my bearings, she assaulted me with a hard spray of water from a rubber hose. *What was this?*

I backed up and growled, but she laughed and shook her head. "You've got barf on your head!"

She grabbed my neck, immobilizing me like Mama and sprayed me down again. Water ran into my eyes and dripped from my chest. From the driveway I heard Aileen screech.

"Who's cleaning up this puke? Dammit, Lana, I told you not to get the dog!"

Lana stopped spraying me and sighed. "She's miserable, isn't she?" I shook myself. She grabbed a towel from a pile on the porch, rubbed me down quickly, then set me free. "Welcome to your new home, puppy!"

She unlocked the front door, opened it, and gasped. "Oh my god. What happened?"

She entered and I followed haltingly, sniffing the air and treading cautiously. Mama had gone in and out of Roger's and Sara's house, but I'd never been allowed. Would I be staying in this house now? Would I be allowed to come and go freely like Mama?

My heart clenched. Would I see Mama again?

I needed water. All that puking made me thirsty.

I began to search, nose to the ground. The room reeked of smoke sticks, like Lana's fingers. Pervasive throughout the room, it reminded me of the box in the back of the beast, and my hackles slowly raised.

The ground beneath my pads felt thick and soft. I lifted my feet carefully, placing one paw down firmly before lifting the other, testing the strange surface. It bounced and smelled delicious. Stale body smells, dirt and food – sweet and salty scraps – leapt out at me. I discovered a little piece of something hard, fatty and delicious in the carpet and began sniffing for more. One morsel after another. A nugget of dried meat, a peanut, a moldy crust of bread, I lost my hesitation and began a search in earnest.

I entered a room with a strong scent of food – old food, new food and in-between. A short narrow room with open cupboards, the counter had uneven stacks of dishes, cans, boxes and half-empty plastic bags leaning this way and that. A faucet dripped into a metal sink. Thirsty, I headed toward the sink but pulled up short in front of a round white metal container with a ripe-but-rotten, sour-but-sweet, cornucopia-of-juicy-goodness scent.

I could barely reach my paws to the rim to peer into it. Garbage! Just as I craned my neck for a bite, the container tilted over and upset in a delicious cascade– food remnants stuck to wax paper wrappers, plastic bags and aluminum foil – everywhere!

Law #1 kicked into high gear, and I scarfed up anything and everything. Thirst forgotten, I needed food! I snatched a bite of a stiff white roll, crunched on some small bones, and licked up an oozing brown mess of some type. I'd just begun cleaning a container of a very savory soup when I heard a loud wail behind me. Lana stood at edge of the room, hands on hips, looking around, face red and eyes glistening, breathing short and fast.

"I left for two weeks. Two weeks!" She motioned towards the

counters and the dripping faucet. "He couldn't put the dishes away? He couldn't take the garbage out? And I'm supposed to clean this up while he's on the road for a week?" Lana's face screwed up tight and she wailed. "We have a dishwasher for Christ's sake!"

She sat down hard on one of the chairs and covered her face with her hands. I reached for a round piece of meat that rolled out of a stale bun, tasty, with the slight tang of a dried yellow substance. I searched for more. Delicious! Lana's breath became heavy and ragged.

Aileen entered the room as I stuck my nose into a paper cup coated with a sweet, sticky white substance.

"Welcome to real life, Lana," she said as her feet landed heavily on the floor. "Just because you've cleaned the place up real good you think that that Roy's going to suddenly become domestic?" She walked towards the sink and grabbed a broom sitting in the corner. I dove headfirst into the upturned container and ravaged a pile of small bones, somewhat spicy with a touch of sliminess. I loved this place.

"You're not the first little princess who's had to clean up after my boy." Lana gasped. Aileen approached as I licked a white plastic wrapper that had stuck to my lips. I shook my head to wriggle it loose.

"He's a man, not a housekeeper. You can't take off for two weeks then come back crying because the house isn't clean enough. Roy works hard and shouldn't have to take on your chores too."

Whack! Something clobbered me, and my head smacked into the metal container. I yelped and shook my head. I struggled to see beyond the stars circling in front of my eyes.

Lana shrieked. "Aileen! What the hell?"

"You've got a lot to learn about dogs in our family."

My eyes stopped spinning. Aileen stood over me with the broom. Her blue eyes glared hard and narrow, framed by a round ruddy face. Her hair hung in a frizzy red and white halo. My eyes still watered from the sting of the first blow when the second one came fast and hard. The bristles smashed down on my nose and the broom head clocked my forehead.

The air whooshed out of my lungs, and I couldn't breathe. I gasped for breath. *What the heck? Why did she attack me? Was I eating her food?*

Lana rushed towards Aileen and yanked the broom angrily out of her hands. "Don't hit my dog, Aileen."

I'd never been hit with an object before. I lay stunned and quiet, blurrily and warily eyeing the broom and the two women. Lana's assault with the water hose had been shocking but not painful. But the two blows from the broom hurt. I didn't want to spend any time around Aileen.

She exhaled noisily, and I watched the broom carefully. Lana carried it back to the corner, and I caught a whiff of the white can as she walked by me. My stomach flip flopped a few times as I got up and padded towards the can. I didn't feel so great. I stopped, head down, and began to pant. My guts clenched and tightened. My back heaved once, then twice and my head lurched down and forward. Suddenly all the food I had eaten spilled out onto the floor in slimy, chunky colorful puddles. I took a few steps and began again, stomach churning, guts heaving, back contracting. I vomited onto Aileen's foot.

She jumped back and screeched, taking her soiled sandal off quickly and chucking it at my head in a wild throw that missed. The sandal ricocheted off the wall and landed in the upturned garbage on the floor.

I backed away from Aileen and barked twice, hackles high and teeth bared. A low growl rumbled out of my throat like the steady hum of an engine. My head hurt. I didn't know why she kept attacking me or how to stop it. I crouched low, bared my teeth as wide as I could and snarled. I did not like this woman one bit.

"Goddammit, Lana, I told you not to get the dog. He's trashing the kitchen, and he's aggressive. And dogs SHOULD NOT be in the house."

My head hurt, my legs trembled, and I needed water. But I couldn't turn my back on this woman. I quickly glanced at Lana then back at Aileen. Lana considered me for a second then looked around at the messy kitchen.

"Thank you for the ride home, Aileen," she said stiffly. She walked to the sandal and picked it up out of the garbage then carried it to the sink and rinsed it off before handing it to Aileen. "The dog hasn't trashed this house any more than Roy's two-week party when my aunt was dying."

Aileen wiped her foot off with a paper towel before putting her sandal back on. "It's a shame about your aunt. It's always tough to lose family. But I tell you, that dog's a mistake. He's going to cause problems for you and Roy."

Lana shook her head. "Roy's not hard-hearted like you, Aileen."

The older woman walked rigidly to the front door. "You're young. Maybe that's what Roy sees in you. He's always liked young. I certainly don't understand it. But you've moved into our world, so you'll grow up fast." She paused and narrowed her eyes. "Don't get too attached to this dog. Or do. I predict that neither of you will last long."

She stepped out the door and let it slam shut behind her. Lana slumped her shoulders, hung her head, covered her face and started to cry. I retreated to the upturned container and rooted around for something to drink.

CHAPTER 6
LANA

L ana and I worked together to clean up the place. I ate up the food leftovers on the carpet and floor, while Lana swept and mopped and picked up the mess everywhere else. I found it easy enough work, but Lana grumbled about it. Well, she grumbled about the man Roy who had caused it.

"Ooh, that man!" she said as she scrubbed several tacky clear puddles off of the coffee table with a wet rag. "I can't believe he left the place like this. He knew I'd be coming home!"

Her face reddened, and she scrunched her eyes shut, threw the rag down then hopped up and out to the porch. Lana often quit mid-scrub, followed by a smoke and a weeping session, as she called it.

"My mom used to get these weeping sessions, too, pup." She lit her smoke stick and took a long drag followed by an even longer sigh. "She'd retreat to her bedroom for hours, and we weren't allowed to go in."

I sat down on the steps at her feet. Lana smoked two different types of sticks. She liked the strong, bitter smoke sticks the most. They gave off a thick choking smoke, the scent of which stuck to Lana like a wet leaf on the nose (trust me, wet leaves are tenacious). She broke out these smoke sticks regularly. When she pulled out the pack, I readied for a sit down on the porch.

Sour smoke sticks, on the other hand, gave off a lighter scent that dissipated more quickly. She usually broke out those out at the end of the day during quiet times when she'd sit and stroke my belly with the tips of her fingernails. The scratching felt divine, though I developed up a very strong hind leg reaction that sometimes broke Lana's concentration.

Lana puffed on her smoke stick. The ash built up on the end where the stick emitted a thick curling twist of smoke. It curled around her beautiful face.

"You wonder how I can put up with him, don't you?" Lana's conversations never made sense, but I loved listening.

I tried to lick her nose.

She pushed me away and tapped the ash off the smoke stick, "He doesn't remember to come home for dinner. He apparently doesn't miss me when I'm gone for two weeks." Her eyes were red and her face splotchy. She rubbed her eyes with both hands and started to cry.

"You should have seen him when we met. I'd been working checkout at the Mart at Aines Junction for two years, but I'd never seen him before. He came in for a case of beer and twelve frozen pizzas." She shook her head and sniffled softly. "I'd never seen someone so handsome. I felt tongue-tied! I didn't know why he would buy that many frozen pizzas, so I asked if he were having a party. He said that he'd never learned to cook anything but frozen pizza. So cute, the way he said it. I told him that I'd never met anyone who lived on frozen pizzas and that I couldn't imagine how he didn't get sick of it."

She took another drag of her stick. I spied a squirrel on a tree trunk across the yard and shifted my hips anxiously. I'd seen squirrels at my old home but hadn't been able to get close. They are tricky, fast little buggers.

Lana's eyes were far away. "Well, he looked at me for a real long time. He has the most beautiful blue eyes, and I felt enraptured. I just stood there staring at him, at his eyes. Finally, my manager came up and asked if I needed help. When I looked around, I had a lineup of customers, and I hadn't even rung up his pizzas! I felt like I'd been in a trance."

She trailed off and took another puff. The squirrel looked as if it were about to leap to the ground, and I tensed my muscles, ready to shoot off the porch.

"He asked me out for dinner before he even knew my name." She sniffed and rubbed her eyes with the neck of her shirt. "We went out that night, and every night after that for the next two months. He opened the door for me. He ordered for me in restaurants. He gave me his jacket when I got chilled. I've never felt so important. Or cared for. By the time he asked me to move in with him, most of my clothes were already here, and I couldn't wait to get out of Dad's house. I fell head over heels in love with him, and I moved in the weekend after I graduated, the first of my friends to leave home, if you can call forty miles away leaving home. I always liked to do things first."

The squirrel stepped onto the driveway, and I shot down the stairs and off of the porch after him. He stopped halfway between two trees, and I beelined towards him, certain he couldn't beat my speed. But not only did he make it to the tree, he turned just out of reach and scolded me with his loud chittering. I paced underneath, huffing and panting and glaring at the squirrel until I tired and curled up beneath it.

At the end of the first day, Lana sat down on the porch steps. "You need a name," she said as she lit a smoke stick. "Luke's no good... too passive, too religious." She grimaced, took a long drag, tapped her ash and squinted at me through the smoke. Her face suddenly lit up and she smiled broadly, wine-colored lips framing broad white teeth.

"We'll just change a letter... how about Duke?" She leaned forward and rubbed my ears. I relaxed into her hands and groaned happily. She scratched my chest, and my foot thumped on the porch.

"Yes, Duke. A solid name for a strongman. Like John Wayne." She stopped scratching my chest, and my foot slowed. She stood up, smoke stick clamped between her lips.

"Duke, you've got to learn some household manners before Roy gets home. Six days. Do you think you can do it?" She looked at me expectantly, and I wagged my tail. I didn't know what she said, but that look that usually preceded an ear rub. Sure enough, she reached down and rubbed my ears. Household manners sounded great to me if they involved ear rubs. She threw her butt into a tray on the porch then went back into the house, and I followed close on her heels.

CHAPTER 7
ROY

Lana's energy– nervous and excited – floated in the air around us as the time neared for Roy to come home. Lana cleaned, and I ran circles around her, throwing in a few snarls to keep her guessing. She mopped the floor, and I grabbed and tugged at the furry stick. She scrubbed the toilet, and I bit at the brush.

"Duke, let it go!" I yanked it. She yanked back. I slid towards her on the smooth floor then tugged as soon as I stopped. It came out of Lana's hands. Her eyes widened as I backed out of the room with the brush and ran down the hall. We had great fun until she caught up with me and marched me to the front door. She grabbed the brush and quickly shut me out of the house.

Huh? I yelped and scratched at the door until I noticed a movement in a tree halfway up the driveway – *squirrel!*

I tore down the stairs barking and ran under the tree. He chattered angrily. I volleyed with my loudest round of barking, but he didn't back down – irritating, cocky little thing.

My nails scrabbled at the bark and his chittering rose into an angry squawk as I hurled myself at the trunk. He climbed higher, and I reassessed my strategy. I curled my lip at him and panted below the tree. *This is my home now!*

A loud whoosh and metallic knocking suddenly filled the air. A massive, monstrous black truck turned onto the driveway. Red lightning bolts ran down the side of the shiny black body. A red face with horns, fiery eyes and a wide mouth filled with jagged teeth glared malevolently from the front grill. I'd never seen such a beast. It was heading towards the house!

Law #4: Protect the Pack kicked into gear. I ran to the middle of the driveway and braced myself, barking, hackles high.

Intruder! Intruder! The massive truck advanced, hissing and clanging. I froze, unnerved by the demon and a sense of impending doom.

"No! Duke! Duke, no!"

Lana screamed, a horn blasted, and I dropped to my belly, nose and eyes assaulted by dust. A deafening mass of sound and heat rolled over me and sucked the air out of my lungs. I gasped, inhaling dust and dirt as it swirled in the air around me. I coughed and gagged, pinned to the ground by the force of the engine and a suffocatingly hot blast of air.

It moved over and away from me. I bolted forward blindly, a loud ringing in my ears and a wild thumping in my chest, running until I could hear sound again. When I finally stopped, I found myself on a large unpaved road that stretched out in both directions as far as I could see. I had no idea where I was. Or Lana.

I whined. Guilt washed over me. I'd abandoned her. Had she been overcome by the beast? I hadn't protected my pack at all. I sat down on the road, lifted my head, and howled.

"Duke!"

Huh? I stopped howling.

"Duke!" Lana ran towards me from far down the road.

My heart leapt.

She's alive! Lana!

She called me again, and I streaked towards her as fast as I could. She knelt down as I neared, and I leapt onto her legs, then her arms, then her shoulders. Somehow she ended up on her back, and I scrabbled around her and over her, whining and sniffing and licking her face. I rejoiced at her impossible resurrection and smothered her happiness.

"I thought you were a goner." She hugged me tightly. I licked her cheeks. "You were so tiny out there in front of the truck. He must not have seen you."

She turned and carried me down the drive, squeezing me and kissing my nose. I licked her face and chewed on her fingers. The black truck rested in front of the garage, the demon's face hidden from view. Halfway down the driveway, the cab door opened, and a 'man slowly got out and looked our way. Lana set me down and quickened her pace. I hurried at her heels.

She reached him as he hefted a large duffel bag onto his shoulder. Lean and wiry with a weathered face, thinning brown hair and a full, thick brown moustache, he studied us as we grew closer. Everything about him appeared hard and unyielding: his steel blue eyes, the set of his jaw, the look he shot at me as we approached. As Lana drew near however, his eyes relaxed and his mouth softened into a smile.

"Hey baby." He steadied the duffel with one arm, looped the other around Lana's waist, and drew her firmly into him. I barked, not sure how to fit in. She laughed happily, and I wagged my tail.

"I missed you, Roy," she said and wrapped her arms around his neck.

This hard man from the belly of the beast was Roy? He nuzzled her ear, and I barked once. "You feel good, babe."

I sat to watch them, tilting my head to and fro. She didn't appear in complete control of herself but didn't appear to be suffering.

I barked.

Roy began smashing his face to Lana's and I barked again. She gave a quick, quiet gasp, and I became alarmed. I barked louder and jumped on her leg, scrambling to wedge myself between them. *What was going on here?*

She sunk into him and seemed to be losing muscle control. *What was he doing to her?* I pushed my head into the shrinking gap between their bodies, but she kept me away with her leg. I jumped up again, and her hand pushed me down.

I leapt again, but Roy's fist clubbed my right eye socket. Light exploded behind my eye, and I fell to the dirt surprised and in pain. I writhed on the ground and yelped, unable to see as my eyes watered and head throbbed.

Lana tried to speak, but Roy cut her off.

"Shhhh, baby, let's go inside. I've been waiting for you to come back."

My head ached, and not knowing what to do, I gave myself an ear scratch. When all else fails, a good scratch usually clears the head.

"I hate when you leave, babe. I need you." Roy wrapped his fingers around her hair and pulled Lana's head back to look at him. "Promise you won't leave me again, baby." He brought her head to meet his and smashed her mouth forcefully against hers. I barked. "You promise?"

Lana made a strange noise and nodded slowly. An odd scent filled the air between them, a strange musk-like 'man odor. Roy carried her away from the black truck, and she didn't look back at me once. I whined and ran after them as he carried her into the house. Just as I tried to push through the door behind them, it slammed shut.

I sat alone on the porch. I whined at the door then returned to inspect the now-silent demon beast. The duffel bag lay on the ground. It smelled like smoke sticks, diesel fuel and unwashed 'man bodies. I marked the bag with a quick leg lift then went back to the porch, circled three times, curled up and waited.

WHEN LANA CAME out in the late afternoon, I bolted out from under the squirrel tree. *Lana!* I ran to her and leapt and yelped until she knelt down and wrestled me to the ground. She smelled flowery, and her hair was wet. Roy stepped out and I wagged my tail. He was part of Lana's pack. Thus, mine.

"Lana, why do we have a dog?"

Lana was stroking my belly, but her fingers paused when Roy spoke. I leapt on her, biting and licking her hands.

"This is Duke." She stroked my head, and I rolled onto my back. "He was the sweetest little thing, sitting outside the grocery store in a box, all alone! He looked so sad. He's really smart and he's already figured out that this is his home now."

She stopped petting me, and I threw myself at her face again. Her breath carried a new scent – intensely sweet, sharp and slightly suffocating. It flowed around us.

"He's a great guard dog. Super brave. Did you see him challenge your truck when you drove down the driveway?"

Roy frowned, hands on hips. "I don't want a dog." He looked at her then scowled at me. "Barking. Dog crap. Dog hair everywhere. Another mouth to feed. Take him back."

He reached a big hand down, and I caught a strong whiff of smoke sticks as he picked me up by the scruff of the neck. I froze at the sudden height and the long drop to the ground. His breath had the same thick sweet smell as Lana's. Our eyes met, and his narrowed. A nasty smile twisted over his face.

"One eye's blue and the other's brown. He's butt-ugly, Lana. No wonder he was left all alone. You're a sucker. He's no guard dog."

He put his face close to mine and growled. He growled! The sickly sweet scent of his breath smelled like Trouble and I drew back my head. I wanted to like him, but Roy made me nervous.

I growled back at him. His eyebrows shot up, and his hand pinched my neck tightly. He shook me, and I yelped. "Screw you, dog. You're at my house." He swung me low to the ground and dropped me abruptly. I stumbled and yelped then ran to Lana who picked me up quickly. I tried to lick her face, but she held me out of reach.

"Roy, baby, don't be like this. He's just a puppy! He's only been here a week, but he's smart and catching on real quick." She put me down, and I trailed them to the black truck. A small bird caught my eye on top of the shed as it turned its head back and forth on the roof. "He's almost housebroken."

The bird flew off, and Roy picked up the duffel bag he'd left lying in the driveway earlier. As he swung it to his shoulder, his nose wrinkled and he cursed, dropping the bag quickly.

"Housebroken my ass. He pissed all over my bag." He turned towards me suddenly, and I crouched low to the ground. Lana put her hand on Roy's arm, and he stopped.

"Roy, don't act crazy. He's just a puppy. I can't take him back. I have no idea who sold him to me. Just some lady in front of the store." She wound her fingers through his and pulled him towards her, running her finger down the hard line of his jaw.

"He's still learning how things work around here, sweetie." His face tightened and she kissed his cheek.

"He's not going in the house." Roy's eyes flashed cold and hard.

"But Roy...." He put a hand up and stopped her.

"Our bathroom smells like dog piss, and I'm not, in any way, shape or form, going to share it with a dog." He released his hand from hers and ran it through his hair. "Let's have a baby, Lana, if you want to take care of something. But a dog? Count me out. If you want it, you can keep it, but it lives outside in its own house where it can bark and crap and do whatever else it does, away from me."

Lana opened her mouth to speak, but Roy stopped her, his face rigid, his blue eyes cold and narrow. "I love you, Lana. I've given my world to you here, this house and property. Heck, you don't even have to work. We have a good life. We don't need a dog." He voice rose into a whine as he continued. "And what makes it okay to change things while I'm away? This is my house, and I don't want a dog in it."

Lana shook her head and squeezed his hand. Her voice was quiet and soft. "Babe, he's no trouble at all. And it gives me something to do. I get lonely out here. You're gone so much. I just miss you."

She tugged gently on his hand. He yanked it back hard, and she stumbled forward.

Lana! I barked angrily. *Who did he think he was?*

"Duke, no!" She grabbed me firmly. I growled.

Roy held his hands out and walked over to Lana. Lana's grip on me tightened, and I smelled her fear.

"What are you doing, Roy?" Her voice softened, whisper-like, and Roy shook his head.

"I'm not the bad guy here, Lana. You can keep your dog." He spoke in a low, measured voice. "But hand him over to me right now."

Lana's grip loosened, and she offered me to Roy without speaking. He grabbed me by the scruff of the neck and carried me at waist height. My stomach twisted. Lana squeaked but didn't say anything as she shadowed us, flitting like a bird from one side to the other. Roy marched, and I swung limply.

"Where are you going, Roy? Where are you taking him? It's not safe for dogs in the shed, with all the fertilizers and broken glass. I think the porch is too small. Will he even fit up there? Roy, where are you going?"

She chattered like a squirrel. Roy didn't say a word but carried me from the porch to a small, gated enclosure across the driveway nearer to the road. I'd never seen a fence like this on the farm, heavy and linked together, chain-like, as tall as Roy himself. A large wooden box sat flat on the hard packed gravel, surrounded by dirt clumps and weeds. The box had a large square hole cut into the front but was otherwise dark. Large black bags on the ground lay open and overflowing with cans and bottles.

He walked into the cage and let me drop. The wind knocked out of me, I yelped. Lana squeaked.

"This is where your dog belongs, Lana. He's got his own yard, his own house. He doesn't need to be in ours."

"But, Roy, he's just a puppy. He can't live out here all by himself." I recovered my breath and started exploring. The box itself had rotted where the corners came together, leaving small gaps. Dark and dank, I turned my back on it until Lana kneeled in front of it and peered inside. I scrambled to stick my head in along with hers. Except for a few leaves, some mouse droppings and shredded cardboard, the box was empty. Mold grew in the bottom corners.

"Yuck, Roy. It's disgusting in here. We can't leave him here."

"Then take him back where he came from." Roy lifted one of the black bags and heaved it out the gate. It landed on a stump and upended, cans rolling everywhere. "Do what you want to fix this place up for your dog, Lana. Go for it. He's got a fenced yard and a pen. That's all he needs."

He tossed another bag out of the yard then picked up the final one and dumped it outside the gate. Lana stood with her hands on her hips, looking doubtfully around the small enclosure.

"I don't know, Roy. He's so little, and it's far from the house." She stared at me. I wagged my tail and stuck my head back into the box. Decay filled my nose. Squirrels, yes, and a family of mice or two had visited, but nothing lived here. The wood smelled wet and sharp, and the mold lent it a sweet but rotten scent – a palace of putrefaction.

"He stays in the pen or finds another home." The gate slammed shut, and I pulled my head out of the box to see Roy stomping off towards his truck. Lana squatted next to me and cupped my chin in her hands. I wagged my tail and put my paws on her knees, reaching my tongue up as far as I could to lick her face. The smile on her face crumpled. She grabbed me tight to her chest, and her shoulders began to shake. Her grip hurt, and I whined but couldn't free myself.

"Lana!" She jumped then set me down and stood up. She wiped her eyes with the back of her hand.

A fat beetle walked through the dirt in front of me. It waddled towards the fence, and I sniffed behind it as it picked up its pace. I reached for it with my teeth but missed, and it scurried faster. My heart skipped as I pounced and tried again. Its crooked legs latched onto my tongue, and I spat it out, smacking my lips. It waddled to the corner of the fence, and I growled as I followed it.

The gate slammed shut, and I turned to see Lana walking away from me. *What the heck?* I called to her, repeatedly. *Hey, Lana! Don't leave me. I'm back here!*

I barked. I yelped. I cried. I whined and scratched at the gate. I walked the perimeter. I dug holes along the fence. I paced the pen – 15 paces wide by 30 paces long – but found no way to escape.

I stood at the gate and stared at the house. Each time I saw Lana walk past the window, I went crazy with barking. *Come back!*

I grew hungry. Finally, after dark, Lana stepped out the front door wearing a thin purple coat fastened with a cord around her waist. I barked. She ran over, coat billowing out behind her, white legs flashing in the dark, wet hair hanging limply along her neck. I jumped up and down on the gate, whining and yelping with relief.

"Duke, stop barking." She reached through the gate. I smelled the familiar, suffocatingly sweet scent on her breath again. Trouble. I kicked the barking up a notch and whined and licked her hand through the fence. "Roy's going to lose it if you don't quiet down. He's been threatening to come out here with the hose."

Lana made no moves to open the gate, and I desperately wanted out of the cage. I could barely control myself. I barked louder and jumped against the gate.

"No, Duke!" She looked back over her shoulder, cracked opened the gate and slipped through. She sat on her haunches, and I threw myself at her, knocking her onto her backside.

"Duke, stop it! Stop!" She pushed at me with her hands, and I grabbed her fingers with my teeth. She pushed me away harder and tried to stand. A panic rose inside me. *She's going to leave.* I pounced on her neck and shoulders, then flipped over her head and onto my back. She stood abruptly, wet hair streaked with dirt.

Roy stepped out of the house, shirtless and holding a large bottle. His white, wiry torso glowed in the moonlight. "What are you doing, Lana? What's taking so long?"

"Coming!" Her voice lowered as she walked to the gate.

"Shoot, Duke, just stop already. Now I have to take another shower. My hair is filthy." I whined and jumped on her. I grabbed the belt hanging from her coat and tugged.

"I love you, cute thing, but I have to get back."

"Lana!"

"Coming!" She tugged her belt free of my teeth with a rip, left me with a small square of thin fabric, then opened the gate and slipped through, latching it solidly behind her.

I yelped and barked as she ran to the house. Roy held the door open, and she gave me a quick look before she entered. Roy stared at me from the doorway. He lit a smoke stick and shook his match before he shut the door. The porch light went dark.

I paced in front of the gate and barked. Would she come back? My throat hurt, my belly ached, and my mouth felt parched and scratchy. My voice broke and became a loud whining over which I had no control. Eventually I curled up in front of the gate and tucked my head under my legs. I lay there shivering and hardly slept at all. For the first time ever, I was completely alone. I thought of Mama and Lila and my stomach hurt. I vowed to escape.

CHAPTER 8
VISITORS

L ife fell into the "Home" or "Not Home" categories. That is to say, Roy.

When Roy took his demon beast on the road, Lana and I had a good time. She introduced me to a leather strap around my neck – a collar, she called it – and attached a longer strap – a leash – to the collar. I bolted out of the cage that first day and was surprised when I couldn't run free. I chafed and fought and flipped around and around until I ended up in a tangled mess. After a lot more flipping and turning, Lana finally untangled me. I walked alongside her uneventfully, until I burst after a squirrel and got yanked onto my back.

We took long walks together, my favorite place to walk being the other side of the creek behind the house. When the water ran high, we walked up the driveway, down the road, then crossed a bridge that took us onto the other side. When low, however, we could cross the creek directly from the house and into the broad meadow and the forest of trees that climbed up the mountain.

As soon as I heard the click of Lana releasing me from the leash, I shot away like a bullet. I loved to run a few laps, turn tightly and speed back to her after every pivot. I threw in a snarl or two as I passed to keep her on her toes, sometimes even snapping as she laughed and threw sticks, which I chased and crunched in half with a head shake and jaw snap.

I showed off my speed and dexterity, plowing headfirst into the creek to chase the bugs on the water's surface, leaping through the tall grasses after mice or crickets, or in winter bounding after snowballs that confoundingly disappeared as soon as they hit the ground.

I couldn't imagine a more perfect life. Lana talked to me constantly, and her voice sent a shiver of anticipation down my spine every time she asked if I wanted to go on a walk.

I'd catch the scent of other animals, sometimes dogs. Though our neighbors mostly remained unseen, we'd occasionally encounter a deer or rabbit which I'd chase until ready to drop.

When Roy was gone, I roamed free on the property and stood guard on the porch where I'd rein in the squirrels, announce any untoward activity, and preside over the abode. Not infrequently, Lana left me outside at night, and I cruised the neighborhood and introduced myself to the ladies, and a few gents, in a joyous burst of noise. Sometimes a light switched on and a 'man opened the door yelling. Or, worse, a dog or dogs would fly out of the house on a beeline towards me. I left those houses quickly, if not quietly.

Lana's friends stayed over when he wasn't home. Female, young, two to three of them who coasted down the driveway in a large car – visits full of laughter and loud music. They brought me treats, and I impressed them my speed and agility, turning tight circles in the meadow as they whooped and cheered. We'd spend the night at the firepit near the creek, with them drinking and singing, and me howling in unison. I loved seeing their car roll down our driveway.

Lana's brother Alex, whose young face and serious gray-green eyes didn't smile, visited on occasion. His visits left me disappointed and Lana disturbed. Not once did he offer me a treat. And when Lana showed him the treat bag, he shook his head and pushed it away. *Pushed it away!*

Some people, like Lana, are dog people, but others, like Roy and Alex, most certainly are not. His visits were brief and infrequent. They didn't carry any of the laughter and loud music of Lana's friends. In fact, his visits agitated Lana. The ferocity of her voice put me on alert. "I'm never going back there, Alex. I don't care if Dad's sobered up or not. Is he still with that nasty woman? Carlene?" Her voice, angry and curt, made me glance up in concern.

"Nah, she's gone. He's with another woman, Angie. Nearly a year now, I think. She seems nice. I think they'd like it if you came back."

"Oh, I'm sure she's a doll, just like the rest." Lana's voice rose. "No way in hell I'm going back home. Honestly, Alex, why would I leave my own place to go back to Dad's? I've got enough to take care of."

"This isn't your place, Lana." His voice hardened as he motioned angrily towards the house. "He's ten years older than you. You've got no car, no income, and you're home alone for weeks at a time. How about a job? Why doesn't he let you drive his car? What about money? How can you take care of anything?"

Lana frowned. "I don't need a car, Alex. And if I do, Roy's mom is twenty minutes away to take me shopping. There's enough work for me here trying to keep the household operating. Roy may not be here all the time, but I keep busy with the house and Duke."

I barked when I heard my name but had other things on my mind. The squirrel on the fallen spruce tree, for one. We'd reached the field, but she hadn't yet let me off the leash. As she leaned over to stroke my head and unbuckle it, I prepared to bolt away.

"Roy wants to have a baby."

She unhooked me, and I exploded into the meadow. But Alex's angry outburst startled me and ruined my stride. The squirrel whipped around and climbed up a birch. I turned quickly to stare at them.

"Why the hell would you do that? You're only nineteen! You're going to be tied to that man for the rest of your life, Lana. You're too young to have a baby."

"Roy and I love each other. I'm not a child, Alex. I've got a home and a man who loves me. I'm not saying it'll happen soon, but when we want to start a family, we're ready. He brings home good money, and I like the quiet of this place." She picked up a stick, and I hopped up and down beside her. She cocked her arm back, and I quivered, ready for the throw. She looked sideways at her brother. "Roy looks tough, but inside he's a little boy. He needs me."

She chucked the stick. I raced into the creek, grabbed it and snapped it in two. Whoops! Guess it wasn't as strong as it looked! I continued to shake and snap the stick as the two of them argued. Eventually the stick disappeared into nothing, so I tracked squirrel scents into the edge of the forest until Lana whistled. When all else fails, chase squirrels.

CHAPTER 9
FRIEND OR FOE

Whenever Roy returned home with his beast, Lana greeted him by leaping on him and wrapping her arms around him. I didn't. I had initially joined in the leap and greet, but Roy didn't appreciate my enthusiasm and ordered Lana to "lock that damn dog up and out of the way."

They'd inevitably disappear into the house after his arrival, and if Lana hadn't already relegated me to the pen, I'd circle the beast and try to identify the scents drifting off of the engine block. They hinted at a different world – tar, gasoline, engine oil and, once, the very strong, enticing smell of a dead deer.

Lana's friends and brother never visited with Roy home, and she spent most of her time with him in the house. We still took walks to the meadow daily, but she didn't let me loose in the yard. Most of the time I paced back and forth in the cage, watched the house, growled at squirrels – all too aware of my impotence, those buggers – and waited for something to happen. I wanted to get out. I needed to be with Lana.

Seasons passed. I grew larger and larger. As my strength and size grew, I tried digging holes under the fence but found the hard packed dirt difficult to break through. Winter arrived, cold and lonely, and my paws were unable to break through the frozen turf.

I sat on the flat roof of the plywood dog shelter and stared at the house, barking whenever I saw Lana through the window. Then spring brought sunshine, warm temperatures and thawing. My spirits lifted. I dug into the ground with relish, mud and dirt flying all around the cage.

"You're a mess!" Lana didn't appreciate my digging. "Down, Duke!" She batted my head away as I approached for a head rub and stiff-armed me when attaching the leash to my collar. I snuck in a good swipe on her legs as she opened the gate, however, and she shook her head and gritted her teeth, almost growling.

Despite my efforts, I couldn't dig a hole deep enough or large enough to get under the fence. Then in the summer Lana started filling the holes with gravel, making the fence even more impenetrable.

By my second fall, I'd stopped digging and began planning other means of escape. Not because I was going stir crazy in the pen – though I was – but because Lana needed me. She and Roy battled in the house regularly. Shrieks and cries blasted out of the thin walls, and though I barked and raged, I couldn't get to her. Locked up and stuck, I ran back and forth, frenzied and snarling through the chain links.

One night as the yelling got louder and louder, I grew frantic. I stopped barking, leapt up to the roof of my house and studied the fence. Could I leap to the top and jump down to the other side? I eyed the gap. I knew I could reach the fence. But I'd have to get my front paws over the thin edge and pull myself up before I could get over. I shifted back and forth on top of my dog house and crouched, my legs trembling beneath me.

I eyed the distance and jumped. My paws slammed into the fence short of the top, and I turned my face away just before the rest of my body smacked the fence and slid down. I shook my head then jumped back onto the house and readied myself again. I nearly got my paws on top this time but still ended up crashing into the chain link. This fence had no weaknesses. It stood tall despite the weight of my body hitting it, and I could find no holes or gaps large enough to exploit.

The noise in the house eased, but I didn't feel better. A quiet rage is often more dangerous than a screaming one. I swung my head back and forth and tried to catch a sound or scent that could tell me what was going on.

Nothing. I again threw myself at the fence and once more slid down the inside to the hard packed ground. Useless. My attempts were useless. I was useless. I jumped on the house then back off again. I whined and tried to dig into the gravel that Lana had used to fill in my previous holes. The rock chewed up my paws and scraped my nails.

I couldn't get out. I lay down at the gate with my nose to the largest opening I could find and whimpered until the deepest dark of night.

The scent of Trouble floated like a cloud around Roy and his anger, and Lana too fell victim to Trouble more than once. One night, she stumbled slightly as she set down my dinner dish and crouched low to the ground. After I'd finished eating, she wrapped her arms around my neck. I licked her face, and she giggled. "You're such a good boy, Duke." Her voice slurred.

My tail swished through the dust in the pen, raising a small cloud. I nuzzled her ear and licked her eyebrow. "I wish Roy liked you. My friends like you. But they don't like him. Alex hates him." She stared at the ground and sniffed, then wiped her eyes with the back of her hand. She wobbled. "Sometimes Roy's not very nice, but he loves me."

"He's all I got. Except you, Duke. You're mine. You love me too, don't you boy?" I had no idea what she was saying, but I loved Lana's soft voice. I twisted around to chew on her fingers then licked her head and ended up with a mouthful of stray hair.

Roy and I had never gotten along. I'd used my best tricks to make friends with him – sitting politely by the gate with my tail wagging in the dirt when he approached, rubbing my head against his hand as he walked by, or grabbing a stick for him to throw. But he didn't want anything to do with me.

And, honestly, something about Roy ramped me up. Not only was his face somewhat crooked, with his left eye lower than the other and his nose slightly pushed to the right, but he'd also returned from his last trip wearing a small furry patch above his lip that scared me. Frankly, he looked infected by the same fungus growing in the corners of my dog house. I barked in alarm then backed away as he got out of his beast. As he neared Lana, I jumped back into action and wedged myself between them. I didn't trust that furry lip.

But Roy kicked me, and Lana chastised me, and I growled nervously when they smashed faces upon his arrival. The furry lip didn't seem to bother Lana, so I relaxed a tad. Just enough to settle down and try to disappear into the background before they went into the house. I always tried to extend my time outside the cage before I got locked up again.

With Roy home, different visitors arrived. Some wound slowly down the driveway in their vehicles, peering around the property as I announced their arrival. Roy greeted these 'mans outside the house where they circled around his demon beast and disappeared into the shed. They'd emerge quickly then leave after a short word or two. Though most paid me no attention, some occasionally glanced my way, and I'd jump on the fence with a full-throated, full body greeting.

"That's a big dog."

Roy would reply with a grunt and a growl. "My old lady's. Barks fucking nonstop. Loud and uncontrollable."

They eyed me suspiciously, though some looked friendly enough. Most visitors didn't stay long, and I'd bark good-bye just minutes after hello.

Other visitors arrived in the evening for firepit parties near the creek with Roy and Lana. Roy tended the fire and drank as people came and went. The drinking, laughing, shouting – sometimes fighting – excited me, and I hated being locked up and away from the fun and Lana.

At the first firepit party, I barked and barked, and Roy yelled at me to shut the fuck up. Finally he marched over to my cage and shook the fence with one hand, a nearly empty bottle in the other. He glared through the gate, bottle hanging loosely, and curled his furry lip at me. He spoke in a low voice tight with anger, and I knew I should quiet down. But there were too many strange people at the property, and I couldn't keep track of Lana. I wanted to stick by her side and keep her safe – *Law #4*. Plus, I could smell meat by the fire, just saying.

I didn't like it when I couldn't see Lana. But Roy blocked my view. He glared at me, unspeaking, reeking of Trouble, until Lana came up behind him and wrapped her arms around his waist. "C'mon, babe, let's get back to the party. Duke'll quiet down. He just wants to be part of the fun."

He stiffened angrily, turned quickly and slapped her face hard. Lana gasped as she stumbled back, and I threw myself at the fence.

"Don't tell me what to do, Lana." He hissed. "You're embarrassing me in front of my friends." He grabbed her elbow and roughly led her down the driveway back to the fire.

I raged from the top of my house. No good at the long game, I couldn't settle and wait for what I wanted. If I wanted Lana, I wanted her now. If I wanted that bone in the corner of my pen, I'd take it immediately. Good things may come to those who wait, but better things come to those who take.

Roy kept his arm around her by the fire, and it reminded me of my collar, somehow. More than once, when things became so loud and crazy that I grew agitated, she rose and gazed at my cage with a frown. But Roy's arm pulled her back, and she fell into the chair with a frozen look of worry that twisted into a smile when she looked at him. My chest tightened when she went into the house, and I launched myself at the fence. Roy chucked a half-opened beer can my way which fell shy of my pen. When she emerged and settled again by the fire, I relaxed.

Roy reveled in the action, a king in his courtyard. He sat on his throne in front of the fire and shouted across the yard. "Your aim sucks, Johnny!" he'd say. Or "Angel, lose twenty pounds before you complain about men."

Lana shushed him, and he turned on her. "Did I ask you?" Her voice lowered to a murmur, but his voice rose as he shook his head and yelled. I jumped at the fence with all my force, earning a second beer can hurled my way. Lana grabbed his arm, and he jerked it free, yanking her forward with it. I railed against him, throwing myself against the fence and pacing the perimeter. I dug furiously, knowing that it was useless, but pushing forward, none-theless.

Roy stood angrily at something she said. Lana started to rise with him, but he pushed her back to the chair. Her face widened in surprise then creased with worry. She rubbed her shoulder where he'd pushed her.

He can't do that!

I exploded with rage and slammed my body into the fence as she got up quickly and moved towards the house. Roy intercepted her, looped his arm around her neck, drew her face close to his and whispered. Pretty soon they started dancing slowly around the fire together. I stayed on high alert, locked up, powerless, furious. I paced back and forth impotently.

More than the yelling and more than Roy's temper, however, I hated the guns. Roy loved guns as much as his demon beast. He set up targets in the meadow across the creek – a line of bottles or cans, a stump with a circle painted on it - and he and his friends would shoot at them. Some of the men carried small guns in their waistbands, pulling them out, crouching and shooting quickly at the targets as if under attack. The sharp crack of these guns hurt my ears and drove every clear thought from my head. Each shot echoed inside my skull, and I couldn't escape it. I felt mad, bombs exploding between my ears, and I barked until hoarse.

But while those small guns hurt my ears, the big guns struck terror into my heart. The sound of them turned me into a quivering, slobbering mess. Each shot ricocheted through my head, a thundering, huge inescapable booming. My body trembled. I slobbered. I felt like throwing up. I could find relief nowhere, and I'd wind up collapsed in a corner of my pen, shuddering and drooling until long after the guns had stopped firing.

The parties ended when Roy fell asleep on his throne. His head would fall to his chest, the bottle would slip from his hand. When he slumped over or rolled out of his chair into the dirt, someone would help Lana carry him inside, and everyone packed up and left.

CHAPTER 10
IMPOTENT

R oy had just returned from an early summer road trip with his demon beast. I'd found a soft spot on the ground in a corner of the pen where the ground sunk and the gravel was light. I was digging at it furiously when Roy and Lana began shouting at each other in the house. Just another a part of the day with Roy around.

On this afternoon they shouted a while, then Roy emerged and paced angrily outside the house and smoked. I barked, and he looked at me and glared darkly. Smoke stick in hand, he marched towards my pen, eyes flashing with anger. The reek of Trouble reached my cage first as he leaned on the chain link with a sneer and practically spit at me.

"If you could talk, you could tell me what she's been up to. But you'd cover for her anyways, wouldn't you? Fucking dog. No respect in my own house."

I whined and craned my neck to look for Lana. He moved to block my view. I don't know why I was startled by the hatred in his eyes. It shouldn't have been a surprise. But the true surprise came when he opened my gate and stepped inside. I fell back into the corner, didn't know what to do. Roy never came into my pen.

He held his smoke stick loosely in one hand and clenched the other in a fist. His eyes looked wild, and he stuck the smoke stick between his lips and mumbled through it as he approached. "Goddamned dog, I don't know why I let her keep you."

I watched his eyes, beadier than normal and flashing with anger. Everything in me screamed RUN, but he'd shut the gate behind him, and I was trapped. Then his right hand grabbed my collar, and he yanked my head down as his left fist clobbered my eye. Pain thundered through my head, and I shrieked in surprise. I thrashed my body but couldn't get from his grasp. "Shut the fuck up!" He twisted the collar in his hand, throttling the collar around my neck so that I could barely breathe. I quieted and lay, gasping for air.

"Roy!" Lana suddenly spoke from the gate. I hadn't heard her arrive and couldn't see her. She was crying. "Roy, leave Duke alone. Come back to the house, babe. He didn't do anything."

Roy's grip tightened, and he slammed another fist into my ear. A blackness passed over me. I yelped but it sounded far away, as if I were in a tunnel. "Don't tell me what to do, Lana." He leaned over me, his fury rushing over me like a wave. My eye throbbed, and a roaring in my head made it tough to focus, the collar tight around my throat. "Know your place, dog. And shut the fuck up." He let go my collar, and I gasped for air. By the time I'd found my legs, he'd left the cage and shut the gate. He held Lana's arm roughly and pulled her back to the house.

If I'd hoped things would quiet down, they didn't. The yelling started again then continued on and on. I paced back and forth, big enough now that I could only take about ten steps before having to turn back the other way.

Suddenly Roy bellowed. "Goddammit Lana, give it to me!" Lana screamed, then I heard a loud thump, and glass breaking. I barked sharply and jumped onto my box, straining to see through the open windows of the house. In the main room, Roy was standing, hands on hips, looking down at the floor.

Lana popped up and dove at him, shrieking, her hands flailing wildly until they grabbed hold of his shirt. "It's mine! Alex gave it to me!"

Roy grabbed Lana's arms then twisted them around and yanked. She flipped over his shoulder like a duffel bag then fell out of sight. The house shook, and Lana screamed loudly. Seconds she later burst out the door whimpering and holding her arm close to her chest. I barked and snarled as she stumbled barefoot towards me on the gravel driveway. Roy chased her to my cage. He reeked of Trouble and sweat. Lana smelled of fear. He kept the gate shut with one hand and dropped his head low to talk to her.

"C'mon, Lana. I'm sorry." His voice slurred slightly, and he staggered against the gate. Lana sobbed. I barked wildly. Roy sneered at me and curled his lip.

Law #4. Protect the Pack.

I couldn't see straight. I needed to get out. I had to keep Roy away from Lana.

"Lana, look at me. I'm sorry. I didn't mean to do that. But you can't hide things from me, especially not money. Why did Alex give you money, anyways? You get everything you need from me."

He dropped his hand to her shoulder, and she flinched, crying harder. I jumped on the gate and barked angrily. He punched the fence, and I drew back. He pulled her into him, and I leapt again. Front paws on the gate, my head reached her height, and I tried desperately to get her to look at me. But she turned away and buried her face in his shoulders.

"Roy, it's for the baby. The money is for the baby."

"Wha-at?" He looked confused. He lifted her head to look in her face. "A baby? You're pregnant?" His face twisted ugly for a split second before he wiped it clean and kissed her forehead. "Lana, when did you find out? You already told Alex?"

"Just last week." She sniffed again and cradled her arm. She whimpered. "You were on the road, and Alex came to visit. I only told him because he wanted me to move back to town again. He thinks I'm too lonely out here. I told him that we were starting a family. He said to keep this money for the baby and to save up for something special."

She started crying again and couldn't stop. "It's my money, and I'm saving it for the baby. Why the hell did you flip out? I'm not hiding it!" Her voice rose shrilly as she sobbed and held her arm gingerly. "You hurt me, Roy. How could you do that? What if you hurt the baby?"

"Shh, shh, Lana, calm down. I told you I'm sorry. I didn't know where the hell the money came from. Two hundred dollars is a lot of money for someone who doesn't work. What am I supposed to think? You could have been turning tricks while I was on the road or something."

She gasped. "How could you say that? I'm not my mom. I've never cheated on you, and I'm not a whore." Her sobbing grew, and she buried her face in her uninjured arm.

He lifted her chin and ran a bony finger along her face. He stared at her. I snarled. His eyes flashed angrily at me and narrowed, then he placed his arm around her shoulder and turned her away from me. "Let's get into the house and take care of you, baby. I made a mistake. I misunderstood. I get jealous, babe, you know that. I thought maybe you had a man on the side, someone who left you money. Why else would you hide it?"

"I wasn't hiding it!"

"Okay, sure." He stroked the back of her head as they walked to the house. "You gotta ice your arm. You did a number on it. I love you, baby. I don't want to see you hurt." She nodded then leaned her head onto his shoulder as they climbed the porch steps.

I didn't get dinner that night. I barked until long after they had shut the door and turned off the light.

ROY REDUCED his road trips and stayed home for so long that I doubted he'd ever leave again. Our daytime visitors increased –

men who met Roy outside, visited the shed briefly, climbed back into their beasts and left – and the nighttime parties got bigger and louder. Roy still presided from his chair by the fire, commanding attention and directing the goings-on. Lana stayed by his side unless fetching food and drink from the house.

"Lana! Go find the chips and salsa. Lana! Bring me another beer. Lana! Show Jerry your beautiful baby belly. Jerry, look at those titties she's got now!" Lana did his bidding without protest, including letting guests put their hands on her belly, which I didn't like.

She didn't argue with him when friends were around. She saved that for nights when they were alone, nights when the trailer overflowed with cursing and yelling, nights when I barked myself hoarse, paced around the cage and jumped on and off my house trying to catch sight of her. I worried about Lana alone in that house with Roy. An angry man who ended arguments at the fire by pulling out a gun, she couldn't match him. His anger shook that trailer, and, while Lana screamed in anger too, she was the only one in tears when the shouts and curses subsided.

I waited for Lana's visits to my pen, my sole source of happiness. When the turbulent nights became more commonplace and Lana spent more and more time with Roy in the trailer, I felt her loss keenly. She seemed to have trouble getting out of the house now, our walks dwindling to just a few every week. Sometimes she only came out to check my water and bring food. Roy followed her and watched from the porch, glaring and smoking. I growled.

Her belly grew in size, and she couldn't stop touching it, rubbing it and placing her hands on either side. "Duke, I've never had a belly before! And my boobs are so big!" I wagged my tail and licked her face. Her belly, round or not, was perfect. I nosed her hand onto my forehead. She laughed again.

"I wish you could come into the house with me, Duke. Roy's gotten crazier and crazier." Her voice grew soft, and she cradled her belly with her hands. "He acts like I'm cheating on him, but I would never. I can't predict if he's going to be angry or nice. It's like he's two different people."

One day, towards the end of winter, another argument started. When the thumping and breaking began, I lost control and raged helplessly inside the pen, pacing, jumping and leaping onto the fence. I tried scaling it again. No luck.

Roy threw open the front door then ran outside with a wooden drawer which he turned upside down, scattering clothes on the snow. "Happy now, Lana?" He threw the empty drawer against the trailer where it cracked and lay shattered on the snow then ran back into the house and came with more wooden drawers that he dumped then shattered. Lana's clothes lay scattered on the snow. "Goddammit, bitch, are you happy now?"

Lana wailed in response, but I couldn't see her. He ran back into the house, and she screamed loudly. Roy dragged her out the front door by the hair. Her swollen body stumbled out behind him, her belly enormous, her face puffy and red. She held her hair below his hand where he yanked it, and she struggled to keep her balance. She pleaded and cursed, and Roy yanked her hair hard and shoved her. With an ear-piercing shriek she flopped like a rag doll down the stairs. Her head hit the bottom step with a thud, and she fell quiet.

The world went silent with her. No crickets, no owls, no wind whispering through the trees. I couldn't breathe.

Lana didn't move, her body on the snow like a fallen angel.

Roy stood, panting and sweating, glaring down at her, hands on hips, breathing heavy. He turned furiously to the door and punched it. The trailer shook. Finally, he walked down the stairs and knelt down next to her.

As soon as he touched her, I exploded. I lunged and snapped and threw myself against the chain link fence. She lay crumpled on the ground. Roy slapped her cheeks softly and moved her hair out of her eyes. She moaned then cried out. I yelped and growled and paced as Roy put his arms under her, lifted her up and carried her to his small town beast. He lay her on the back seat, and I heard her whimper.

A savage fear rose in my chest. Panic shot through me as Roy started the beast, and my barks turned to yelps. *He's taking her away.* I howled as they turned around and drove up the driveway and out of sight. My throat grew hoarse. I shivered on my house and whined.

CHAPTER 11
ABANDONED

R oy didn't come back that night. I never got dinner. Early the next morning, Aileen arrived. She went into the house then came back outside to put Lana's clothes, still scattered on the snow, into black plastic bags. I barked nonstop. A gnawing ache twisted in my stomach. Aileen looked up and narrowed her eyes before she carried the black bags into the house. I continued to bark.

She eventually came out with a large bowl and walked towards my cage. I hadn't forgotten Aileen's fondness for brooms, but my need to eat weighed heavier than any personality preferences. *Law #1* prevailed, but my satisfaction was short-lived. Instead of the crunchy, meaty kibbles that Lana served me, the bowl held leftovers from a 'man supper – potatoes, bread crusts and vegetables. Apparently Aileen couldn't tell the difference between 'man food and my food. I hoped she wasn't eating my kibbles in the house! I gobbled it down anyways and kept a wary eye on her.

Aileen left the property then returned in the late afternoon followed by Roy in his small beast. I greeted his arrival with a frenzy of barking, but he didn't look my way, just went into the house and disappeared.

Every day I waited for Lana to return. My house became a watchtower, my eyes peeled to the top of the driveway, my ears tuned to the sound of any beast slowing on the road. One day Alex drove slowly towards the house, and I jumped and barked crazily. I didn't see Lana, but even if he weren't with her, he could take me to her. He parked next to the black demon beast and got out slowly. I jumped on the gate, barked and wagged my tail.

Alex! Hey boy! I got a stick! I didn't know if Alex would want a stick, but I picked one up for him and pranced around with it. 'Mans always got excited about sticks.

He ignored me and walked stiffly, shoulders squared and back straight, up the porch steps. Aileen peered out the window as he arrived, but Roy opened the front door, bottle in hand and smoke stick hanging off his lips.

I barked and barked. *Alex! Over here!*

The two men talked. Alex motioned inside the house, then pointed to his beast. Roy responded, and Alex shook his head. Roy spoke again with more emphasis, and Alex responded angrily. After a few final words from Roy, Alex shook his head angrily and turned around quickly.

Alex! Take me to Lana! I leapt on the fence. I barked and barked and barked, but Roy looked up, not Alex. Roy shouted at Alex and pointed at me. Alex paused and studied me.

Yes! Yes! Take me with you! I begged him. My throat hurt from barking.

Alex shook his head, got into his beast and left. An ache deep in my chest throbbed as he disappeared. I threw myself at the cage and howled.

A day later, a beast appeared with a headdress of flashing lights and painted stripes on its sides. Two men with black matching outfits, big belts and guns strapped to their sides got out of the beast. I growled at the guns and began to pant. They appraised me and scanned the property before heading up to the porch and knocking on the door. Aileen opened it and spoke to them then disappeared when Roy came to the door. He folded his arms and glared as the men spoke. Periodically he nodded, but when they took out a piece of paper and held it out, he backed away and shook his head.

One of the men motioned to their beast and then back to Roy. Roy ran his hand through his hair. The other man held the papers out again, and Roy took them. Aileen came to the door with the large black bags and handed them to one of the men. They turned around with another glance around the property and at me, and they got into their beast.

Roy remained on the porch, his body tense and angry. I yelped and howled as they drove away, watching the beast climb the drive. Suddenly a beer bottle broke against my cage. Glass and liquid flew into the gravel of my pen. I leapt onto my box and barked until my throat grew hoarse as Roy slammed his fists repeatedly into the door of the trailer.

Aileen came and went daily. I didn't get a lot of meat or any crunchy kibbles when she fed me, nothing like the food that Lana used to serve. Sometimes Aileen's dinners filled my belly; most times it didn't.

Hunger and I became good friends. Aileen and I, not so much. I tried everything to get a nice word, a soft touch, more food. But a soft lick would end with a hard slap, a playful head butt with a fist to the ear.

I backed off, stayed wary and barked at everything that entered the property. I kept guard, watching and waiting, alert to danger within and without. Roy spent most of his time in the trailer, and when he did come outside, he staggered through the yard reeking of Trouble and throwing bottles at my cage randomly. He left the house in his beast once or twice, and I waited hopefully for Lana to come back home. She never did.

CHAPTER 12
BREAK

The darkness of winter gave way to spring and with it the light came back into my life. Months after Lana disappeared, I gazed out at the open field across the creek behind the mobile home and saw a dog. Not unusual. I saw animals in the field periodically: deer, skunks, coyotes, sometimes even stray dogs. I didn't want them around while I was stuck in a cage, so I barked loudly and aggressively until they moved away.

But this dog stayed near the creek, so close that when the wind shifted, I caught her scent. Sap, mixed with cedar and earth. Her scent told me two things: first, she was female, and second, she was young like me, perhaps two or three years old. When I barked, her head whipped up and her tail wagged slightly. Smaller than a shepherd, compact and lean, with red and white markings, she had short wiry fur and teardrop ears.

Roy ran outside when I barked. He yelled at me, beer in hand, and she spooked. She ran away quickly with no backwards glance, leaving me barking at her retreating form, hoping she'd return.

I was so focused on her departure that I didn't notice Roy until his foot crunched on the gravel and his closed fist clubbed my face.

Whoa. I shook my head, backed away and bared my teeth. I

couldn't believe I'd lost control of myself for a minute, watching that dog.

"Shut your fucking trap." He kicked at me with his boot. I jumped onto my house to avoid the kick. He feinted with his left and then released the beer can from his right. It caught me above my left eye. My eyes flashed like lightning, my legs went limp, and I slid off the house. He spat on me and walked out of the cage. I growled a low deep growl and got back to my feet as stars swam in front of my eyes. A slow drip of blood trickled into my eye, and I blinked. It stung, but it hurt worse to shake my head.

"I oughta get rid of you," he said as he latched the gate behind him. I stared at the spot where the dog had been.

As the weeks passed, she continued to visit, coming closer and closer to the house. She came most often in the early morning, trotting to the creek then sitting down on her haunches, tilting her head and wagging her tail. I begged her to come closer.

One afternoon, she wagged her tail and for the first time barked back.

She barked at me.

Roy saw her when he came out to yell at me. He threw a rock across the creek, but it fell short. She barked one last time and ran out of sight.

He sauntered over and poked at me through the fence with a shovel handle. I growled quietly. He sneered at me. "I hope that dog's not a friend of yours. It comes near again, it gets the coyote treatment."

Roy shot at every coyote he saw in the field across the creek. My growl grew louder, a low rumble in my chest growing in volume. He jabbed the handle through the fence again before he walked away and into the mobile home. I turned to stare at the empty field where she'd disappeared.

Then I smelled her. Nearby. She'd crossed the creek. I whirled around, circled around. I jumped on my house, swinging my nose in the air until I located it – her scent – sap and cedar and earth, coming from behind a rose bush at the corner of the trailer – my Rose! I whined. She stepped out, and I yelped and quivered.

But my yelps attracted Roy, I realized, as he pounded up the driveway towards me, attracted to my noise like a fly to a pile of scat. He marched two steps in front of my Rose and hadn't seen her yet. I ran back and forth in front of the gate and snarled in rage as he approached. I couldn't let him turn around and see her. I locked eyes with him and hurled myself at the fence, sliding down and snapping. He picked up the shovel and held it like a baseball bat then sidled forward, holding the spade end of the shovel high as he reached the gate. I launched myself towards the gate and crashed into it then hurtled myself into it again.

"Roy!" Aileen shrieked from the porch. "Roy, what the hell are you doing?"

"Teaching this dog to stay quiet," Roy yelled at her as he undid the latch. "He's out of control."

I backed up in my enclosure and crouched, ears back, hackles high, a loud snarling rumble in my throat. I hated this man. I hated what he'd done to Lana. I hated what he did to me. I wouldn't let him hurt my Rose. Roy flipped the gate handle and balanced the shovel. He pushed open the gate, and Aileen shouted.

"Roy, watch out for the other one!"

Roy turned quickly and saw Rose trailing behind him. He swung the shovel at her, and it clipped the right side of her face. She yelped and fell to the ground.

Fury surged within me. Roy stumbled with the swing of his shovel, and I launched myself onto his chest and knocked him to the ground. He reeked of Trouble. I stood over him, this monster who hurt Lana and now Rose. His eyes widened, and I bared my teeth and grabbed his wrist. I clamped my jaws down hard on the bone and shook my head violently. Roy screamed and I felt a crack, then a snap. Aileen yelled, and Roy shouted at her.

"My gun! Grab my gun!"

I felt a cold nose wet in my ear and looked up to see Rose, one eye red with blood. She trotted to the open gate, looked towards the creek then beckoned me to follow. I dropped Roy's mangled wrist, and we ran across the yard and past Aileen emerging from the trailer with the shotgun.

We picked up our pace and leapt across the shallow creek. The gun boomed as the tree stump next to us exploded. We ran through the open field, fifty feet from the nearest tree. I zig zagged, shoulder to shoulder with Rose, waiting for the next shot, dreading the sound of the gun more than anything else. It came as we were midway across the field. My left hip exploded with a searing pain as the buckshot hit it, and I cried out then plunged jaw-first into the razor-like grass. I picked myself up, ignored the pain and pushed myself to reach Rose. Together we took a sharp left towards the woods and sped up as the gun cracked and the ground burst open behind us.

We ran side by side, dodging in and out of trees until I finally dropped. I couldn't run anymore. I hadn't been out of my cage in the months since Lana left, and my body throbbed with pain. I collapsed, exhausted, at the foot of a tree, and Rose nudged me into a hollow in the root system. I circled the leaves into a nest and curled into a ball. Rose sat next to me, alert, as my eyes drooped and my head fell, heavy.

What came next?

No Lana. No Aileen. No meals. No cage. No Roy. I shut my eyes and breathed in deeply... cedar, sap, earth. The scent of freedom.

PART THREE
WOLF

CHAPTER 13
JOURNEY

I awoke as if on fire, with flames licking my hip, burning and pulsing hot, hot, hot through my bones. I yelped. I tried to run, to escape the heat, but I couldn't move. Was I chained? I yelped again. I kicked my feet to get away, and pain exploded throughout my body.

Something soft touched my nose, and my eyes flew open.

Rose.

Her gaze – beautiful, soft, brown eyes – met mine. Despite the ugly swollen gash and matted blood on her forehead, her eyes were calm and soothed me. My panic subsided. I was in the forest, unchained and untouched by either smoke or fire. She nudged my nose again, and I shuddered. I couldn't see it, but I could feel it burning inside me, this fire. I felt aflame.

I lifted my head, and my body screamed. I inspected my wounds. My back leg looked like meat remnants on a bone – chewed up flesh swollen and caked with blood and dirt. The shot had blasted my hip and thigh, and pellets sat lodged just below the skin. I licked the area and yelped. Red and angry, a flaming pain.

My head hurt, too. My jaw was stiff. I tasted blood. The left side of my head throbbed with a sharp ache, and sound had disappeared from my left ear entirely. I lay my head down, willing the pain to leave me.

Rose stood up and whined softly. I whined back. She wanted to move. I didn't.

I had no idea where we were. I'd never been this far away from the house. My head felt too heavy to think. My body screamed at me to stay put.

She nudged me in the ribs, and I growled. She did it again, and I lifted myself up. Pain exploded throughout my body, and I nearly buckled. But I didn't. Panting and trembling, I stood.

I lowered my head, and Rose licked my face and ears. As I closed my eyes, a fireball erupted in my guts. I heaved once, then twice as I emptied my stomach, swaying on my feet. The nausea passed, and I gathered my strength. Rose trotted away and stopped once to look back at me.

I didn't want to move. But I would follow Rose. *Law #3: Know your pack.* Rose was now my pack.

I took a painful step forward. Then another. My injured body screamed at me. I wanted to lie down but followed Rose. I pushed through the pain to stumble after her.

We left as the sun broke over the mountains. I wondered, briefly, if Roy would come after us.

MEMORIES of that day are fuzzy – creek crossings and fences, pastures and forest. It all streamed by me in a blur despite our slow pace. I hopped heavily on three legs, using the injured one only for balance when stopping. I had no thoughts other than to keep up with Rose. *Follow Rose.* She set a fast pace, and whenever I lost sight of her, I'd stop and sink onto the forest floor, surrounded by cedars and spruce, the familiar scent of squirrels, bears and the quick smell of fox. Several times I dropped to the ground and closed my eyes then found myself jerked awake by Rose's cold nose on mine. Hunger and pain consumed me. I whimpered. I didn't want to walk anymore. But when she walked away, I staggered to my paws and followed.

I saw no 'mans or their beasts during our trek. Perhaps I heard their calls once or twice, but, given the fog of pain and my singular focus on Rose, I couldn't be sure.

In the early evening that changed. We exited the forest, climbed up out of a gully and stepped onto a hard, paved road, solid and unyielding on my pads. Beasts raced each other along six lanes in either direction. With no tree cover, I trembled and sunk low to the ground, nervous. I watched Rose run undaunted across the wide road. Beasts bugled and swerved around her. I staggered to my paws and stepped onto the road, trailing her red and white body, a beacon in the dark.

A beast approached, and I crouched, blinded by its bright eyes. It squealed loudly and screamed just past my head, spitting pebbles into my face as a blast of heat pushed me backwards. My hip gave out, and I stumbled and fell. I wanted to follow Rose, but she had disappeared. The beasts had taken her place.

My head sunk to the ground. Rose barked from far, far away. She barked again. And again. I moaned.

Another whining metallic beast approached, but I couldn't move. It came upon me fast and at the last second swerved with a loud shriek. Its breath ruffled my neck, and it too spit hard pebbles. Eventually, one of these beasts would eat me, or crush me. I didn't want to die.

I took a deep breath and stood. From the far side of the road, Rose barked. My legs quivered. Head low, I staggered across the pavement, eyes locked on Rose. Beasts blasted past me, screeching and blaring on one side or the other, but I reached her, finally, on the far side. She touched her nose to mine before she led us down into a gully, then up into a wooded area that faced a clearing. She slunk under a chain link fence.

I stopped.

I'd spent the past few years inside a fence like this. I lifted my head to sniff the air but withdrew at the pain in my head. Rose trotted away.

Know your pack.

I dragged myself under the fence.

CHAPTER 14
REFUGE

We entered a clearing that was nothing like Lana's meadow of wildflowers and grasses and rabbits. Instead I limped into a barren hard-packed dirt littered with patches of cement. Fires burned in metal barrels, and colorful tarps hung from small stands of trees. Flimsy fabric structures tilted sideways. I trailed behind her slowly, warily. My head thumped in a sharp ache, low to the ground. A loud whine reached my ears. When I realized it was mine, I shut it off and focused on Rose's body. I needed relief, a break from this long day, a place to close my eyes, somewhere to rest and cool this burning inside me.

We wove through shadows and in and around fire sites and bodies thick with clothing. No one spoke to us. An unseen dog growled. We reached a yellow shelter, and Rose approached three 'mans standing around a small fire. They carried strong scents. Even from the shadows I could smell unwashed bodies and the strong, sweet scent of Trouble. As she neared them, a 'man with a scraggly gray beard bared his teeth in a broad, gap-toothed smile and leaned over to pat her head.

"Suzy Q! Where have you…." His mouth turned downwards, and his brow wrinkled as he bent over her. "What the heck?"

Rose danced away from him and turned towards me. I growled. My eyes blurred, and my legs crumpled under me. I fell to the ground. Rose barked.

"Ah Suzy, Suzy... you hurt?" He followed her, holding a bottle wrapped tightly in a paper bag. "Who done this to you?" I struggled to keep my eyes focused on him. They felt heavy; my eyelids drooped. My body trembled. I burned hot, so, so hot.

The 'man reached out slowly towards Rose, and she lay down beside me, ears back. His body stiffened when he saw me, and he sat back on his haunches and whistled, lifted the bottle and swigged. Trouble trickled down his beard. Putting down the bottle, he rolled his eyes over me then put his hands on his knees and heaved himself up to lean over and peer down at me. I growled weakly. His faded gray eyes winced as they passed over my jaw, and they widened as he saw my hip.

"Jacky... Tank...." he called out over his shoulder. "Suzy brought back a boyfriend, and he ain't in good shape."

"Too fat?" A 'man laughed with a cackle that turned into a wet, ragged cough, a female with a large broken smile. She appeared behind Rose's bearded 'man with a messy head of brown and gray hair that looked as if it were trying to escape from beneath a black knit cap.

"Suzy Q, what's you got into?"

She reached her hand out to Rose who gave it a quick lick. My eyes tried to close on their own, but with the smell of Trouble all around me, I couldn't dare let them.

"Your man's been beat to shit, Suzy. Looks like he's been ate up and spit out by something."

"No animal did this." A low, deep voice spoke as a dark hooded face with solemn brown eyes appeared above Jacky. He was a large 'man, dressed in thick, ragged clothing, with a sphere of curly gray hair peeking out of the hood surrounding his face. The smell of Trouble floated off of him, and his movements were slow. "That's a shotgun blast right there. Someone shot Suzy's boyfriend."

"And they bunged up Suzy's face, Tank." The bearded man wiped his eyes with a sleeve and took another drink of Trouble. "My poor Suzy, she don't deserve this." He reminded me of Lana during one of her weeping sessions.

"Quit your crying, Critter," Jacky said as she grabbed Rose's jaw and looked at her wound. "Blubbering don't never help no thing."

"Who shoots a dog?" The man named Critter dropped his head to his chest and sniffled, wiped his eyes, then sat down on the ground, setting his bottle next to him. He tried to pull Rose into his lap with his free hand, but she resisted and yelped when he missed the collar and instead yanked her by the scruff of the neck. He wrapped his arms around her. I growled and struggled to get up. *Protect Your Pack.*

"Critter, let go that girl." Jacky said sharply. "She don't need no cuddles. She need a dog doctor. And her friend too. What we gonna do with him?"

Critter let go of Rose who licked his cheek before coming back to my side. She curled up next to me, and he stared at us. The tears running down his face got lost in his long beard. He drank again from his bottle then shook his head. "Who'd do that?"

Tank moved forward and dropped a silver packet on the ground in front of me and Rose. It flopped open to reveal a soggy mass of mushy yellow and brown food which I swallowed in a heartbeat. Rose licked my jaw. *See Food, Eat Food.*

Jacky whistled. "That'un's a hungry creature. He dint even save none for Suzy." She turned to Tank. "Got more?"

Tank shook his head slowly. "That's my breakfast from the Mission this morning. Was going to be my supper. He needs it more than I do."

"You're a good man, Tank," sobbed Critter. "I never known anyone as generous as you." He took a swig from the bottle and threw his arm out expansively. "Take the dog, Tank. You deserve him. He ate your food."

Jacky glanced sideways at Critter and then at the large man

named Tank who stared only at the ground. "We need to clean his wounds, or he's not sticking around for anyone."

I gave up. I closed my eyes and shuddered, curled into Rose as closely as I could, and lost track of everything.

CHAPTER 15
ASSAULT

R ose's scent kept me grounded through the fog of pain that first night. The scent of her 'mans, on the other hand, terrified me. When they surrounded me and poked at my wounds, only her nearness – the scent of cedar, sap and earth – settled the panic that flashed in me like lightning. I warned everyone off, wouldn't let anyone else touch me. My body ached.

Rose licked my jaw. The touch of her tongue sent spasms of pain through my body, and I yelped. I whined even before I opened my eyes. When I did, a foreign landscape greeted me. No fence, no creek, no house on blocks. What had last night been a clearing filled with people and fires and shelters was now mostly empty of the first two. Here and there figures wrapped in blankets lay underneath trees or near barrels with smoke rising faintly from them.

I sniffed the air passively and recognized Critter's and Jacky's scents in the yellow shelter beside me. I could see and smell the 'man Tank sleeping to my right under a tree. The pungent smell of Trouble from last night had dissipated, though the scent lingered as if woven into the environment.

Rose got up and stretched slowly. The gash above her eye flashed red and angry, but she moved as if it didn't matter. She looked at me expectantly, teardrop ears lifted and head cocked. I didn't want to get up. She moved towards me and nudged my nose. It hurt like hell. I growled. She backed off and barked at me. I lifted my head and took a breath then tried to stand.

I'd been injured before. Roy had clocked me with beer cans and tools, and some of those wounds had taken weeks to heal. Just yesterday I'd walked for hours through jaw-clenching pain, and I'd willed myself from each step to the next. But now I shuddered, dropped my head to my paws and looked at Rose pleadingly. *I can't.*

She whined and touched noses with me. I inhaled her scent, licked her nose, then watched her turn and trot through the shelters and into the trees on the other side of the clearing. My eyes followed her until she disappeared, then I closed them. I could do nothing but sleep.

I awoke under attack.

Large hands – Tank's – held my mouth while Jacky looped a rope around my nose, binding my jaw shut before I knew what was happening. I growled and tried to stand just as she circled the other end of the rope around my neck and pulled it tight against my chest. Suddenly, my chin was tied tautly against my chest. I was muzzled. I couldn't lift my head.

Rose danced nervously around me, licking my face, getting in Jacky's way and yipping and yelping. I kept trying to rise, but with my head lashed to my neck and pain exploding throughout my body, all I could do was writhe and growl.

"Critter, come git Suzy Q," Jacky yelled. She held a bottle of Trouble in one hand and Rose's collar in the other. Critter came out of the shelter rubbing his eyes. He stopped.

"Whatchu doin with my bottle, woman?" His eyes flicked to me and widened. "Whatchu doin to that dog?"

"Cleaning him up." Jacky spoke like a sergeant. "Critter, take Suzy. Tank, keep holding this'un's neck." Both men obeyed her. I thrashed and growled violently as Tank's large hands pinned my neck and head to the ground. Jacky put her weight onto my legs. Pain and terror flared around me. I snarled as much as I could with my mouth tied shut. Roy had been a mean cur with many tricks but this was not one of them. These 'mans were unknown, and I didn't know what they were dishing out. More pain, from the feel of it.

"Hey!" Critter exclaimed. The smell of Trouble stung my nose, and I felt the fiery liquid splash over my hip. My flank flamed, and I yowled and struggled harder. Tank pinned my forepaws down with his arm.

I began shrieking, as much as possible with my mouth tied shut. Jacky jabbed her fingers into my hip, pouring Trouble on it, and poking and prodding at the hard little pebble balls. With every jab I saw Roy ramming the shovel handle through the fence, and I thrashed and wailed, delirious. Rose yelped from Critter's arms. Together we cried as they tortured me.

Finally, Jacket sat back. She coughed then spoke in a raspy voice. "That's as good as I can do. Let's hope it's enough." Jacky lifted the bottle once more, but this time she put it to her lips and drank. Nearly empty, she handed the bottle to Tank who tilted it above me and finished it off.

"Hey!" Critter yelled again. He whined softly. "My bottle...."

"Ready Tank?" Jacky moved, and the weight left my legs. Her hand undid the bindings near my neck. Tank released my paws. The rope dropped away from my head, and I snapped at the air as I rose with all my strength to stand, wide-legged and swaying. My hip burned, and I felt sick. I heaved a few times then reeled in place, lurched a few paces forward, and lay down, keeping my eyes on the 'mans.

Critter released Rose who rushed me, then he snatched the empty bottle from Tank. His voice wavered then whimpered. "It's all gone."

Rose sniffed my hip and head then licked my face and sat down next to me. My eyes darted from one 'man to the other. I didn't want them near me but couldn't move. Tank carried a bowl of water to me, and I showed him my teeth and growled a low threat. He retreated but left the water. As Rose kept guard, I drank until my stomach filled and bloated. It soothed the heat inside of me. My eyes grew heavy. "You kilt him, Jacky." I heard Critter sob before I lost consciousness.

I awoke in the cold absence of Rose's body. My eyes flew open, and for the first time in days no crack of pain jolted through my skull. Critter's and Jacky's scents flowed out of the shelter, but I couldn't locate Rose's. I lifted my hips and managed to stretch mildly for the first time in days. Only residual pain. I gulped the water that was still in the bowl in front of me. I was hungry, very hungry.

I began to search the clearing, gingerly weaving through the flimsy shelters filled with sleeping bodies. 'Mans and their things surrounded me. Tarps and ropes blocked the sky and covered the containers and shelters of the 'mans' world. Shopping carts stood motionless on tiny round feet under burdens of multi-colored bags and blankets and assorted belongings, enticing but out of reach. Empty bottles and cans that smelled of Trouble lay sentinel by the carts. Various sizes of shredded white plastic bags scuttled past me with the breeze.

The steel barrels that had lit up with fire at night smoked gently. Bodies curled around them, stretched or curved under dirty blankets or sleeping bags, sometimes newspapers or cardboard. Twice a bleary red eye opened from a mound of fabric and followed me as I sniffed the side of a tent or bag. Both times I stopped and locked my eyes on it until it closed. I encountered three other dogs in the camp, whom I smelled long before I saw them or heard their warning growls. I backed away, not ready to determine friend or foe.

The sleeping structures were flimsy and flapped in the light wind. Debris lay everywhere, but food seemed to be in short supply. Though my hip ached dully, the fire in it had subsided. It felt good to move again, but I was hungry. The days of sickness with no food left me weak. After a complete circuit of the camp, I found only some cold soggy sticks in a cardboard cup which, of course, I ate.

The loop around the camp exhausted me. I returned to the yellow shelter where Rose rushed me with a happy bark and ran her shoulder into mine, nearly dropping me. I yelped and staggered, and she whined and flattened to the ground, ears back, tail whipping up dust. She crawled towards me. I woofed softly and collapsed by her side, wiped out from the brief search for food. Still hungry.

Rose's 'mans, like Lana and Roy, didn't rise with the sun or even shortly after the sun. No stranger to hunger, having learned to eat lean in the past months when Aileen managed my meals, I waited. I lay next to Rose who jiggled beside me. She wagged her tail, put her nose in my ear, licked my lips, pawed my shoulder, then all of a sudden she was on my back attacking me! I turned over to scrape her belly with my paws, and then, despite the pain, the hunger and the exhaustion, she and I wrestled together on the ground like puppies.

CHAPTER 16
KNOW YOUR PACK I

My jaw took a season to heal – it stopped itching by mid-fall – but my hip stayed tender through to the next spring. The hard pebble-like shot under my skin became tough knots that ached in damp weather. Except for the first month when my hip throbbed painfully, my injuries didn't limit my mobility too much. I adjusted to life in camp.

Rose floated through life naturally happy with a wagging tail, and I stuck close to her. Every morning she'd wake me with a cold nose and a playful head butt, and I'd growl or nip in return. No matter how many times I snapped or warned her, her cheerfulness overcame my grumpiness, and we'd end up tangled together in a wrestling match, rolling and jumping and yelping around the shelter site. Only occasionally did we land on Tank and just twice collapsed the shelter on Critter and Jacky.

Rose reminded me of Lila, though she didn't fight with the same ferocity. And rather than competitive and pushy, I felt warm and tingly with her. This warm sensation swelled from my chest and tingled all the way down to my paws, but it wasn't like the arousal or the pressing urge to couple I'd felt when I'd encountered other females during my midnight ramblings near Lana's. From my first scent of her, I knew that Rose could never have puppies, but that didn't change my feelings. In the universe of the 'man camp, Rose was the sun around which I revolved.

Like the sun, Rose shone her light on everyone, 'man and dog. She threw herself happily at her pack, no hesitations.

I didn't understand. The 'mans didn't deserve my trust. I'd broken out of Roy's prison to escape 'mans and in no way wanted to rely on Rose's pack. If Rose would leave with me, strike out on our own, we could make a life for ourselves. But she loved her 'mans. Wouldn't leave.

When I'd been injured, Rose had spent every night curled up next to me under the stars. But as soon as I recovered, she left to sleep on the pallet with Critter and Jacky. Why was she in league with them? Her devotion didn't make sense. A member of their pack, yes, but surely her allegiance must be food-based. I'd certainly grown attached to those foil packets that hit the ground with a satisfying splat.

I missed her, wanted her body curled around mine. Instead I had Tank, who lay down next to me every night, too close, so that I huffed and groaned and removed myself. Way too close.

I could have joined her in the tent, I suppose. But anything with four walls, even flimsy fabric, felt like a cage. I couldn't sleep in there.

I looked forward to the early mornings, which we often had to ourselves, when we braved the loud roars and screeching beasts to cross the asphalt highway. Most mornings we left only for a quick stretch and recon mission, but on some days we'd be gone from sunup to sundown. We spent hours roaming the mountains and creeks that bordered the city.

Eyes only for Rose, I followed her everywhere. Occasionally I sensed an odd familiarity to the land, as if I'd been there before. Perhaps during my injured trek with Rose, or perhaps close to my homeland where Mama and Lila might still live. I could never tell exactly; I'd left Mama's home so long ago and had only foggy memories of the journey to the 'man camp.

When one morning we emerged from a stand of trees and into

a clearing, a familiar scent of rotten garbage and food, rusty iron, and motor oil swept over me in a wave and stopped me dead in my tracks. I stood in the field where I'd played with Lana. Across the creek lay the home on blocks and the cage where I'd been locked up.

I sniffed the air, hackles high. No scent of Lana. The cage was vacant of all but dead weeds, the gate flung open wide. No Black Devil Beast, no Roy. His face leapt into my mind, ugly with rage the last time I'd seen him.

I snarled. I paced stiffly and remembered Lana at the bottom of the porch. I whined. I growled again. Suddenly Rose shoulder-checked me, licked my face, and tore off into the woods. I followed her, my beacon, slowly and heavily at first, and then, as we moved into the trees and she bounced through the shadows like a coyote hunting mice, I shifted into an easy lope, caught up with her and started a game of chase.

Our day trips were simply larks. We'd follow a fox scent, then happen upon some deer, splash through a few creeks, and roll on a dead animal if we were lucky. We explored aromatic compost piles, plastic bags loosely tied and tossed on the sides of roads, the discarded bones of creatures long dead. I spent our time together trying to earn her allegiance. Rose was the reason I stayed in camp; I felt no loyalty to her 'man pack. 'Mans be damned, I tried to get her to leave with me. But she always returned to camp, and I couldn't quit her.

We'd trot back in the late afternoon or evening, and she'd wriggle with happiness to greet Critter or Jacky. I'd watch from a safe distance to see if dinner were forthcoming. Even if I'd eaten well, which, despite the diversity of offerings was rare, I always wanted food. We never had food in such abundance that I could skip a meal, and I never knew how much I'd get the next time or when it would be coming.

The 'mans attended feedings at the Mission, a large somber cement building near the camp where they'd stand in lines with crowds of other 'mans, all waiting for food. Rose and I weren't allowed inside. We'd hang out with the other dogs and search for scraps in the shadows of a large metal container ripe with decaying food and 'man waste.

Once, after the 'mans had gone into the Mission for a meal, I led Rose into a park far from the 'man camp. A large park with tall trees, large green fields and scattered benches occupied here and there by city 'mans, we found a large hole, a den of sorts, big enough for both of us to climb inside and sniff around. Tucked into the thick hedging that bordered a small fountain, it smelled of pine needles and the stale waste of a mammal that I couldn't identify.

I lay down and curled into a ball. The ground felt soft and warm compared to the chill in the air, and I whined for Rose to join me. *Leave your 'mans,* I wanted to tell her. *Let's stay here.* She sniffed my head then looked back towards the camp and whined softly. I grumbled and shifted. She pranced around me nervously in the tight space then lay down behind me and began nibbling on my ear. I leaned back into her, content.

I had the only thing I wanted. Rose. No 'mans. No 'man shelters. No Trouble.

I drifted dreamily off to sleep but woke to the cold piercing my back. Rose had gone. I sniffed the air and whined. She appeared before me and barked once then leapt away and looked back invitingly. She pranced towards the camp then returned and barked once more. My stomach growled, and as I watched her turn and trot away again, I slowly rose to join her. She wasn't going to leave her 'mans. I followed her back to the 'man camp.

Critter, whose scent of damp leaves and soot paired well with omnipresent camp 'man smell of urine, Trouble and unwashed bodies, didn't like to share the food he brought back from the Mission. He made a show of eating in front of us and giggled at the drool that dangled from our lips. He acted almost puppy-like despite his long gray beard, leathery face and missing teeth. He poked, happy and laughing, at Jacky or Rose, until they turned on him or left to find another place to sleep.

When one of his moods struck him, Critter threw tantrums that put any pup to shame, yelping, weeping and whining to anyone or anything that'd listen. It didn't take much to set him off – a hard word, a noisy neighbor, a dog that looked at him the wrong way. Sometimes, however, he'd act up to the wrong person, and he'd come back battered and beaten, as if his mouth weren't already missing enough teeth. He'd whimper and cry and fall asleep curled around his bottle.

Critter wasn't violent or cruel, despite his taunting and tantrums. He loved on Rose. She never growled when he clasped his arms around her neck and never snapped when he dragged his face close to hers. I couldn't understand how she let him wrap himself around her like that. On occasion, I tried to separate them, wielding my nose like a wedge. But Critter pushed me away, and even Rose snapped at me, annoyed. I paced around them, huffing.

For all that Critter was small, Tank was big. And where Critter chattered noisily like a squirrel, Tank lurked silently like a bear. His size drew attention. If he were walking, 'mans reacted to him in the same way they reacted to me, with wide eyes and a tight grasp on their bags or children. They'd swing wide in an arc around us rather than pass by directly.

Tank carried a silent pack inside him that only he could see or hear. One minute he'd be sitting silently, then suddenly he'd be on his feet arguing, gesturing wildly, no one else around. His pack mainly stayed hidden, but once they got out, it took a while for Tank to come back alone. He'd sit and whisper with his shoulders hunched, frown, shake his head and wrinkle his brow. He'd shout out loudly and make a fist, ignoring other 'mans around him completely. He became unpredictable, and everyone in camp left him alone, even Critter, who usually got in the way.

Though Tank had the size advantage, no one questioned that Jacky led the pack. She barked, and both 'mans and dogs sat up and listened. A top heavy 'man, built like a tree trunk, she balanced on stick-like bony legs swallowed by baggy pants. She walked as if one leg were shorter than the other, leaning to one side as she swung the other forward. Deep lines etched her rough face. Her voice, when she spoke, reminded me of a frog's croak.

"He ain't pretty, Suzy Q, but you hand-picked him outta some-where, dintcha." Jacky spoke loudly and laughed even louder. "I got me one of those too." She rapped her knuckle on Critter's head and cackled when he jolted up, a quick cackle that turned into a long bout with a thick, wet cough. She hacked and sucked air alter-nately, bending over as she braced herself on the ground where she sat, her hair a ragged veil over her eyes. After a while she cleared her throat, spit into the dirt, then sat back and ran her hand across her mouth.

"Y'all gonna give us some babies, Suzy? I got some babies, Suzy. I got six babies. But they's all grown now. My babies all grown." She lifted a bottle of Trouble from between her legs and drank heavily, grimacing as she finished. She wrapped her arms around her knees and rocked back and forth, quiet, except for the wheeze of her breathing.

Each day Jacky gave the pack marching orders, sending us out to earn money or food in the city. "Critter, you 'n Rose work the park. Tank, try 'n find a new tarp, it's beat to shit." She made sure that all gains of the day – be they coins or bills, food or Trouble – were distributed fairly.

One evening Jacky didn't come out of the shelter at feeding time. Critter begged her to get up, but he came out alone shaking his head. "She says she ain't eatin' tonight," he told Tank. He ordered us to sit with her then left with Tank for the Mission.

Rose and I stayed behind as Jacky took ragged breaths through her sunken, sallow face. She didn't speak but lay her hand on my head and every so often let out a low moan. Rose licked her face; I licked her hand. I tasted smoke and sickness and the layers of camp life. Despite being nested in cardboard and blankets, her hand felt like ice under my tongue. She mumbled unintelligibly.

Tank and Critter returned, and Rose and I left to scrounge for food. A wailing police beast with red flashing eyes greeted us when we came back, two gun-laden 'mans standing thick and rigid beside it. A larger flashing beast – an ambulance – pulled up as we watched, and two 'mans exited quickly, leaving its mouth gaping open. They swarmed the yellow shelter and moved quickly around Jacky's prone figure.

I growled quietly and wanted Rose to leave camp with me. These new 'mans could only bring trouble, but she wouldn't follow. She ran to Critter, standing red-faced and lost, in the middle of the yellow shelter, surrounded by the invaders. He grabbed the arm of one of the 'mans. "She don't want to go to the hospital. She want to stay here."

The 'man looked at him and frowned. "Take your hand off of me." Critter removed his hand quickly. "She needs medical care, and she's not going to get it here. How long has she been sick like this?"

Critter's face crumpled. "She tol me she dint want no hospital. She want to stay here. Don't take her." His voice whined and pleaded.

The 'man shook his head. "She needs medical care to stabilize. Then she can decide what to do and where to go. But without help right now, she won't be making any decisions. She needs a hospital."

Critter shook his head and started sniffing. His voice sounded high and desperate. "Don't take her." He fell to his knees and grabbed hold of the man's lower legs. "Let me come. Take me too."

Another 'man took hold of Critter's forearm, pulling him up and away from the tent. Critter yanked his arm free and ran back to Jacky. He crouched by her feet and eyed the 'mans warily. This time the two 'mans with guns each grabbed him by an arm and lifted him away as he struggled. Rose barked and yapped in circles around them as they moved. I paced on the edge of the crowded shelter, growled and kept an eye on Rose. As two of the 'mans lifted Jacky onto a rolling bed, she moaned. Critter cried out and struggled. Rose danced around him, whining and yipping and tripping the 'mans up as they moved around the tiny space.

One of the 'mans kicked out at Rose, and *Law #4* kicked in.

Protect the Pack. I barked and charged them. A wooden club slammed into my shoulder, knocked me to the ground and stole the breath out of me.

I gasped for air but got back to my feet. Roy had dished out worse. I crouched and readied to launch again. Before I could spring, Tank grabbed my collar and yanked me up by my neck. He dragged me away from the tent as I gasped and hopped uselessly beside him. Critter screeched and wailed and Rose yipped and yapped, but Tank held firm until we reached a half wall where he let my front feet down but kept hold of my collar. The 'mans packed Jacky into the jaws of the ambulance beast and drove away.

Without Jacky, the 'man pack drifted aimlessly apart. Critter had eyes only for Trouble and pursued it in and out of camp with every staggering step through every waking minute. His good cheer disappeared into a melancholic gloom, and he sunk in on himself, curling into a ball on his cardboard bed and drinking heavily.

Tank left the yellow shelter and didn't return. Rose and I, out searching for food, found him sleeping in a doorway near the Mission, one foot bare and filthy. I nosed it – icy. He slowly opened one eye, then the other, and he stared at us, glassily, from underneath the cardboard and newspapers. "Keep it down," he said, though we were quiet. He frowned. "Shut your screeching. Momma says be quiet." He lay back down and whispered to himself until he quieted and his body twitched with sleep.

I wanted to leave but instead stuck by Rose, always Rose. She split her time between Critter and Tank, both drowning in a flood of Trouble. I didn't understand it.

We could do better on our own, without this 'man pack. Admittedly their smell made them more attractive than most, but in my experience, 'mans caused pain. And there was a shortage of food. I couldn't get enough, never enough. I knew Rose must be hungry too, and I tried to convince her to leave. Time and again, I'd lead her to the edge of the 'man camp and implore her to follow me out of there, but she never did. She'd just bark at me with a quick tail wag and turn back to the 'mans.

We scrounged for food, cruising neighborhoods at night – hit and miss as we knocked over silver metal cans in back alleys. We found enough to keep us alive until the day that Jacky limped slowly back into camp.

She clutched a plastic bag, wore a new heavy red coat and carried a distinctly sharp and sterile smell. Critter saw her and covered his face with his hands. Jacky limped into the yellow shelter and sat down gingerly on the blankets. Critter crawled over to her, put his head in her lap and began to sob with deep gulping breaths. "I thought you weren't coming back."

Tears rolled slowly down Jacky's face as she stroked his head. She lay down gingerly next to him. "I aint goin back there," she said. Rose licked both of their faces as I inspected the bag she'd brought. It held a pair of fluffy socks and several small plastic bottles that rattled when knocked about. The bag and its contents smelled like the new scent Jacky carried – strong and sharp. She closed her eyes, and Critter's gulping sobs slowed as they both fell asleep.

Once back, Jacky spent most of her time sitting in the yellow shelter or under the green tarp and again ensured that our spoils – whatever was gained from the day, be it the money that street 'mans threw into their cup, food from the Mission, or bottles of Trouble – were shared equally.

I cared nothing for the Trouble or money, however, focusing only on Rose and the food, the distribution of which was mostly reliable, and mostly enough.

CHAPTER 17
LEARN AND OBEY

Despite the importance of *Law #1*, and though I excelled at it, I quickly learned not to grab food out of the 'mans' hands. Critter talked like a squirrel between bites – nonstop chattering – and threw his arms out for emphasis, spitting crumbs and gesturing with his hands full. A quick lunge, and I could easily knock it down and scarf it up.

However, Critter would roar and chase me through camp, slapping my haunches with his bony hand, and banishing me from the shelter he and Jacky shared. Thus, food in-hand became off-limits, though any food on the ground was fair game. I kept a close eye and watched each bite intently, waiting to capitalize on any momentary lapse of focus.

Rose and I separately accompanied Critter or Tank onto the streets of the city adjacent to camp. For hours we lay on cardboard or a thin blanket in winter, expected to remain silent beside Tank or Critter. If someone threw a coin into the cup, Tank nodded his head, and I wagged my tail. I applied myself to this task easily; I'd spent a lot of my life at Lana's sleeping and waiting.

I found it tricky, however, to learn when to hold back my growl. Most 'mans around us lived in the camp themselves and carried the layered scents of camp life – grimy skin, unwashed clothes, Trouble, sickness, and a variably strong scent of urine. Following Rose's lead, I growled at anyone with camp scents.

But outside of camp, growling at the non-camp folk – those reeking of perfume or food, those who threw money into our cup or walked by us on the streets – was expressly forbidden. Critter and Tank had a no-tolerance rule for growling at the sparkly sweet people who swarmed the streets around us.

I lived with a sense of unease for another reason; I hadn't been able to apply all my laws. *See Food, Eat Food* always applied, of course. And *Law #3* was clear – Rose, was my pack. Thus *Law #4 – Protect the Pack –* was automatic.

But *Law #2: Know Your Name* remained elusive. Critter called me Big Dog. Tank liked Sarge, and Jacky preferred Suzy's Boyfriend. I wanted a simple name, a reliable one. Without it I felt ungrounded, on alert at all times in case they threw one of my names into conversation. However, when I finally received my name, it came at such a moment of confusion that I didn't realize it at first.

I lay curled, a damp cold soaking my bones, on a blanket on the sidewalk next to Tank who was leaning against a cement wall beneath a large overhang on a drippy gray and wet day. Dozy after an early morning jaunt with Rose, a familiar scent shocked me awake. Smoke sticks, lilac and a mild scent of apples.

Lana.

I whipped my head up to sniff the air but she stood in front of me, holding a wriggling 'man pup in her arms, her mouth open and her eyes wide and fixed on me like an unguarded hamburger in a bus stop. My heart exploded with happy yips and body wiggles, and before I could think, I leapt on her.

Lana squeaked. She stumbled backwards on the sidewalk, and the 'man pup in her arms shrieked. Tank yanked me roughly by the collar and pulled me to the pavement. His fear filled my nostrils as he scolded me and held me flat to the ground, glancing from me to Lana.

"What'chu doing, hound? None of that." He held me firm to the cement and shook his head. "None of that."

I whined and whimpered. *Lana.*

I struggled and twisted, ears flat on my head. *Please let me touch her.*

He kept me pinned to the ground, then Lana suddenly dropped to her knees in front of both of us, eyebrows pinched, eyes shining. She gazed at me then smiled at Tank. The 'man pup struggled in her arms and struck her ear with a thrashing hand. She grabbed his hand and pointed at me with it. I panted.

"Duke." Lana's voice shook.

I whined. The little 'man in her arms kicked her in the ribs as she gazed at me with a stricken face. Her eyes shifted to Tank. "He was mine," she said quietly. "He used to be my dog."

Tank stiffened, and I caught a second whiff of fear. His hand tightened on my collar. Lana smiled, shook her head and touched my heaving ribcage. It felt like fresh straw under my body – soft, comforting, warm.

"Don't worry," she told Tank softly. "He's not mine anymore."

My writhing stilled when Lana's hand stroked my ribcage. She scratched my ears at the base where they itch so badly. The 'man pup pulled his fingers from his mouth and kicked his legs again as he reached for me. He patted my head with hard baby taps. I closed my eyes.

"I couldn't go back," she whispered. She ran her hand along my scars, the pocked and faded wounds on my hip, the jagged scar above my eye, the long thin line across my jaw. She looked older, weathered. Her face had filled out, less angular, almost puffy. Her eyes hadn't changed – a friendly and kind brown flecked with green. My heart flipped as they met mine. I whined.

Do I go with Lana? What do I do? Who's my pack?

Tank's grasp loosened slightly and his fear scent receded. I wriggled forward, belly on the cement. I put my nose on Lana's thigh and licked her arm as her hand stroked my head. We sat there, Lana stroking my head, Tank holding my collar, the 'man pup kicking and patting both Lana and me.

"He's a good dog, isn't he?" Lana looked to Tank who nodded solemnly and ducked his head. He kept his eyes on the pavement. "I called him Duke. What do you call him?"

Tank pursed his lips and frowned but didn't say anything.

"Wolf!" The 'man pup kicked his feet excitedly.

"He's not a wolf, Carl."

"Wolf!" The 'man pup screeched the word.

Tank stared at the ground and spoke quietly with his deep voice. "He gets called lots of names. Wolf ain't a bad one."

Lana's knees were wet from the pavement, her back damp with rain dripping from the overhang. Carl wriggled and fussed in her arms, and her eyes shifted from me to him then Tank. She carried a tattered bag across her shoulders. Her clothes looked worn and smelled like stale bodies and smoke sticks. I tried to wriggle closer to her, but there wasn't much room on the sidewalk to move without pushing her and the 'man pup out into the beast path. 'Mans streamed behind Lana in loud groups or quiet singles.

Lana looked at Tank, her eyes filled with tears. I whined again. The 'man pup threw himself towards me as Lana shifted him onto a different hip, but she held fast to him.

"Mine!" He reached his arms out, and Lana struggled to keep him still. He smelled a lot like Lana but carried a bit of camp smell on him – urine and unwashed skin – overlaid with his own spicy scent, something like pepper. I sneezed, and he jolted in her arms then started to cry.

Lana laughed, a beautiful, bubbling sound. She wiped her eyes as she stood then sniffed and rocked Carl who fussed and fidgeted on her hip. Twisting the bag round her shoulders, she rummaged her hand around inside it until she came up with a small zipper pouch which she pulled out and opened.

Treats?

I hadn't smelled any, but what else could it be?

I writhed frantically. Tank loosened his grip but maintained his hold. As I rose to my feet and nosed her thigh, she reached into the pouch and pulled out a green bill. I lifted my nose to sniff it then dropped my head, disappointed. *No treats.* Money.

Lana held her hand out to Tank who stared unmoving at the folded green bill. "Take this, please. For him. For you."

Tank didn't speak or move. He looked at her silently, and I was confused. Our whole purpose on the streets was to gather money. *Why didn't he take it?* Granted, paper money was rare. Maybe he wanted coins.

She thrust her hand closer to him. Tank sat rigidly on the sidewalk. His jaw shifted back and forth, and his forehead creased as if in concentration. I licked his hand, and his body jumped slightly. He slid his eyes to Lana and the 'man pup, and his big hand released my collar. I leaned into Lana's legs.

"He got a girlfriend." Tank spoke slowly, gazing slightly away from Lana, still not acknowledging the token in front of his face. He patted my mangled hip with the buckshot scars and ran a finger along the scar on my chin. "She brought him to us, bunged up like this."

Lana's hand lowered, and her upper lip trembled. Her hair lay wet and flat on her head; her breath caught in tiny sobs. "I couldn't take him," she whimpered. "I had to leave, and I couldn't go back."

Tank nodded slowly. "Life don't always give us no choice."

Lana pinched her eyes shut, and she shuddered. Carl kicked his feet and bounced his body up and down on her left hip. "Wolf!" he cried as he threw his body sideways in her arms.

"Carl, stop!" Her voice held anger and sorrow, and it broke as she thrust the token at Tank. "Take care of him. He's a good dog, and he deserves a good life. A good family."

Then she crouched down once more, and I leaned into her shoulder and winced as the 'man pup patted my head heavily. Lana wrapped her arm around my neck and kissed my jaw. My body hummed happily. I licked her mouth, and we touched foreheads until she stood suddenly and shook her head.

"You're a good boy, Duke." She crumpled up the token and threw it at Tank. Then she turned her back quickly and walked away. I got up and began to follow, but at Tank's soft whistle I stopped. My heart clenched. Confused, I watched her leave. Carl's head swivelled back so that his eyes locked on mine as he retreated, and I whined.

Tank stood and watched them walk away. He stared at the token on the ground then studied me. He picked up the token, threw our blanket over his shoulders, and led us back to camp slowly as the rain continued to fall. Jacky and Critter sat under a tarp tending a fire, and Tank tossed the earnings to Jacky. Her eyes widened as she lifted the green bill.

"Wolf," Tank pronounced. "His name is Wolf."

CHAPTER 18
GRETCHEN

My empty, grumbling stomach woke me early, but it was the feel of Tank's body curled up against mine that jerked me awake. I bolted away, turned and stared. He slept on. Why had he been there? I felt more settled with my new name, but close contact still made me nervous. Lana had wanted companionship. Roy had wanted me gone. What did Tank want? Or Critter, or Jacky?

I stretched slowly and left Tank lying on the tarp behind me as I stuck my head into the tent. Rose wagged her tail and stood up, licked my muzzle and stepped outside. I leaned into her shoulder. We trotted quietly through the camp, the sun not even a suggestion in the sky.

As Jacky stayed sick and got sicker, our food supply had become hit or miss, mostly miss. Last night I'd heard the clanking of metal cans in the neighboring streets, and I woke knowing that we should hit them first thing. Hitting the food cans at the right time required proper timing. Too early, and there might not be enough to make it worth our while. Too late, and we risked sacrificing the cans to the loud, gaping-mouthed garbage truck that cruised the alleys. To add to the risk, the 'mans living in the houses weren't friendly, even those with their own dogs. Getting in and out quickly was essential.

Two cans sat on the first corner – one metal, and one softer and pliable. The metal cans had proven too loud for stealthy dining, so I rose up with my front legs on the softer can and sniffed the lid.

Bones!

I pushed the can over roughly. Rose danced around me as it rolled, waiting for the lid to fall off. It stayed fixed. I pounced on it, and my weight caved the side in. Rose pounced on it once, then twice, then a third time. No luck.

I sniffed the can. Definitely bones. If we couldn't get the lid off, we'd have to try another. My empty stomach rumbled. Rose whined. A dog barked nearby. I paced back and forth before jumping again on the can. This time the lid popped off and rolled down the alley. Rose dove into it headfirst and rooted around then emerged with a chicken carcass. I lunged into the can and withdrew a large mass of meat and fluff wrapped in paper.

We took turns, ripping apart bags and searching for goodies. Exhausting the first one, we headed to the next can in the alley and repeated the process in a rare morning of abundance. By the time we finished the first line of cans, the sun peeked above the horizon and the big beast clanked several blocks down the alley, its gaping mouth heading towards us and swallowing up the cans' contents.

As I lifted my head out of a can, mashing down on the remains of a delicious type of sandwich, the back door to the house behind us opened. "Damn dogs!" A 'man in a fluffy loose garment burst off the porch and ran across the yard towards us. "Out! Get out of here!" She yowled like a cat doused with water and carried a broom above her head as she ran.

I bolted away and barked at Rose who jumped to my side. The 'man opened the yard's back gate and ran at us. We headed towards camp. As we passed the next house, a back door opened, and a large black dog came running out barking.

A challenge! Large and black, with short fur, a round head and droopy ears that flew behind him, he confronted us at the back fence. Rose and I tore down the fence line with him, the three of us barking and snarling and snapping and having great fun. We reached the end of his yard, and he stopped, his face sad. I turned back and looked at the fence line. The 'man in the robe, her face red and twisted, had gained on us. We ran back anyways, much to the joy of the black dog who ran with us, growling and barking. As we neared the 'man in the fuzzy garment, she took a swing with the broom but missed. Quickly we turned back and ran again, the dog snarling alongside us.

We left him where his fence ended, his cry following us as we tore through a gauntlet of dogs trapped in their yards and hollering their frustrations. A long-haired skinny dog ran shrieking off his porch to challenge us at the back fence. A tiny dog with a smashed face joined in as we approached the next yard. The neighborhood rose to the occasion, and we raced as many dogs, snarling and snapping, as we could. The yowling was deafening and exhilarating, a neighborhood alarm clock for the ages.

We panted at the end of the alley. Behind us 'mans were bending over fallen cans and picking up scattered items. The large beast clanked and rumbled, consuming everything thrown into it as two 'mans in blue ran to and from its gaping side. Rose leaned into my shoulder, and we trotted away from the alley, a howling of loss in our wake.

After a mid-afternoon nap, I pushed a large grasshopper around the camp with my nose, following it around the shelter site. Rose had gone to the streets with Tank, and I'd been waiting for her return. So much of my life involved waiting. For the past few years I'd been waiting for Rose to leave with me for a better life, but a recent event had made me question myself.

We'd suffered an invasion, the camp attacked by 'mans who rolled through like Trouble-filled torrents of destruction. They erupted off the streets, flowed into our camp like lava and destroyed everything in their path. Carrying iron bars and rough wooden clubs, they swung them into tents and smashed them into shopping carts. Their sole purpose seemed to be destruction; they didn't take anything. They tread on belongings and spat at, or worse, attacked the camp 'mans as they crawled out from under the shelters as they fell.

As the invaders approached our site, *Law #4* kicked in. I ran to protect Rose, my pack, standing stiff-legged in front of the tent with bared teeth and raised hackles. She snapped at me with a frustrated whine, and I fell back in surprise. Why did she push me away?

She ran over to Tank as the attackers drew nearer. I followed and took a defensive position near her. She again gave me a frustrated bark then moved back to the tent where Critter and Jacky slept.

I started to follow but saw two attackers, hoods pulled tightly over their heads, inching towards Tank. A surge of anger rose in my chest, and something loosened inside of me.

Tank. They wanted to hurt Tank.

I suddenly realized that my pack had grown bigger than Rose. Tank had never hurt me; in fact he'd been kind. Critter and Jacky had never hurt me.

Tank was my 'man! Critter and Jacky were my pack!

I puffed out my chest and snarled savagely in front of Tank wrapped like a sausage in his blanket. One of the attackers looked like a toad, with big blue eyes, a sweaty face and wide thick lips, while the other resembled a fox, with a sharp nose and a thin face.

"Not worth it, dude," fox-face said, looking me over. "Plenty of others. Remember, hit and run. Time to get out of here."

Rose and I charged, and they bolted quickly away from us and our 'mans. She returned to the front of the tent, and I went back to Tank, sniffed him and lay down cautiously. My tongue darted out to lick his hand, and I curled up next to him and inhaled his earthy, Trouble-laden scent. For the first time in years, I felt at home.

. . .

"Good afternoon."

My head jolted up from the grasshopper I'd been tailing around our shelter. A young 'man, her hair pulled into a tail on the back of her head, stood at the outer edge of our shelter site, a clipboard in her hands and small pack tightly affixed to her back. Grasshopper forgotten, I barked a warning then approached her stiff-legged with a low rumble in my throat. She wore jeans and a puffy jacket that looked like a 'man's sleeping bag. Her eyes widened and she stopped.

I circled her.

"Goodness, ha ha, he's a big dog. Is he friendly?" The new 'man held her hand out, and I sniffed it quickly – flowery with a twinge of citrus. I saw an opening for a good two-legged face massage and thrust my nose into the gap between her legs.

"Whoa! Hah!" The 'man laughed and backed away from me. "Really friendly!"

She pushed my head down as I moved towards her again, and Jacky shouted from inside the shelter. "Wolf, back off! Keep your nose outta her nasty!"

Jacky called me into the tent then slapped my hindquarters. I huffed at her and growled quietly while she patted the pallet on which she lay. "Wolf, git down here." She coughed roughly, her breath catching in a wheeze. Critter had wandered away, and she sat alone in the small space.

"My name's Gretchen," the 'man said.

I ignored Jacky and circled the stranger again, sniffed the air and discovered a delicious scent floating down from the pack on her back. I lay down between them and kept an eye on her, particularly the pack.

The 'man looked at the board. "I'm looking for Jacqueline Williams. Is that you?"

Jacky ran her eyes up and down the 'man. "Who's askin? Are you a cop?"

The 'man smiled. "No, I'm an outreach worker with Hospice.

I'm following up on a referral from the hospital. Can we talk about the next few months?"

Critter stumbled over me as he entered the shelter and sat at Jacky's feet on the pallet. He reeked strongly of Trouble and wobbled upright. "Hotspits? Wazzat?"

Jacky's eyes darted to Critter. Her mouth twisted. Her shoulders shuddered, and she sank lower on the pallet. She looked at the 'man, and her eyes flashed an emotion that brought Lana to my mind and made me uneasy – *fear*. I looked at the stranger with a new wariness, and, low and soft, my growl filled the silence.

Jacky nodded. "Okay. Let's talk. But call me Jacky." She looked at me. "Wolf, cut it."

I cut off my growl. Critter hooted. "You call her Jaqueline, and no one's gonna know who you talking about."

Gretchen looked at them seriously then nodded then smiled. "Thanks. Are you Ronald Waters? Or," she looked at the board in her hands. "Gerald Mackay?"

"He's Gerald!" Jacky snorted. "But everyone calls him Critter."

Critter smiled happily and patted Jacky's leg.

"Sure thing." The 'man looked around the shelter, took the pack off her back and set it on the ground. She unstrapped a small, folded, metal contraption from the side of it then snapped and clacked the contraption together quickly. I stood up and backed away. *What new beast was this?*

She stopped. Her contraption had become a small metal stool with a webbed seat. I circled behind her, angled closer to the bag with the delicious food scent then lay back down.

"I hope you've recovered from the attack last week." The 'man unzipped the pack, and I fixed my eyes on her.

"I dint see nothing in the attack," Critter looked around the shelter and shook his head. "When I woke, all the tents were down and folks were beat and cryin."

"Shi-it. You and Tank never roused." Jacky chuckled. "Wolf and Suzy protected me while you two bozos slept it off."

"I ain't no bozo." Critter narrowed his eyes at Jacky. "I just sleep hard."

Jacky cackled. "Sleep hard? Passing out ain't sleeping!"

Critter started sputtering, and the 'man with the tail interrupted. "The newspaper said that they destroyed a number of tents and caused several injuries. Did you lose anything in the attack?"

Critter looked confused. "Lose anything?"

"Yes, did the attackers take anything of yours? Or destroy anything?"

Critter's eyes widened. "Ooh, now that you mention it, I lost a mickey of vodka."

Jacky guffawed, and the 'man smiled. "I was thinking more along the lines of personal belongings. I heard that tents and belongings were destroyed."

"Vodka is very personal to me," Critter said with a rise in his voice.

"Oh, leave it, Critter. She ain't bringin you no vodka!" Jacky shook her head sadly. "Shameless."

"Hee hee," Critter laughed and slapped his knee then stared at his hand. Then he looked up at the stranger and narrowed his eyes. "Why you here again?"

Jacky spoke in a gravelly voice. "We din't lose anything from the attack. I was awake but stayed in the tent and didn't see anything. I heard the dogs fighting and men yelling, and I know'd something was wrong. Dogs fighting ain't never no good."

"So you didn't lose anything either?"

"Nah, none of us did. Tank neither."

"Would that be Mr. Waters?"

"Yeah, that's Tank. He's out with Suzy right now."

"Suzy? Do you know her last name?"

"Hah! Suzy is Wolf's girlfriend!"

The 'man's eyes shifted to me. I met her eyes then shifted mine to the pack and back again. She looked down at the board in her hands.

"I guess that's why I don't have her name on my list." She smiled brightly and shifted some papers before lifting her eyes to Jacky.

"Jacky, do you remember talking to the doctor about hospice?"

Jacky's eyes shifted nervously to Critter then back to the 'man. "I was doped up, but I remember something about it."

"I'm part of the hospice team that you might have talked about. I'm here to follow up. We've got a lot to cover, but we can stop whenever you want to. And I'll be visiting regularly."

Jacky nodded and Critter whined. "What is she talking about?" He hiccupped and tilted his head back to regard the 'man suspiciously.

"Critter, this sickness ain't gonna get no better."

"What? Jacky you shut up."

"Critter, I ain't goin nowhere. I'll be here as long as I can. That's what this lady is for. If I don't talk to her now, they'll just take me away when I can't stand up for myself no more. And you'll never see me again."

Critter put his head in his hands and leaned forward on his knees. "No. No. No. No. No. NO!" He shook his head and looked defiantly at Jacky. "You talk to her all you want, but you ain't goin nowhere. And I'm leavin." He stood up too quickly and fell back onto the pallet, landing on Jacky's legs with an *oof*.

I jumped up as Jacky swore and slapped Critter's shoulder. The 'man stood up and held her hand down to Critter. I inched closer to the pack to sniff it and give the outside a quick lick. Definitely meat, maybe chicken, inside. But impenetrable. I snuffled the pack and nosed it around a bit to see if there was a hidden opening. No luck.

"I'm going to take notes while we talk," the 'man said after Critter tottered outside. "There are a number of things that I'd like to talk with you about. The first of which is that you are in charge of your care. As long as you are not incapacitated…."

"Inca-what?" Jacky interrupted, and I startled. I must have been falling asleep.

"Incapacitated. Of sound mental status. As long you're of sound mental status, I can help you put together a Care Plan including directions for your care in case you can't make those decisions later. So it's important that while you're still healthy enough, you make decisions about the future.

My eyelids grew heavy. I set my chin on the pack and closed them.

CHAPTER 19
FLASHING BEASTS

I woke to the whoosh of red fur and Rose's waggling body tumbling around me. Her paw swiped my muzzle, and she leapt onto my shoulders. Straightening my legs beneath me I shook, and she fell to her back then quickly jumped up and sprang onto my head. I dumped her again and growled while she bunny-kicked me from below. Side to side, I lunged at her throat, and she twisted and turned until she scrambled out from under me. She grabbed a red, knotted t-shirt, looked in my direction, wagged her tail once, and ran away.

Chase!

I vaulted over Tank. Rose and I zig zagged through camp - she the prey, I the pursuer. Each time I narrowed in on her, she'd jolt into reverse, and I'd shoot past her, growling and scrabbling and unable to stop until she'd already switched directions. We ran through other shelter sites. Leaping over prone bodies became part of the game. A few other camp dogs joined in the scramble, and there were soon four to five of us chasing each other through the shelter sites, leaping over bodies and scrambling for purchase on slippery tarps.

On one of Rose's reversals, I snapped my teeth around the fabric in her mouth and yanked it free. It flew in the air over my shoulder and landed at the feet of a sharp-nosed dog named Spider. I roared and took off after him as he picked it up and ran.

I pulled alongside him and had almost grasped the fabric when the ear-splitting wail of a beast sounded and stopped us all in our tracks. Its sharp sound pierced my ear drums. Spider dropped the rag and howled. Rose yapped, and I lifted my throat to the skies and joined them.

A wailing beast jerked to a stop on the outskirts of camp and flashed its eyes angrily. Its yowl screeched to a halt as two 'mans exited. They swarmed like ants around the back of their beast and opened its mouth. I snuck over to snatch the rag back from Spider who looked at me in surprise but didn't put up a fight. Ears flat, he ducked his head then skulked back to his shelter site.

Gretchen, who had been a regular visitor to camp for several months, had arrived earlier and ran out quickly to speak with the 'mans at the back of their beast. Rose and I followed her excitedly. She ignored us and led the two 'mans towards our shelter. One carried a bag, and the other led a flat metal gurney with long rolling legs. Tank stood outside the shelter, a deep frown creating furrows in his brow. He shook his head and held his hands over his ears.

Gretchen looked him in the eye. "Mr. Waters, Jacky asked me to call for medical care. I'm taking them into the shelter."

Tank nodded, side-eyed, but said nothing. He walked away from her and the shelter entrance.

"Sick, sick." He muttered and stared blankly as I approached. "No medicine."

I wagged my tail and licked his hand. He jolted and looked at me with his brows furrowed and mouth pursed.

"It's no use, Wolf." He said quietly. "No use." He sat down under the tree near the shelter, wrapped his arms around himself and began to rock back and forth slowly. I lay down at his feet and put my head on my paws.

Critter's voice rose in a high pitch from inside the shelter. "It's too early. She's not ready. It's not time."

Gretchen responded in low, gentle tones. Her voice was sooth-ing, but Critter's continued to get louder.

"Jacky. Jacky! Tell them. Tell them you stayin here."

Jacky moaned, and Critter cried out. The tent shifted as figures inside the small space moved around.

"Jacky, tell them."

"No, Critter." I barely heard Jacky's whisper over the commo-tion in the shelter.

"Jacky!" Critter gasped and a whimper caught in his throat.

"I'm done, Critter. I ain't good no more. Let me go."

Critter shrieked, and his pleading turned into a ragged sobbing. "No, Jacky. No! Don't leave. Please, Jacky. Please, Gretchen. Gretchen!"

Tank moaned softly next to me. Gretchen exited the shelter, her arm around Critter whose body shook and trembled. Rose ran to him and whined as he collapsed into a pile. Gretchen turned back to the shelter as one of the 'mans started backing out, wheeling the metal bed.

Jacky lay on it, wide straps circling her shrunken body. The 'mans stopped as they exited, and Jacky turned her head. Her eyes were open but dull. Her face softened as Tank and I rose to approach her. Critter beat on the ground with his fists.

"I got nothin left, Tank. I can't fight no more." Her voice rasped in a heavy, tired whisper.

Critter groaned, and I nosed Jacky's hand lying on the beast beside her. She scratched my nose with one finger but kept her eyes on Tank. Rose nudged her way into the circle and licked my face before licking Jacky's hand.

Tank nodded and when he spoke, his deep voice broke.

"We all got a time to go." He said softly. "You know better than any of us."

From the ground, Critter sobbed. Tank looked down at Jacky and wiped his arm across his face.

"This world is full of hurting, Jacky, but you ain't never hurt me. And I don't want you to hurt." He sniffed and leaned down to kiss Jacky's forehead. "Go, sister. Don't hurt no more."

Jacky's face was wet and pinched as Tank stepped away.

"Critter," she said.

"No." he whimpered from the ground. "Why? You hurtin me now, Jacky. What do I do without you?"

"Critter." She repeated. "Get up."

Critter got up slowly, his face wet and red, his beard streaked with dirt. His shoulders shook and his mouth formed a jagged gash in his face. He wrung his hands and looked as if he might crumple in on himself.

"Critter, I know you."

Critter pinched his eyes shut and shook his head back and forth. His breath came in ragged gasps. Tears ran down his cheeks and into his beard.

Jacky shuddered then took a raspy breath. "You a big man inside that little body, Critter. And I love you big man." She coughed and caught her breath. "I aint leavin you for good. I'm gonna wait for you on the other side, that's all. And when you get there, we gonna party."

Critter's face squeezed tight; his body shook with sobs. He grabbed Jacky's hand then brought his lips to it and kissed it. He laid his head on Jacky's chest. "You my world, Jacky. What do you want me to do?"

"Let me go, Critter." She put her hand on Critter's head and closed her eyes. "I gotta go now."

Critter whimpered but lifted his head and took a step back. Gretchen nodded, and the 'mans moved Jacky away. I followed and watched as they loaded her into the mouth of the ambulance. Rose joined me as the other 'man climbed into the beast and woke it. It grumbled, flashed its eyes then began wailing and left us standing on the edge of the camp.

We walked slowly back to our shelter site. I spied the knotted shirt that we had tousled over just a short while ago, and I walked past it. I didn't want it anymore.

CHAPTER 20
AFTERMATH

Critter devoted himself to Trouble and the pursuit of it. That wasn't unusual – I'd witnessed it for years. But I'd also been in camp long enough to know that the search for Trouble required money, and that money came from work on the street. But neither Critter nor Tank had ventured out on the street for money in the aftermath of Jacky leaving, and it created problems. Immediately after Jacky left, most camp 'mans shared Trouble willingly with Critter. A few days later, however, they began complaining.

"When you sharing with us, Critter?"

"Hey, how come you only asking for booze but ain't bringin' any?"

Critter stumbled from one site to the next and one afternoon found a pack of young 'mans willing to share a bottle. It was a younger and rowdier pack than usual, not one he or Tank normally visited, but he sat down with a happy smile.

"I 'preciate it." Critter nodded at the young 'man pack. "I miss the old lady." He sniffed, and his eyes grew red and watery.

"Sure thing, old man," one of the 'mans spoke and handed Critter a brown bag wrapped around a bottle. "Have a swig of our special sauce."

Critter grabbed the bag eagerly and tipped it to his mouth,

throwing his head back to drink. Almost immediately he spit the liquid out in a wide spray, threw the bottle to the ground and dropped to his knees, retching. I sniffed the empty bottle – urine – and drew my head back sharply. I'd seen a dog or two sample the stuff, but I'd never seen a 'man drink it. Nothing wrong with the practice, just not a fan myself.

Critter sputtered. His face turned a mottled purple as the 'man pack howled with laughter. Critter frowned and clenched his hands. I tensed. He shouted angrily then dove, fists flailing, on top the 'man who had handed him the Trouble. The 'mans formed a circle around the two on the ground.

I barked in surprise but didn't know who to target, so I hopped around the outside of the circle growling and barking while trying to figure it out. Fights in camp could start and end quickly. Lots of bark but usually not a lot of bite.

Critter stumbled out and landed on his back in the dirt. I ran to him. His face was red and splotchy, his beard wet. He pushed me aside, leapt back into the middle of the circle and lunged at the pack leader who shoved him hard with a shout. *Law #4* kicked in, and I dove into the circle next to him. Critter lurched sideways, and the circle of 'mans widened as he staggered and fell.

"Shame!" Critter looked tiny. He spit at them from his hands and knees. I prepared for an attack and stood next to him, curling my lips and flashing my teeth. His head came to my shoulder. "Shame on you!"

Critter stood up, and a 'man shoved him. Then another. I grabbed a pant leg. He toppled and fell. As he went down, the circle closed in, and he and I were trapped below a mass of moving legs. A foot kicked him, and he shrieked. A hard elbow crashed into my nose, then a boot kicked me in the ribs. I snapped at the hand then grabbed the meaty flesh of someone's calf and bit down. The 'man screamed as if I'd grabbed him by the throat.

"Agh! Get him off me!" He fell to the ground and kicked out at me with his free leg. I let go and growled. "The dog! Get him away from me!"

The circle of 'mans separated, and a second boot kicked me in the ribs. The wind rushed out of my lungs, and I gasped for breath, my eyes on the 'mans. I growled and snapped in their direction then headed towards Critter who was curled up on the ground moaning with his hands over his head. He didn't look up. His face was splotchy and wet, his beard full of snot and dirt. I growled and licked his face.

The 'mans backed off. One 'man rocked back and forth on the ground and held his leg. Another held a wooden bat in his hands and silently watched me.

Critter lifted his eyes, shook his head and patted my neck.

"I got no use for humans no more, Wolf. I'm done." He pushed himself up to his hands and knees. His body shook, but he stood and looked sadly at the silent, staring 'man pack. His face, red and puffy, glistened with sweat and tears. Streaks of dirt had turned to mud in his beard.

"You ain't no better than me." He shook his finger at the 'man pack and blinked his eyes. "Just younger. You all shit."

"He bit me." The 'man on the ground pointed at me with an angry jab, his face ruddy and bloated. His finger shook.

I growled.

Critter ignored him. "You shit." He pointed at the 'man who had handed him the bottle. "You shit." He pointed at the man that just spoke.

"You shit, too. Fact is, you all shit. And you all stink. I'm done with you."

"Don't come back here looking for booze, old man," the pack leader said. "We got our own troubles and don't want your cryin'. We're tired of you."

Critter limped out of their site with his head down. I followed slowly, nursing my ribs which ached. Other packs watched us silently as we made our way back through camp to our shelter site. I tailed Critter into the tent where he lay on his pallet, curled into a ball and shook. I paced in a circle then lay down next to him and watched the camp as the sun's shadows grew long.

. . .

Rose's cold nose in my ear woke me. *Food!* I lifted my head with a quick shake, sniffed the scent of Mission food on her lips then tasted it – a salty, smoky residue with a tinge of sweetness. She wriggled around me, and I finished and went to find Tank. He had food. I nudged his arm and licked his jacket. He laughed.

"Hungry, Wolf?" He chuckled and stared at me until I sat down. My back legs were trembling, and I licked my lips. My favorite part of the day. He told me to stay, so I sat straight up and watched him bend over and walk into the tent, Rose at his side.

What if he gave it all to Critter? What if he gave my food to Rose? I whined and shifted. As he backed out and turned towards me, a line of drool dripped slowly from my lower lip and fell onto my foot.

He opened a silver packet and threw it to the ground. I dove into the packet and inhaled. Salty, smoky, with a dash of sweetness, just like Rose. I licked the wrapper while Rose sniffed the ground around us. Tank sat on the ground and stroked my back, and my licking slowed. His fingers and hands were broad enough to knead both of my shoulders with one hand while the other worked my hips – a double doozie that made my knees weak.

I leaned into Tank's shoulder. He put his arm around my neck and rubbed his face against mine, nose to nose, eyes closed. I sighed and collapsed, my upper body on top of his legs, my haunches in the dirt. I rolled my back onto his thighs and bared my belly. My head hung backward over his knee, throat open to the sky.

"You okay, Wolf, you okay." His voice was deep but soft, a low pleasant growl. He scratched my stomach. "You big and you ugly, just like me." His legs shook as he laughed, and I rolled off my perch.

I got to my feet and shook off the dust. We stared into camp together. Small lights moved about shelters and tarps. Occasionally someone laughed or cried.

Rose danced out of the shelter and ran up to us. She sniffed my nose and jaw line carefully. Critter emerged. His face looked puffy and purple, his beard stiff. He threw a crumpled silver packet to the ground, which Rose and I ran over to inspect. I'd tried to chew these balls in the past but couldn't get through the metal. It hurt my teeth, and I could never reach the food. I left it. If Critter had left real food inside, he wouldn't have crushed it.

"Needin' some vladdy." Critter's voice was scratchy. He rubbed his face, eyes watery and red.

Tank nodded slowly. "Got enough for a fifth." He patted his pockets as if searching for something. I sat alert and watched his hands intently. Good things came from pockets. He stopped patting himself and stood stock still. My mouth began to water. His eyes widened, and he reached up to remove a small stick that had been carefully tucked behind his ear. He put the stick between his lips, cocked his head sideways, then held a lighter up and puffed in and out a few times.

Sour smoke drifted through the air past me. "Man dropped this in the cup today." Tank handed the stick to Critter whose hands shook. I kept my eye on Tank's hands and pockets but lost interest. He and Critter passed the stick back and forth and smoked, but no treats appeared.

I sighed contentedly, lounging under the tree with an almost-full belly, watching the lights and bodies of the camp twinkle and rustle. Rose napped beside the tent and whimpered quietly as her feet jerked. After these past few years trying to get Rose to leave with me, I'd finally realized that this was home. My eyes grew heavy and were slowly closing when a beast approached the edge of camp.

Its flashing eyes roused me, but I heard no accompanying yowl. A sneaky police beast. I disliked these sneaky ones even more than those that rushed into camp with their ear-piercing shrieks. The 'mans who arrived with these silent beasts usually cruised the camp shining bright lights in faces and taking away one or more camp 'mans when they departed.

Critter and Tank stood above me, watching the police 'mans walk into camp. I sniffed the air but couldn't detect anything unusual. Just the same old camp smell of unwashed bodies, disease, and Trouble with a hint of Tank's sour smoke stick.

Next to me, Rose roused. A moth flew across her line of vision, and she whipped her head and snapped it to the ground with a sudden lunge. It struggled to right itself while she nudged it up and over several times. It wriggled its legs and beat its wings furiously against the dust then sat still. Rose nosed it again, and the tiny legs gripped her nose so that the moth clung to the tip of it when she lifted her head.

Hah! I leapt forward and barked as she swung her head in circles until the moth fell to the ground.

"Why the hell they going there for?"

I followed Critter's eyes and saw the two police 'mans talking with the group of 'mans that Critter and I had visited earlier in the day.

"No good," Tank muttered. "Those folk are no good."

The moth was fluttering weakly now. Rose poked at it, and I shifted my gaze between the quivering wings and the police 'mans.

Police 'mans always traveled in twos. They reminded me of beetles – small heads and thick, stiff bodies that creaked like leather saddles. An assortment of heavy objects hung from their waists and swung as they walked. One of the 'mans held a long metal flashlight that he swung around the camp. It blinded me as it passed over us and was glad when it moved on. A short-lived happiness, however, because it returned and glared into my eyes.

Rose pushed at the moth a few more times, but it didn't move. She licked it, and I watched in surprise as it stuck to her tongue. She too seemed surprised because she shook her head and spit it out rapidly. It lay still on the ground. I sniffed it – musky, and slightly sour –and then sniffed Rose's mouth as she stretched it wide, licking her lips repeatedly. I sniffed the moth again and thought about eating it but wasn't encouraged by her reaction.

Wouldn't she have swallowed it if it were any good? I'd never tried to eat a moth. I scooped it up on my tongue.

"Good evening, men."

I turned quickly around and spit the moth to the ground. My tongue tingled, and I licked my lips then growled. The police 'mans walked into our shelter site. One was big, though smaller than Tank, with a broad face and what looked to be a dark caterpillar under his nose. The other was younger than his partner, with a swagger that belied the scent of fear he carried. It concerned me. Fearful animals attack, and I'd seen the damage that these police 'mans could do.

They approached Tank and Critter and cast their light around the site, flashing it over Tank's sleeping pallet and across Critter's tent and the tarps and circling back to me and Rose.

"Officers." Critter nodded and spoke stiffly.

I felt the eyes of the camp upon us. A small group of camp 'mans formed a wide circle of spectators. Tank said nothing. He flicked the lit end of the sour smoke stick to the ground then stuck the dead end in his pocket. He shifted from one foot to the other and looked down. He put his hands in his pockets.

The younger police 'man took a step back from Tank. His fear scent spiked. He put his hand on his belt and narrowed his eyes. "Please remove your hands from your pockets."

Tank hunched his shoulders and frowned. The 'man repeated himself louder. Tank's hands went to his head and clutched it like a basketball. His frown deepened.

The caterpillar police 'man spoke. "We've had several complaints about loose dogs in the neighborhood, and today we received a report that one of your dogs bit someone."

"How do you know they're our dogs?" Now the fear scent came from Critter.

The 'man looked at Critter. "Are these your dogs?"

Critter's voice rose as he responded. "Those dogs ain't bit no one." He shook his head back and forth quickly.

"One of those men has some pretty severe bruising on his leg."

126

The police 'man looked at both Rose and I, then settled his gaze on me. "He told me that it was this big dog right here." He pointed his light at me, and I blinked and growled. "The one with the scars."

Get that light out of my eyes.

Police 'mans didn't bring good things to camp.

Critter waved his hands at the 'man camp. "They attacked me! They's shit! My old lady is gone." His voice whined like a mosquito and ended with a wail. "They don't have no respect...." He sniffed.

"Did you get into an altercation with the complainant?" The beast 'man shone his light at Critter.

Critter stared at him with confusion, his mouth open. "What?"

"You got in a fight with him?"

"They beat on me! Me!" He pleaded with the caterpillar 'man. "I ain't done nothin'. They's losers. Piss drinkers."

The 'man shook his head. "Have you been drinking, Mr. uh..."

"No!" Critter's voice was shrill. "I can't get no drink! And they beatin on me!" He started to shake his head, swinging it back and forth between the two police 'mans.

"My dogs never bit no one." Critter's face turned red and pinched. Spit gathered at the corners of his mouth. Tears started rolling down his face, and his shoulders slumped as they shook. "Those men were beatin' on me."

The police 'mans looked at each other, and the shorter one spoke. "What's your name, sir? You're pretty upset." He reached a hand out to Critter's shoulder. "It'd help if you calmed down."

Critter shrieked and twisted his shoulders away from the 'man. "Why you here? I ain't done nothin'. You don't know nothin'." He stumbled and tripped over Rose, who yelped and jumped. I sprung out of his way as Critter fell to his knees. He clutched at me and clung to my neck leaning into me, breathing hard as if gulping for air. I stood, Critter's face against my shoulder. I didn't know what to do.

Rose had darted into the tent and peered out from the sleeping pallet. Tank began pacing, his hands over his ears. He shook his head then whispered to himself and nodded as he walked back and forth. The two police 'mans, with their thick shells and appendages, took up too much space. Suddenly it felt hot. I began to pant.

"Sir," the police 'man turned toward Tank. "Can you tell me what happened this afternoon?"

Tank ignored the 'man and continued to pace. His lips moved, though I couldn't hear any words.

Critter raised his head and hollered at the 'mans. "He don't know nothin'!"

His voice echoed in my ear. I whined.

"Please calm down. We're just trying to find out what happened. Refusing to answer our questions makes this more difficult."

"I ain't refusing nothing. And you tryin' to take my dogs!" Critter pushed off me and stood up. He wavered. "I don't got nothin' to say to you. They was beatin' on me, and you blaming my dogs."

The police 'mans murmured to each other. The younger one took a few steps back. He turned his head to speak into a black object that hung from his collar. I looked up in alarm when the box talked back.

The caterpillar 'man held his hands out to Critter. "Listen, you're very agitated. And your friend here isn't any better. You haven't even been able to tell us your name." He looked at me and then at Rose. "We've had multiple reports of dogs running loose in the neighborhoods near here, knocking over garbage cans, acting aggressively towards other dogs. A big, scarred mixed breed dog with a limp, and a skittish, medium reddish spaniel mix... they fit your dog's descriptions.."

The 'man looked from Rose to me and ran his eyes along my body. "Sure sounds like these dogs. And we received a complaint that one of these dogs bit someone this afternoon." He looked Critter. "Does this ring any bells?"

"No." Tank's was loud and firm.

Caterpillar man's head snapped around to Tank. "Care to explain that?"

"He don't know nothin'!" Critter stamped his foot, and spit flew out of his mouth.

In the distance, a beast wailed. The second 'man finished his conversation with the box and approached his partner. "We got animal control and a second cruiser on the way."

Tank roared. "No!"

The police 'mans stiffened and stepped back with their hands on their belts. Rose came out of the tent and whined. She stood next to me. Tank paced and gestured wildly. "Our family. These are our family."

I barked. The 'mans looked at me then back to Tank.

"Sir, stop moving." Tank pounded his fist into his flat palm. His head and shoulders rocked back and forth as his pacing became tighter and his turns quicker. The beast's wailing sounded closer.

"Please calm down."

"Calm down?" Critter spit as he shrieked. "You harassing us. You!" He pointed a shaky finger at the 'mans. "You don't listen. You can't take our dogs!"

Critter grabbed Rose's collar. "Grab Wolf and let's go, Tank."

The camp 'mans who had formed a circle around our shelter suddenly backed away, leaving a gap. Critter hurried through it, his hand grasping Rose's collar. She panted and trotted beside him. Tank grabbed my collar, but the caterpillar police 'man stepped in front of us. The other 'man went after Critter and Rose. A new wailing beast arrived, and I heard its jaws snap open and shut as more police 'mans exited.

The caterpillar 'man reached down to his belt and brought out a long, thick club. He slapped it in his palm and waved it menacingly in my direction like Roy about to throw a beer can. "Stop now and control your dog."

Tank frowned and shook his head. "No. Don't do that."

I saw Critter and Rose break away from the camp. Tank groaned. "You causing pain." His voice shook.

"Sir, I need to you look at me."

"Leave me alone." Tank's voice was deep and pleading. He looked down at the caterpillar 'man, his eyes sunk in sadness. "Why you doing this?"

The 'man's eyes hardened. I growled. He took a step forward and drew back his club, and I tensed to jump.

Suddenly something slammed hard into me. I yelped and collapsed into Tank's knee. He wobbled and turned just as a new police 'man clubbed him on his shoulder. With an oof, he staggered a few steps then reached out and grabbed the 'man who'd struck him. He shoved hard, and the 'man stumbled to the ground. Tank turned to the 'man who struck me and reached out.

The 'man's baton came down on Tank's forearm. Tank clutched his arm to his chest then ducked his head and used it like a battering ram to knock the man to the ground. From the edge of the camp, I heard Critter screech and a 'man shout. Rose barked. I turned to face the two police 'mans.

Without warning, a coil slipped around my neck and tightened quickly. I couldn't breathe. I struggled. A shot cracked through the night. Critter screamed, and Rose's voice rose in a loud, wet, strangled cry.

Rose!

I snarled and snapped and twisted in the coil. A police 'man held the other end of the pole. Rose's cries rose to a sharp pitch and then began to fade. Critter's shrieks were unintelligible. Beasts shrieked and skidded on the wide hard blacktop. I couldn't breathe.

Rose!

Tank grabbed the pole and yanked it so that the 'man on the other end had to jump forward to keep his balance. As Tank reached his long arm toward the 'man holding the pole, the caterpillar 'man rose up behind him and pointed a black object at his back. He pulled the trigger.

Tank went rigid. Ra-ta-ta-tat! Ra-ta-ta-tat!

Tank bellowed and released the pole. He grimaced and swung his arms wildly behind him. As he turned, the noose tightened on my neck again and dragged me backwards. Two thin metal wires hung from Tank's back. He moved towards the caterpillar 'man, and the other police 'man rose and pointed a similar object at Tank. He fired at his chest.

Ra-ta-ta-tat! Ra-ta-ta-tat! Tank went rigid again, and his shoulders shook. This time he collapsed forward onto his hands and knees.

The police 'mans rushed him and knocked him into the dirt. Two kneeled on his neck and legs while the caterpillar 'man knelt on his back and struggled to bring Tank's arms together. He succeeded and locked them into metal collars then leaned back, straddling Tank.

I writhed and twisted as the caterpillar 'man's partner dragged Critter into our tent site holding him roughly by one arm. I couldn't see Rose. Critter screamed hysterically, his hands collared behind him like Tank's.

Where was Rose?

"You shot her." He sobbed in big shuddering gasps. "Suzy never hurt no one."

"The other dog ran off, sir." The 'man held Critter who sobbed and sputtered.

The caterpillar 'man stood up from Tank's back. Tank's face was in the dirt, his cheeks blowing in and out as he struggled to breathe. The 'man kicked the dirt next to Tank's head and looked at Critter.

"Goddamn crazy." He looked at me and spoke to the 'man behind me holding the pole. "Find the other dog and take them to the shelter."

Critter howled. Tank bellowed and struggled to get out from under the weight of the two 'mans kneeling on him. He moaned. The noose choked me and dragged me backwards. I fought and snarled, my head pounded as if it would explode. My feet tangled, and I fell to the ground. For a second, the noose loosened, and I gulped in fresh air. Then it tightened again. I turned on the pole to attack it but could find no weakness. I yelped and pleaded and growled; I twisted up and over the pole, trying to bite it and free myself.

All in vain. They hauled me to a large metal beast with a ramp that led into one of its gaping mouths. I tried to go under but was dragged out. Every time I got close to the ramp, the noose loosened. When I skirted in a different direction, it tightened.

"That's it, big guy, just take the ramp."

The 'man with the pole talked to me as I fought him and my terror. I could no longer hear Critter or Tank. His voice calm, I heard few of the words. He finally forced me up the ramp and into the beast's mouth, slamming it shut behind me where I huddled in the corner of the hard, cold cell and felt my body lose control of itself. I sunk into my stench and shuddered.

Rose.

PART FOUR
SHADY

CHAPTER 21
ALONE

My body shook uncontrollably. I hunched in the corner of the cold metal box. It smelled strongly of the cleaning fluid that Lana used. But underneath lay the faint scent of animals. And death.

The beast stayed silent, but more beasts arrived and 'mans moved quickly outside.

"Did you find her?" A voice spoke outside my cage.

"Nah, she took off across the highway. I thought she'd get hit, but she made it across. We'll probably get a call later." A metal handle clanked, and I watched my door, but it didn't open.

Outside, Critter shrieked. I leapt at the closed mouth of the beast and struck at the metal with my forelegs. I scrabbled against it with my claws, bit it and hurtled myself into the closed mouth. I slammed my shoulders against it.

No use.

My legs buckled. I collapsed to the floor gasping like a fish yanked from a pond. My heart pounded, and I saw a vision of Rose in the field behind Lana's house, her red, teardrop ears lifting as I barked a greeting. I saw Tank throwing us silver packets of food. I heard Critter laughing, saw his beard filled with crumbs. I felt Rose's body curled up next to mine.

My Rose.

I lifted my head and howled.

The beast began to grumble and shake. I growled. As we began moving, the metal box jostled and jolted me back and forth, just long enough for me to puke my Mission meal all over it.

I retched again.

And again.

When the beast finally stopped moving, I huddled in my own mess. I didn't care. I didn't move when the beast's mouth opened or when the loop circled back over my neck to pull me out. I didn't object when they dragged me through my mess and into a metal cage. I didn't react when they hosed me down. I wouldn't look at the 'mans and didn't care what they were doing with me. When they were done, I crawled into a corner, curled into a ball, and closed my eyes.

Like Critter, I was done with 'mans.

CHAPTER 22
DESPAIR

"What are they planning to do with this guy?" The young 'man swept the walkway next to my cage while she spoke to another 'man puffing on a smoke stick and sitting on a bench. Both 'mans wore the same dark blue pants and light blue shirts. Black ink drawings – animal faces, flowers and images I didn't recognize – covered the arms of the 'man with the broom. She smelled of coffee, sawdust, and rabbits. Normally those rabbit smells would intrigue me, but right now I didn't care.

The other 'man, larger than the first, had a scent like a pond – organic with a slight rot. Though not young like the first 'man, he didn't yet have the years of Tank or Critter and moved well enough.

"Apparently he's a biter. He came in last week from the homeless camp near the highway. Dr. Weathers is trying to figure out if he's going to be put down or put up for adoption."

"Who'd he bite?"

"Another homeless guy, I think. But apparently that guy wouldn't confirm that it was this same dog, and now they can't find him at all. Dr. Weathers wants to do some behavioural and health assessments."

"Poor guy." The 'man leaned the broom against my cage then

squatted down at my height. "Are you a biter? You look a bit shady. Maybe that's your name. Sound good, Shady?"

She studied me for a long time. I stared back without moving. The floor and walls of my cell were gray, cold cement. A chain link gate climbed to the ceiling and trapped me inside. Across from my cage sat a row of other cages, just like mine, a wide cement walkway between us. When I'd arrived, they'd given me a blanket on top of the metal sleeping pallet, and I'd shredded it the first night. The next morning a 'man strapped a leash to my collar, led me out of the cage and gave me a chance to stretch my legs. We went to a soft green grassy area, like those in the parks I'd trotted through with Rose.

Rose.

It hurt to think of her. Worse than a police baton. Worse than a beer can to the eye. Her scent had disappeared from my life, a memory now, like Rose herself.

As if I'd never met her.

Pain stabbed deep in my chest. For the first time in my life, I couldn't eat. I didn't want to move. I just wanted to sleep.

But twice a day a 'man came into my cell, hooked a leash to my collar, and led me outside. I can't say that I looked forward to it, but it broke up the endless ache. I appreciated getting out of the frigid box to stretch my legs, especially my hip, which grew stiff and painful on this cold floor.

Other dogs came out in the yard at the same time. All remained leashed, and we generally circled around each other in big loops. I sniffed each dog for signs of Rose. Some shied away from me or just stood in one place and panted, looking scared. The short leash kept me from socializing or tail sniffing, and I wasn't allowed off-leash. In a separate yard, other dogs ran free while the blue shirts watched. If I had cared, I would have wanted to run with them.

But I didn't care. Each day I returned to my cell and sunk into the cold floor. I ignored the 'mans as they came by and rubbed the floor with their brooms and mops, like those I'd attacked at Lana's house. I refused to acknowledge the food that they slid into my cell. I had no interest in any of their friendly overtures. What was the point of any of this?

My life had been shattered in one quick moment.

By 'mans.

Why should I care what happened next? I didn't have the energy to start again. I didn't want to start again. I saw no way to get Rose back, and that was all I wanted.

"You're not sure about me, are you." The 'man with the illustrated arms stood up and looked at me one last time. "Well, Shady, I don't blame you. But start eating your food." She turned around and pushed the broom away, leaving me alone. I closed my eyes and sunk into my sorrow.

CHAPTER 23
GLIMMERS

My cell door opened. A new 'man held the door in one hand, a leash in the other. She wore a long white coat and hair knotted on top of her head. I wondered if it were piled there to make herself look bigger. Because she was tiny. I mistook her at first for a 'man pup, but as soon as she spoke, I realized that she was fully grown. But like a mouse. Her voice was soft but strong, her scent fresh and citrusy.

She stood at the doorway and waited. None of the other 'mans waited; they just came into my cell, hooked my collar to the leash and walked out of there whether I was with them or not, the end result being that I had to follow or be dragged. Of course, no one dragged me, mind you. I'm not a sack of garbage. When it's time to go, I pop right up and start moving.

"I'm Dr. Weathers. Time to get acquainted, big guy." She bared her teeth, and I stood up and stretched, a long stretch backward then forward, before approaching her slowly and waiting as she snapped the leash to my collar. However, rather than leading me out of the building to the green grassy area as normal, she took me down the aisle between the rows of cages toward a door at the end of the hall. The dogs in these cages exploded with barking and yelping, and I challenged them all, snarling and lunging as best I could against the tight hold of the leash. I swung my head back and forth and snapped at my barking neighbors and panted.

Emotions – fear, sorrow, anger, playfulness, aggression – surged and roared over me as I passed through the gauntlet. A tiny white yapping fluff ball with miniature legs and beady black eyes snarled and spit as I walked past her. A slobbering black block-headed hound with a bellow like thunder lunged at his cell door on his hind legs, his front paws pushing against the gate. A flop-eared rust-colored wiry fellow with a white patch on his face jumped in the air and turned circles before landing and doing it again. I saw them and felt anger. And pity. For all of us prisoners.

I watched for any opportunity to escape, but she led me quickly through the door at the end of the walkway. As it shut behind us, the cacophony faded. This new room was much quieter and filled with mostly empty cages that reeked of animal scents – the tangy and offensive smell of cats (cats are offensive in general), the loamy, flowery smell of rabbits, and even a faint, musty whiff of mice. The 'man with the illustrated arms scrubbed the floor with a mop.

An acrid, skunky scent, squirrel-like, emanated from a creature with a small, long body, mottled brown fur and a brown mask over his eyes. A bandit in prison, he whipped his narrow body back and forth then rushed the cage and bared his teeth at me as we walked by him. His paws scrabbled at the wire as if to shake it.

A challenger! I lunged and barked at him, and he scurried to the far corner where he hissed. The two 'mans laughed.

The tiny 'man and I entered another hallway with doors on either side. We took the first door and proceeded into a small room. A metal table, fastened to the wall, took up the center of the room. Several jars and strange-looking metal tools sat upon a counter which featured a sink and a cupboard above it. The room smelled of animals, as everything here did, but it carried a sharp clean scent that burned my nose. I sneezed.

"Gesundheit!" The 'man bared her teeth at me again as she laughed. She'd talked to me throughout the walk, but I hadn't heard a word, preoccupied by the screeching hounds and other animals. Now she turned to me and asked me to sit, which I did. She picked up a clipboard, similar to the one Gretchen had carried, and stared at me. "You've got your basic commands down, don't you?"

I began to pant.

"Now let's see what kind of shape you're in." She clicked on a button which gave a loud squawk. I cocked my head as she spoke into it. "Ashley, can you come in for the exam?"

The door opened, and the illustrated 'man, Ashley, entered. "Hey Shady." She greeted me with a head pat then grabbed hold of my collar as the tiny 'man pushed a button. The table began to sink to the ground. I backed away.

Is it alive? I stared and leaned forward to sniff it but found no signs of life. Ashley led me towards the table, and I followed. The scent of animals lay like a fog over everything – thick but dissipating upon inspection. I stepped onto the table, and it began to rise.

What the heck? My claws scrabbled uselessly on the metal, and I tried to jump off. But Ashley thrust her hand in my face, and the scent of meaty goodness filled my nose.

Treats! I forgot about the treat pocket!

I'd been around white coats a few other times – once or twice with Lana and a few times when they'd visit camp and look over Rose and me and the other camp dogs. White coats liked to shine lights into my eyes and ears and massage my body. And they always offered treats.

I inhaled the treat and watched Ashley's pockets closely to see if her hand was heading back in that direction. No luck. The table stopped moving, and I stood slightly lower than Dr. Weathers, my head at her shoulder height.

She washed her hands and faced me. "Ashley, I'll need you to hold him still during the exam. He came in with a biting allegation, so if he starts getting twitchy or nervous, we'll muzzle him. So far he's fairly relaxed."

"Will do. John and I haven't seen any aggression. I haven't seen him react to much of anything, actually." Ashley stroked my head which felt good. She obviously didn't know about the magical chest scratch, but I didn't hold it against her.

The tiny 'man opened my mouth and peered down my throat with a tiny light then felt my teeth and gums with her fingers. "His teeth look good, surprisingly. Some plaque buildup, but no signs of periodontal disease. Dogs this age are at higher risk."

"How old do you think he is?"

"I'd say about 8 or 9 years old, but it's hard to tell with these big dogs. They start slowing down sooner than the small ones, and this guy's a biggie. He's starting to turn gray around the muzzle." She tilted her head to peer into my ears. "He looks pretty good. Thin, but nothing worrisome. His ears are clean. No mites or infections." She turned to the counter and jotted something down.

"He hasn't eaten much since he's been here. The first few days he didn't eat anything, but he's started picking at his food more recently." Ashley scratched my chin and tickled my lower jaw with her fingertips. "How do you think he got these scars?"

Dr. Weathers studied me. She touched my chin. "These are clean, like from a sharp edge, but these scars…" Her fingers ran over my left eye, and she pushed tenderly on the rough lumps and ridges left by Roy's beer cans. "are jagged, like from broken glass or metal. And they seem to be older than the others. I can't determine how they happened, but it was quite a while ago. They healed roughly. He probably didn't get any vet care."

She moved her hands over my shoulders and along my spine and stopped at my hips. She ran her hands over the scar on my left hip and inhaled sharply. "This is from a shotgun."

"Shotgun?" Ashley's voice rose and I looked sideways at her. She returned my gaze with furrowed brows. "Why would someone shoot a dog?"

Her hands on my body made me nervous. Maybe if I sat down, she'd give me another treat. 'Mans liked it when I sat.

"Keep his hips up, please." The 'man in white spoke sharply, and Ashley snapped her fingers in front of my nose. I leaned forward to investigate

Treat?

As I sniffed her fingers, she stuck her other arm under my midsection and lifted my hips. I stretched my nose and pushed her pocket, but she didn't catch the hint. I licked her hand as it passed by me.

"People do some awful things. These wounds were likely caused around the same time as the facial scars. There are a lot of sick people in the world." Her voice was tight with anger. She pushed gently on my hip, and I shifted uncomfortably. "The scarring is rough, and there are still a few pellets under his skin, so I doubt he got veterinary care. It looks as if it became infected at some point, but someone cleaned it up. I'm surprised he doesn't limp more than he does."

I shifted again but Ashley wouldn't let me sit.

I groaned.

"Getting a bit restless, are you?"

My eyes moved from her face to her hand.

Check your pockets!

I licked my lips.

I sneezed.

Dr. Weathers laughed. "We're almost done here, big guy. Ashley, can you keep him still?"

The grip on my collar tightened. I whined softly, questions flooding my mind.

What was I doing here? How long would this going to take?

Where was Critter? Or Tank?

Where would I go next?

Where was Rose?

How could I get some treats?

I looked Ashley's hands again and then glanced at her blue shirt.

Your pocket. Check your pocket. I whined again, and Ashley reached to pat my head. I intercepted her hand with a nose shove.

No pats, just treats!

"He's getting a bit restless."

"Try a treat. I'm almost done."

I groaned again. 'Mans could be so dense.

Ashley's free hand moved towards her pocket, and I froze. She brought out a treat. I licked my lips and felt saliva bouncing from my jowls. I inhaled it as soon as she held it out.

Gone! I looked for more. She brought out another, and I ate it.

"Well, his appetite is finally improving. I was worried that he was depressed."

The vet moved around from my side to the table where she again jotted some notes. "That's certainly possible. Dogs experience depression, though we don't know much about it since they can't tell us. It can be associated with the loss of a companion – human or canine – but not usually a long-term condition. If the symptoms stick around, it's typically related to underlying medical issues. But his health seems just fine, considering that he's probably had sporadic veterinary care."

"Is he going up for adoption?"

"We'll wait to see if he's picked up by his owners."

"You'd send him back to the homeless camp?"

"You know, it's a different life for a dog than what we think is normal, but as long as the dog is cared for and treated well, it's not necessarily a bad one. And he's probably very attached to his people. I interned with a vet clinic back east that conducted outreach and vet care to homeless camps. Most of those dogs were considered family and were well-cared for, happy. And when I see the homeless on Bishop Street here, a lot of their dogs are lying on blankets while they sit on cement. Check it out next time you go downtown, and you'll see what I mean."

"I hear the city's going to clear the camp." Ashley stroked between my ears.

"There's been plenty of trouble there, but where will they all go?"

I yawned. The 'man in white turned toward me and put her hand in her pocket.

Hey! Hand in treat pocket!

I stood alert.

"Good boy" she handed me the treat, which I ate quickly in case she offered another. She rubbed the top of my head. "He's in good physical shape despite the old wounds. I haven't seen any signs of aggression, but let's try him out in a few different situations while we're waiting to see if his owners return for him. If all goes well, he should be eligible for adoption within two weeks. He might be tough to re-home, though, given his size and age and what we know of his history. We may have to look for a foster home placement in the meantime."

"What about the biting?"

"No one's confirmed that he's bitten anyone. We're going to introduce him to new situations and watch him closely. He's showing no signs of aggression, so let's wait and see. For now, why don't you take him out to the dog yard and let him off-leash? No one else should be out there right now."

The tiny 'man opened the door.

Freedom!

I leapt off of the table and prepared to make a dash for it, but my legs hit the slippery floor and splayed out when my paws hit it.

"Whoa!" shouted Ashley as she clung to the end of the leash. "Didn't expect that."

I gathered my feet to rush through the door, but the tiny 'man laughed and blocked it with her body.

"Slow down, big guy. You'll get out of here, don't worry."

Ashley grabbed the leash close to my neck, and we walked through the door together.

CHAPTER 24
HOPE

After my meeting with Dr. Weathers, the blue shirts started letting me run free with other dogs inside the off-leash area, a fenced grass field. The first time they unclicked the leash, I'd stood in disbelief and tried to catch my bearings. It had been ages since I'd had the liberty of running loose – life at camp had been one big freedom party in many ways, I realized.

Now, several weeks later, I scouted the lay of the land and stood with my nose in the air when suddenly a large golden dog ran past me with a floppy ball in his mouth.

A ball of rags! My heart leapt. I froze and sunk down in a crouch as I watched a small sharp-eared dog with black and white patches chase the golden dog. They tore around the yard in circles, and I quivered.

I wanted that ball. I wanted to grab it and shake it as hard as I could, to show my fellow canines that I might be down but not out, that I may have fallen but not for long. The ball captivated me, and though Goldie outpaced his small pursuer, I watched with growing unease as my big black hairy neighbor tackled him. They rolled together through the grass in a snarling mass until the golden dog re-emerged with the ball and left Blackie behind.

Three 'mans stood in the grassy area with us, talking and

watching. There were at least twice as many dogs. A few of them stood trembling, tails touching their bellies, heads hanging with wide eyes and a defensive stance, unwilling to engage with 'man or hound. I turned away from the quakers. As Goldie came barreling past me again, I launched myself after him, running parallel until I could administer a good shoulder check. He careened sideways and gave me a wide side-eyed glance. His goofy grin grew larger despite the ball of rags trailing from his mouth, and he picked up his pace until I ran at my limit, struggling to keep up. He started to pull away, and my teeth snagged a shred of the fabric. I bit down hard and tugged. He whined and growled then slowed as we ran cheek to cheek, and I felt a growing elation, a sense of being alive that I hadn't felt since I'd been torn away from camp.

Suddenly Goldie stopped short, and I hurtled past him, losing my footing and my grip on the rag. By the time I skidded to a stop and turned around, he was heading in the other direction. A scrap of fabric flew like a flag from the corner of his mouth, and I aimed for it, cutting the angle between us to make up for lost time. Running harder than I had in months and nearly in reach of the fabric, I leaned forward, legs pumping, and clamped down on it. At that very moment, the large black dog crashed into Goldie from the other side and sent us all reeling and tumbling though the grass. My head slammed into the ground, and my vision blurred as I found myself under the two dogs. I spotted the ball on the ground and snarled and writhed to free myself.

Just as I scrambled to my feet, a small fluffy dog grabbed the ball and shook it. She had a mottled gray face with whiskers that looked like a 'man's moustache. The ball was almost too large for her mouth but soft enough for her to grasp. I ran at her head-on, with Blackie and Goldie flanking me. She pranced around with the ball, wide-eyed and mouth so full that it almost blocked her line of sight. As I drew near, she growled a warning, and I smiled at her, panting. I had faced down grown men one hundred times her size, scrapped with farm dogs four times her size. A battle with her over this rag ball was nothing in the grand scheme of battles. I lowered my head and paced slowly towards her with a single driving thought.

Get the ball.

She snorted and shook her head as I approached. As I closed the distance, she backed up a few paces then suddenly turned tail and darted away, a rabbit flushed in a field, zig-zagging one side to the other until we were once again in a game of chase. Goldie and Blackie were tight on my tail as I pursued her, then Blackie broke off at an angle when the ball carrier reached the fence and turned back. Instead of running in Blackie's direction, however, she turned and ran full speed back at me and then whipped by me on my left! I twisted quickly but my momentum sent me sliding in the grass on my shoulder. I saw Goldie lose her footing, and she too ended up sliding to a stop just short of where I was picking my panting body up off the grass.

The ball!

The rabbit dog had too far of a head start, and my legs were weak and trembling from exertion. Blackie streaked across the yard, but Goldie, like me, was slowing down. I stopped and panted, and Goldie pulled up beside me. He had a goofy grin, vacuous and man-pleasing. We introduced ourselves with a couple of quick sniffs then watched as Blackie overtook the little gray gal and began a tug of war. It ended when a 'man in blue clipped them both to leashes and led them out of the arena. The ball lay near the gate, and I raced Goldie to it. We took up where they left, tugging each other back and forth until we, too, were leashed and led back to our cells.

MY PRISON STAY LASTED for too long. Neither Critter nor Tank came to rescue me, and I sniffed every new arrival in vain for scents of Rose. Lana had never come back for me. Critter and Tank were nowhere to be seen. Maybe this was just how the 'mans ended things with dogs.

I grew tired of the cage, tired of the noise, tired of life in a metal box. Unlike at Lana's, where I'd been caged outside with fresh air and squirrels, here I was captive to the endless complaints of my fellow prisoners. Life droned on with a monotony that I'd never previously experienced. Sunlight was elusive, peeking down the hallway here or there then leaving quickly before its heat reached me. Squirrels appeared only in my dreams. The only warmth in my cement block cell came from my own body.

My neighbors were generally loud and came and went frequently. A few like me seemed to be here for the long haul. Big Blackie, for one, furry and barrel-shaped in a cell across from me, a good-natured blockhead with a massive drooling problem. And then Goldie, large, long-haired and goofy, friendly and happy but with a penchant for barking that made him insufferable.

Feeding time was a raucous event, with almost all of us dogs leaping and barking. Each time I saw the 'mans pushing the food cart down the hall, I howled as good as any hound. Even Goldie couldn't out-bark me when food was heading down the hallway.

Strange 'mans occasionally strolled down the hallway, stopping to stare at each cell and its occupant. The whole jail block joined Goldie in announcing new entries. I and my fellow prisoners raised our voices and competed for their attention. The visitors walked the gauntlet of dogs, examined each of us and talked between themselves.

"Mommy, a dog with different colored eyes!" A 'man pup stood outside my cell with her mama, her eyes wide and finger pointing. I ignored 'man pups unless they were eating food. A confusing mix of 'man actions with puppy attitude, I never knew how to treat them.

"You're right, sweetie! It's common in cattle dogs, huskies and Dalmatians. This guy looks like he's got some border collie in him, like our Josie did. I'd say definitely he's got border collie."

"He's big!"

"Sure is, sweetie, A bit too big for us, I'm afraid."

"And he's got lots of scars! How'd he get those scars, Mommy?"

"I don't know, honey. Some dogs like to fight. Maybe he's one of those."

The 'man cub eyed me suspiciously. She linked her hands with her mama and watched me as they moved towards Goldie's cage. I lay in front of the door and watched with my head on my paws.

Dr. Weathers appeared in front of my cell. A tall figure moved behind her. "This is Shady, the one I was telling you about."

The 'man wore a thick plaid shirt and blue jeans and towered over her. "He looks to be from herding stock and in good shape despite the scars. And he knows his basic commands. He's a hard one, though. Hasn't bonded with any of our staff – a bit aloof or depressed."

"How long's he been in here?" The 'man's voice was clear and strong.

"Six or seven months. He came in last fall. Maybe October? I'd have to look at his records."

He moved forward; I noticed his brown hair was sprinkled with gray and clipped unevenly across his brow. He squatted down to study me and held the chain links as he spoke. "Look at you. Big, aren't you? What's your story, Shady?"

Surrounded by hard, cold cement, the nose-stinging scent of bleach and the despair of caged dogs, I didn't lift my head. 'Mans didn't interest me. They came, they looked, they frowned. They always left with another dog.

Not interested.

But gradually, against my best intentions, my nose started paying attention. My ears swivelled in his direction. From his plaid jacket, a very appealing scent drifted casually my way, reminiscent of the bacon that Lana used to cook. The bacon of which I very rarely, once or twice without invite, got to taste. I lifted my head as he asked to open the gate. My senses rose to high alert level.

"He's been battered, no joke. I don't know that I've seen a dog with so many scars." The white coat opened the gate. "And he's getting on in years, too. But it hasn't slowed him down. He actually puts the other dogs in line quite often."

The 'man stepped into the cage, and I kept still and watched him suspiciously. He approached me with hands out which I sniffed carefully – leather, spring rains and apples – but my interest lay in his pocket. He ran his hand over my head then cupped my chin with his hands, and I angled my nose towards the pocket on his right. I laid my ears back and thumped my tail. When he smiled, the thin lines around his eyes crinkled. Definitely past the midpoint of life. No dark lines or thick wrinkles like Critter or Tank, but not fresh-faced like Lana. The warmth of his hands under my chin made my insides hum pleasantly.

"You're a big guy, aren't you?" He spoke softly, stroked my back and scratched between my shoulders. His hands felt like sunshine on a cold spring day. "You've been through a few battles." He turned his head and hollered over the shrieking of my neighbors. "Any idea how he is with livestock?"

Dr. Weather's face appeared. "Unknown. But he's smart, and he's not easily intimidated. I haven't noticed any aggression towards other animals, though he's not afraid to throw his weight around."

He looked back to me. "An unknown. Where does that leave us?"

My tail flipped once, involuntarily. *Betrayal!*

Despite myself, I liked this 'man. His eyes were friendly, and his hands stroked my coat confidently. He smelled not only agreeable but appealingly. On top of that, his pocket, very close to my nose, oozed goodness. I pushed into it a little bit to gauge his reaction. His face broadened into a smile, and he stood up and reached into his pocket.

"You've found the Porkies."

Porkies?

I'd never heard the word, but I loved it already. When he lifted his hand from the pocket, I smelled two of my favorite human foods – bacon and peanut butter. I fixed my eye on it and stilled myself, though a small line of drool dripped over my lips and bounced from my mouth as I began to pant.

He tossed the treat to me, and I caught it without hesitation, without moving. Good aim, this 'man. And the treat? Sublime. I quivered for more.

He turned to the 'man at the gate. "Can I take him for a walk? Maybe give him a run in the dog yard?"

"Of course. No one's in the big yard at the moment. Why don't you head there?"

She handed the 'man a leash which he clipped to my collar. I stood and stretched, and we quit the cage together.

We walked to the empty yard where he unclipped my leash and picked up a round yellow ball. These balls had a satisfying first bite but split quickly at the seams. I typically didn't care for them, but when he held this one in front of my eyes, then smiled at me and cocked his arm back to throw, I wanted it badly. I longed for the fuzzy feel of it in my mouth and the satisfying, rubbery, hollow pop when it burst. He threw it, and I streaked across the yard to capture it. I snatched it and chomped down, shook my head and growled as it slipped out and bounced away. I pounced on it again and heard a sharp two-note whistle.

I raised my head, and the 'man was holding his hand up in the air. I stopped moving and stared at him. *What does he want?*

He whistled again and waved his hand. "C'mon boy."

Another treat? I dropped the ball and ran to him. He lowered his hand as I neared, and I barely tasted the bacon-y, peanut-buttery goodness that I caught in mid-air.

He laughed and shook his head. "You left the ball." I trotted alongside him as he walked through the yard. He reached the ball and bent down to pick it up, and I barked encouragingly. I knew he could do it! I leaped and wriggled around him.

He told me to sit, and I sat. He held the ball in front of my face. "Stay," he commanded. I cocked my head. Where else was I going to go?

As he drew his arm back, I quivered, ready to chase the ball down. He repeated his command to stay then threw it. I tore away from him, but his whistle pulled me up short. He called me back and gave me a treat when I returned immediately.

This 'man intrigued me. He had the best treats I'd ever tasted. If he didn't want me to chase the ball, I wouldn't. Maybe *he* wanted to chase it again. He was slow, but I thought he could certainly learn to properly follow his throw. We walked to the ball, and again he told me to sit and stay. As he cocked his arm back to throw, I waited. If he wanted to chase it first, I'd let him.

The ball bounced, and I looked at him then back to the ball. He didn't make a move towards it, and it rolled swiftly away from us.

"Break!" He barked the word at me, and I waited, wondering if I'd misjudged this man – perhaps not as quick as I thought.

He threw his arm in the direction of the ball. "Get it."

I bolted towards the ball, grabbed it and shook it hard. His whistle came before I had a chance to really chew on it. This time I brought it with me.

"Good dog," he said as I arrived. "Sit." I sat.

"Drop it." I watched him. When he pulled a treat out of his pocket, I stared intently. "Drop it." He repeated the phrase and held the treat up. I dropped the ball. He tossed me the treat and picked the ball up.

We repeated this a few times. I finally realized that he didn't want to chase the ball at all. He instead wanted me to bring it back to him. I had no idea about the point of this game, but I was made for this! Though I would have preferred to keep the ball and chew it, each time I dropped it at his feet, he gave me a treat. I returned with the same dirty old ball time after time, and he gave me a fresh treat with every trip. What a trade-off!

Having mastered the ball game, we walked out of the fenced yard. I let him lead and glanced up at him periodically as we walked. He took us to the horse pen, which I'd never explored. The strong, rich smell of horses was one of my favorites, a scent that brought me back to the barn of my earliest days. The lone horse in the pen, a silky, golden color with a blonde mane, neighed as we approached, and I greeted her nose to nose through the fence as she lowered her head. The 'man stroked her forehead.

"Good with horses then, are you?"

He crouched down to me at eye level and stared. His hands stroked my ribs and scratched my ears. I began to pant. *What does he want?* I eyed his treat pocket hopefully. He chuckled, and I flopped my tail uneasily. With or without treats, I wanted to please him, this calm, agreeable man with the low, even voice.

"You look like a beast." His nose was inches in front of mine. I reached forward tentatively and licked it. 'Man sweat. He bared his teeth in a broad grin. "But so far I haven't seen anything in you that I can't work with.

"You've been around the block a few times, but you've come out on top, haven't you? Still here, anyways. King of the hill, huh? How about that? King?"

I licked his nose again – a quick dab of the tongue – and sniffed his face before I averted my eyes again. A faint trace of woodsmoke hung about his head, and a peppery, spicy kick to his breath made me want to move closer.

He stood up and scratched my head. "I'm Walter. Let's go home, King."

PART FIVE
KING

CHAPTER 25
WALTER

After a rousing send-off by my fellow hounds, I gladly left the shelter. I wouldn't miss the constant whining and canine complaining.

Getting in Walter's beast presented its challenges, however. Namely, I refused to get in. But Walter's liberal tossing of Porkies proved to be a tremendous incentive, and he opened my window so that I could hang my head out as my stomach churned.

We stopped at a large, dog-friendly building filled with people and dogs and incredible animal scents that stopped me in my tracks. Food. Cedar shavings. Food. Rodents. Food. Birds. Food. I couldn't think straight!

I followed Walter blindly, overtaken by the store and the noise, not to mention the little red cotton fluff of a dog that surprised me at a corner. He barked as we came face to face, and my snarl sent him scrambling straight into the lower base of a carpeted tower, a soft little alcove that he filled with growls until dragged out by his 'man.

I walked out of that building with a new red collar and a brand new bacon-scented squeaky toy that I refused to give to Walter or the 'man behind the counter. Then came a gut-churning ride in Walter's big beast truck, a slow climb up a long valley.

I poured out of Walter's beast on liquid legs, sliding to the ground in a trembling mess. I gained my feet slowly and lifted my head to scent the air. A cool fresh breeze flowed off of the mountains and drifted over me. My lungs gulped in the clear air. Walter busied himself around the beast as I stood and took it all in.

He'd parked next to a small log cabin with a covered porch. Behind the cabin towered three peaks, still snow-covered in late spring. A small orchard of fruit trees extended out from one side of the cabin, ancient fruit shrivelled on the tree. A small barn with several outbuildings – a shed, a chicken coop, and a couple of smaller structures – faced the cabin, and a large pasture and fenced garden ran in front of and beyond the barn. Bounded by a fence of barbed wire, the pasture extended to a large pond and three massive granite boulders. Two horses stood shoulder to hip next to each other under a lean-to covering a feeding trough. They watched us and swished their long tails in each other's faces. From the barn I heard the bleating of goats.

Walter unloaded the front of the beast near the house then sat back down in the front seat without me. The beast quickly roared with intention.

Where's he going? I barked and feinted as he moved the beast backwards then forwards toward the barn. I snarled and chased it as it lumbered away from me with my new 'man inside.

As the beast approached the barn, chickens – maybe a dozen or so – fluttered about and clucked then scattered in all directions as it went through them.

Chase!

Other than the unfortunate incident in my youth, I'd never been up close and personal with chickens. Rose and I had chased geese in the city park, wild creatures who reacted quickly and aggressively when under attack. But chickens apparently had neither the agility nor speed of wild fowl. I zeroed in on one as she separated from the others then grabbed her between my teeth. Her loud squawk turned into a strangled squeal. So easy! I shook the chicken vigorously and marvelled at how simple she'd been to catch.

Once caught, however, I didn't know what to do with her. Soft and chewy, I chomped down a few times. But the feathers stuck to my gums and pricked the top of my mouth. I released her. She tumbled out of my jaws and lay still. I nudged her a few times. I licked her.

Suddenly Walter grabbed my collar with a loud "No!" He pulled me away forcefully but not roughly.

I closed my eyes and lay flat on the ground, ears back, my body tight in anticipation of the blow.

It never came.

I opened my eyes.

Walter clipped a chain to my collar and fastened it to a metal post then walked to the chicken and picked up the limp body. I sat up, watching intently. *Was he going to throw it? Was this another game?*

I shifted nervously, the chain heavy on my neck. Walter stroked the chicken and looked at me darkly. I sunk my head. I didn't like that look. He twisted a loop of twine around the chicken's two feet, leaving a length of it loose. He approached me, the chicken swinging slightly at the end of the twine. I wagged my tail wanly, uncertainly. *What was he doing?*

He looped the loose end of the twine around my collar, cinched it tightly, then stepped away and stared at me. I sat up, but the weight of the dead bird pulled my neck down. I reared my head back and tried to look at it. The chicken hung from my neck. I couldn't see it! I tried to jump away, but it stuck to my neck and flopped against me like an open door on a windy day. I leapt and twisted, but the chicken slammed into my body with each twist. What did this mean?

"Chickens are off limits, King. You need to learn to be around them. Let's see how you do after living with one attached to you for a while." He paused and studied me. I wagged my tail. "It's a trick my dad used to use with our old hounds. Didn't work with all of them, but hopefully you'll learn to leave them alone."

I didn't know what he was saying. The weight of the chicken around my neck dragged me down. I felt crazy. I barked in confusion. Walter unloaded the back of the beast. The chickens followed him in and out of the barn, clucking and fussing noisily. I yelped and barked, chained to the post with the chicken tied to my neck.

What was the meaning of this? I growled at the chicken. It hung heavily and pulled my neck low. I lay down to release the pressure. The chicken lay in front of my chest, and I tried to avoid setting my chin on its feathery body as I lay my head down. Walter finished unloading the beast and approached me. I wagged my tail but remained prone. I pleaded with my eyes to remove it. He unclipped the chain from my collar but left the chicken looped to it.

I stood and took a few tentative steps with my burden. It swung into my chest with each step, slapping me like waves on a windy day at the lake. I turned circles and tried to grab onto the chicken body. Unable to seize it, I sat down and studied my situation.

I'd chased and caught this chicken. Walter had tied this chicken to my collar. If I chased and caught chickens, they became mine. But I didn't want this chicken. I didn't want its floppy body attached to mine. Did this mean that I shouldn't chase chickens? Or only that I shouldn't catch them?

I became confused and stopped trying to sort it out. Walter whistled, and I trotted to him, chicken thumping against my chest. I stopped. He whistled again, and I started towards him. This 'man intrigued me despite my new accessory. I supposed I could go along with this new twist. Just keep those Porkies coming!

The chicken thump, thump, thumped on my chest as I trotted alongside Walter. He opened the door to the cabin, and I halted on the threshold. Inside looked dark and constricting despite the sunlight streaming through the windows and lighting up the front room of the cabin.

"Normally I'd let you in. But not with that chicken. Sit tight." Walter shut the door and disappeared into the cabin. I stared at the door and cocked my head at the sounds of banging metal and water running. He returned with a large silver bowl that smelled of fish oil and meat, and I rose quickly onto my hind legs to sniff despite the weight of the chicken on my neck. Walter knocked me away with his knee.

"Back off, King. You won't normally get lunch around here, but I bet you're a bit stressed. This should help."

He set it down, and I rushed the dish. The chicken swung forward and knocked the dish away from me as I lowered my head. I tried again. It moved again. I chased the dish as it scooted around the porch, until Walter laughed and picked it up. He set it on a chair that was sitting near a table on the porch.

"Try it now."

I could reach the dish without the chicken interfering. Chewing and swallowing required a bit more effort with the weight around my neck, but *Law #1* prevailed, and I ate quickly and heartily.

CHAPTER 26
FOWL

Having a chicken around my neck wasn't the worst thing I'd experienced, but it complicated the search for Rose. Though content to spend my days busy with Walter – he liked to rise early and keep moving – I left the property each night, seeking out signs or scents of her. But the chicken slowed me down; my neck ached and my pads grew sore. Several times I pushed on and found myself too far at daybreak to make it back to Walter's for morning patrol.

Walter greeted my return on those mornings with a scowl and a shunning. I didn't mind the scowl, but when he turned his back to me, as if I weren't right next to him, jumping up and down and greeting him with my happy good morning bark, it hurt worse than a beer can from Roy. Like I'd been abandoned. I wanted to do anything to get back in his good graces. Except stop searching for Rose.

"Where the heck are you going, King? Why can't you stay home?"

I groveled, whining on my back in front of him. Eventually he'd relent and greet me. On one unfortunate occasion, after a piece of fencing had firmly snagged the chicken around my neck, I spent the night trapped under the fence, the front half of my body in the pasture, my back half sticking out into the yard. No writhing or wriggling could free me. Walter found me in the morning and released me with a curse. "Goddamned dog. You're looking for trouble."

But I wasn't. I was looking for Rose.

After the night under the fence, I stuck around. I learned the ins and outs of Walter's routine and that of his livestock. The two horses, Duchess and Big Gray, spent their days in the pasture but returned to the barn at night. Each morning Walter fed them in the barn then released them into the pasture and refreshed their hay. The horses shook their heads at me when I leaned in to sniff their forelegs. Big Gray stomped his foot too close to my head, and I barked sharply. He shook his head and snorted, shying away while Walter steadied him with a hand on his forehead and a soft murmur. I circled behind Walter and sat with a low growl, respecting their size but making sure they knew the pecking order. Walter, of course, held the number one position, but I ran a close second.

The mother and daughter goat duo Dilly and Dally also spent their nights in the barn. Walter released them each morning to ramble around the property. Unlike Duchess and Big Gray, they roamed both inside and outside of the fenced pasture. I sometimes found them on the porch, an unfortunate situation due to the fact that *the porch was mine*. Dally had the nerve to challenge me one day. She stood with her head low and facing me down from the top of the porch stairs, preventing me from reaching the top of *my porch*. I snarled and feinted to one side and then the other, and she stomped her feet and thrust her head (and horns!) at me.

Normally I would have seen it coming. But the chicken somehow blocked my vision, because suddenly Dally rammed me in the ribs! I yelped in surprise more than pain – her tiny head carried more force than I would have imagined. I growled and barked and faced off with her – at a distance – and we remained in a tense standoff. Had it not been for the chicken around my neck slap, slap, slapping my chest every time I thrust forward, I would have quickly removed the interloper.

Instead I paced and grew agitated at the bottom of the porch steps. She was *on my porch!*

I simply wanted to get a drink of water.

Or maybe I wanted to lay down on my bed. *On my porch.*

Or curl up in front of the cabin door. *On my porch.*

It's not important. The main thing is: *goats do not belong on my porch.*

The situation was going to get messy. But just as I'd resolved to use excessive force to remove her, Walter arrived and called her, reaching into his pocket and holding out a handful of peanuts (I sniffed the air to ensure that they were NOT Porkies). Dally shook her head up and down and raced down the stairs towards him. I trotted quickly up the stairs, then turned to gloat. She ignored me and hopped alongside him, joined by Dilly, who'd been munching on some weeds near the garden fence. My satisfaction at winning back the porch subsided as I saw Walter laughing and talking to them. I quickly realized that that was where I needed to be.

I scrambled to his side and squeezed myself into the space between them. He and I led both goats into the pasture where they leapt and kicked and began to play in the wide open space. They preferred hanging out on the large boulders near the pond, and I preferred not to share *my porch.*

The chicken around my neck grew stiff and battered after a week, and the odor infused itself into my activities. Though normally a fan of decaying matter, living with a rotting body strapped to my collar started to overwhelm me. Filled with cold, fresh water, my drinking bowl nonetheless tasted like death. The putrid taste of rot filled my mouth as I ate. The body hanging from my neck began to look like the charred remains of a tree stand after a fire – black and patchy with only small stands of scarred feathers.

I couldn't let a dead bird keep me from exploring my new life, but it did get in my way as I dipped my body in the pond, chased squirrels in the yard, or even curled up for a nap under a favorite tree or the large pile of blankets that Walter had laid out for me on the porch.

Finally, after a week or two, Walter called me to him and narrowed his eyes as I approached. "I hope you've learned your lesson." I shrunk to the ground as he cut the rope binding me to the chicken. The weight around my neck lifted.

Free!

I leapt, exhilarating in the weightlessness of my shoulders and head, then stopped and looked guiltily at the chicken – *did he want me to get a new one*? I sniffed the chicken and looked towards the chicken coop reluctantly. I didn't want a new chicken. If I had to keep a chicken around my neck, I'd rather it be the one that I was used to.

When Walter picked the chicken up and began walking toward the barn, an even greater weight lifted from my shoulders. An incredible lightness and joy replaced the physical weight of the chicken. It spread through me, and I raced ahead of him to the pasture gate and back again as fast as I could. I'd been tied to this chicken from the almost the exact moment that I'd first arrived, and I realized that Walter may have no idea how fast I could run. I decided to show off.

I lowered my head and tore past him and around the gate as quickly as I could. I ran laps in circles around Walter, tighter and tighter until he stopped and stared. Admiringly, I might add.

Finally winded, I finished with a head butt to the back of his thigh, just a small tap to let him know that it was okay to move on. I must have caught him daydreaming, because his legs buckled, and he fell forward to his knees with an "*oof*".

He picked himself up off the ground quickly. "Damn, King. You're happy about getting rid of this chicken, aren't you?" He asked me to sit. I sat. He held the battered chicken by the feet. "Tell me you're done with chicken chasing." He shook it. I averted my eyes. I didn't want this chicken again.

"No chicken chasing King." He held the chicken under my nose. "NO."

Walter's voice was gravy on kibble. Rich and thick, it made a good thing – Walter – even better. But I kept my eyes averted. He had treats in his pocket, and not just peanuts. I'd rather score a treat instead of the chicken.

He turned away and walked to the shed, an interesting room full of tools and some of the big cans that Rose and I used to knock over in the alleys near the camp. He opened up one of the cans and deposited the chicken inside.

I barked. *Good boy, Walter. Let's be done with this chicken business.*

Walking back to the house, I turned my nose up at the chickens as they milled about. They teased me with their clucking and pecking and erratic runs around the yard. However, though I bluff charged them half-heartedly, I didn't dare capture another. I had no desire to assume responsibility for any more of these foul birds.

CHAPTER 27
PATROL

Unencumbered, I adjusted to life with Walter and began to search in earnest for Rose. I couldn't wait to find her and bring her back to Walter's. His ways and his property enthralled me, and I wanted to share it with her.

Between Walter's morning patrol of the property and my night ramblings for Rose, I learned the lay of the land. He woke early, and together we'd cruise the perimeter of the property. The patrols gave me all kinds of insights into the creatures that lived around us, and they also reminded me that Walter, like all 'mans, used few of his senses. He relied almost exclusively on sight to inform him about the comings and goings. His nose was very much useless, and his ears looked too small to be of any assistance.

Early spring, the property burgeoned with life on a level I hadn't ever been able to fully experience. Certainly not when I'd been locked up in the shelter. And rarely in the 'man camp where city life presented an entirely different scent and soundscape. I chased squirrels (always squirrels!) who taunted me from trees when they weren't arguing and chattering with each other in the branches. I shot like a bullet after any on the ground, chasing them and barking madly. They'd scatter quickly and each time escape up and into the branches of trees to taunt me.

Deer ran through the pasture regularly and even jumped the garden fence on occasion. They bolted quickly and changed directions with one quick bounce. They never let me get too close. I scented the occasional passing bear or coyote, their scents hanging from the undergrowth of brush or the base of trees alongside patches of fur or sprays of urine. Sometimes, deeper in the trees, I'd find a depression where a large animal had bedded down. Raccoons came closer to the outbuildings than the bears or coyotes, but though I smelled their fading scent in the morning, I rarely saw them.

My patrols with Walter took us down the driveway to the road. Every time I reached it, I'd stand on the road and lift my head, searching the air for any scent of Rose.

"What are you looking for, King? What do you smell?"

I whined. Not Rose.

Free of the chicken, I began leaving again at night, running far and wide and searching the mountains and the neighboring farms and houses. Even if I didn't make it back home in time for morning patrol, breakfast was always waiting. This 'man didn't use hunger as a weapon, but he wasn't happy about my wandering.

"Why are you so restless? I tell you, King, I've never had a dog that ran like you. It's not safe out there, you know."

One morning, during a routine patrol of the property after Chicken Liberation Day, Walter and I were walking along the base of the mountains behind the cabin. The weather had turned warmer, and the winds of the previous weeks had died down. Following the scent of a rabbit, nose to the ground, the sound of a beast slowing and turning down the driveway made me lift my head.

No cars, trucks, or other 'mans had visited since I'd arrived at Walter's. He didn't share his cabin with a mate or 'man pups, though I could detect the faint scent of a female 'man mixed among his stuff. But the scents were stale and dissipated quickly, leaving me with nothing but the shadow of another 'man in his life.

The beast purred as it came up fast, and Walter groaned. A low, sleek, sparkling blood-red beast, it chewed up rocks and dirt and spit them out in its wake. I challenged it, ignoring Walter as he shouted my name. It screeched to a stop in front of the cabin, dirt and dust flying around it, and I circled, barking and scenting the air. As the beast's mouth opened, a 'man stepped out, and a strong wave of sweet, chemical flowers passed over me. I sneezed. I sneezed again and again then shook my head before I resumed barking.

The 'man's colorful face stretched tightly across high cheek-bones. Despite the taut skin, her scent wasn't young like Lana's. Closer to Walter's age, I figured. Thin brown eyebrows arched as if in permanent surprise above eyes with dark, glittery blue lids. Her puffy red lips lifted into a smile as Walter came up behind me, though she kept her eyes fixed warily on me and stayed close to her beast. Her face, tanned like Walter's, gazed out over a thin neck and arms and legs that stuck out like sticks from under a short navy skirt and a ruffled, sleeveless pink top. If anything could stand out in the mountain forests more than this 'man, I couldn't think of it. Her body blinded me with color.

"Walter! So happy to see you again!" She took a step forward then stopped immediately as I launched a frenzy of barking. Neither Walter nor I had given her permission to leave her beast.

Walter placed his hand on my back. "Easy, King."

I continued with a low growl.

"Hi Cherry. This is a surprise. What brings you out here this early?"

His voice, though cool, held no threat. I stepped down my alert level and lowered my growl to a quiet throat rumble.

"Yes, it's a bit early, but I know you're an early riser. Not enough hours in the day, right?" She talked cheerily and continued without waiting. "I've had some buyers looking for a property like yours."

Walter began to respond, but she held a hand up. I shifted nervously and eyed her with suspicion.

"Now, I know you're not on the market, but this may be an offer that you can't refuse. They're from the city and wanting to buy a small hobby farm. They're well-endowed financially, so money's not an issue. I've taken them to several properties that are on the market, but they're all too big or underdeveloped."

Walter tried to speak, but the 'man cut him off.

"The last time we talked, you weren't interested in selling, but really, Walter, you ought to consider this. These buyers aren't the types who can develop a property. They're looking for a turnkey farm. You, on the other hand, could purchase any number of properties and turn it into a paradise like this one. You could come out with a pocket full of cash and a new horizon!"

"Not interested, Cherry. This is my home. I've been here for 30 years and have no desire to start over. I've told you before. You're wasting your time."

I barked. Walter had my support. One hundred percent. I paced around the vehicle and searched for scents.

"Oh, Walter, you say you don't want to start over, but what about downsizing? Take a look around. You've been all alone out here since Ellen passed – that's ten years. What are you going to do when the day-to-day work becomes too much to handle? You're too far out of town to hire anyone, and you're not going to be able to take care of this all on your own."

Walter groaned and ran a hand through his hair. "I appreciate your concern, Cherry, but I think you'd be better off focusing on your own future. Sounds to me like your Mustang's going to need a new transmission soon."

Her eyebrows shot up even higher than normal, and for a moment her face lost its cheery smile. "Are you serious? Walter, do I have a bad transmission? Oh, Lord, I haven't got time for that!"

I didn't know about any transmission, but I peed on the tires. I marked the front left and back right with a quick leg lift then turned and kicked a bit of dirt behind me to accentuate the effort.

Her smile returned, and she moved closer to Walter, touching his arm and leaning into his shoulder conspiratorially. "The ladies would love to see you in town more often, you know. You're somewhat of a mystery, popping in and out of the feed store and the bank in your dirty jeans and faded flannels. Being cousins, they come to me for information. I tell them that you're an independent bastard who likes animals more than he likes people. They don't believe me, of course, and god knows that they wouldn't make it out here."

I gave a low rumble. The only lady I wanted to see was Rose. Walter put his hand on my back, and I quieted.

"I'm not selling my property, and I'm not looking for a woman. I'm content here. Entirely. Now, if you're done asking me questions that you already know the answers to, and if you're through giving me a headache about relationships, I've got work to do."

"I'll never be done with you, Walter." She laughed, a tinny sound with a forced lightness.

I barked.

Time to go, lady. Walter didn't want her here, and this talk of moving made me nervous. How would I bring Rose to live with me if I didn't have a home?

"Please give it some thought. Not about the ladies, but about your future here. Maybe it's time to start thinking about change."

She handed Walter a small, thin card. "If you decide you want to make a change, call me first. I'm family."

He looked at it and shook his head "I'll keep your card. But don't expect anything. I've got no plans to change."

Cherry leaned in to kiss Walter's cheek. I barked at the bright red mark her lips left on his face.

"Easy, King." Walter's hand stroked my neck, and I shifted. I would be glad when this 'man left Walter and we could get back to our routine. I hadn't gotten my body rub yet.

She left us with her syrupy, chemical scent as she swirled around and back into her beast, starting it with a roar. She waved and left us in a spray of dust and pebbles.

CHAPTER 28
KNOW YOUR PACK II

If not for my desire to find Rose, I'd have been content with Walter. Life with him had a rhythm, which I fell into easily. Each morning we patrolled, and I'd search for Rose's scent. Then we'd settle on the porch for breakfast and a good body rub (well, only I got the body rub; after a few attempts on my part, Walter insisted that I keep my paws off of him) and move into the business of the day. My business meant cruising the property for a second search for Rose while Walter went back into the cabin before heading out into the yard.

The cabin didn't interest me. After I'd been released from the chicken, Walter had invited me inside and placed my sleeping blankets just inside the front door. I'd entered tentatively, memories of Aileen and a broom hovering inside my head. This cabin was tidier than Lana's. It had two rooms – a large open space upon entering, and a small room in the back. A sink and a cooking stove, where I could smell faint traces of Walter's dinner from the previous night, sat adjacent to the back room but open to the main one. A woodstove lay in between the kitchen and the back room; three chairs sat at a small table alongside two soft armchairs (I only guessed that they were soft; I stayed away from furniture in general after a painful boot from Roy had taught me that couches were off-limits). Books lined the walls of the house, and I sniffed deeply into the rich scent of leather to discover a hint of mildew and mice droppings.

I inspected both rooms of the house, which gave off ever so faint scents of another 'man, especially the back room that contained a bed fit for two 'mans or three to four large dogs (one can always dream). A scattering of clothes (the scent of another 'man, though faint, rose from a box) hung in a small closet built into one wall, and a window above the bed opened up to the mountains behind the cabin. Overall, the cabin smelled like apples and wood smoke and Walter.

I imagined sleeping in front of the woodstove or trying out one of the armchairs, but the longer I stayed inside, the more the walls began to shrink in on me. I began to pant and pace. None of it felt right. I didn't belong in the house. I belonged outside.

I padded to the door and stood there with my nose to the frame, breathing in and out through the crack at the door. Despite Walter's scent, I felt Roy's fists slamming into my ribs. I remembered Aileen's broom whacking my head. I needed to get out of there. I couldn't breathe. I whined. I gasped for fresh air through the thin door frame.

Walter held a small towel and opened the door with a smile. "Need a bit of fresh air, eh King?"

I launched my front paws onto his chest in thanks before I scrambled out of the cabin and onto the porch where I stood tall and gulped in fresh mountain air. Walter stepped out with me, and together we surveyed the yard. A woodpecker hammered on a nearby birch. Squirrels scolded each other as they leapt and scurried across branches. I leaned into Walter and his hand stroked my head.

"I've never known a dog that wouldn't just curl up on the carpet or sneak onto the bed. Funny how life turns us certain ways or another. I'll build you a house on the porch. How's that?"

He set his towel down on the little table on the porch and went to the other side of the deck where he paced out a distance with his feet, turned, and tread another few steps. "It'll fit here. That way you're still technically part of the house but also outside and not outcast in the yard. That work?"

I glanced up at him. He looked directly at me, and my heart flipped once. I leaned into his legs, and he stumbled backwards then chuckled. "You're a quirky dog. I guess I've got my own quirks."

He slung the towel over his shoulder, turned to head back into the cabin, then paused and spoke at the door. "One of my quirks is that I like a clean kitchen before I start out into the yard." He snapped the towel at me, and I barked a friendly challenge as the door shut.

For the next two days, Walter worked in one of the outbuildings filled with tools and small beasts. The noise – the high whine of machinery, the buzz of a saw and thwack of metal hitting wood – hurt my ears. I retreated to the edge of the barn where I could watch the open door without suffering from the ear-splitting shrieks of the machines. Every so often the sounds would still, and I felt a small loss and a tiny fear that I wouldn't see him again. Then he'd reappear, holding a piece of wood or a tape measure. Happiness would surge over me, and I'd leap and dance around him as he walked to the porch to bend over, measure and lay out some of the wood pieces he carried to and from the shop.

Toward the end of the second day, Walter loaded up the beast's basket with all the lumber and drove to the porch. He left the basket open and began laying some of the pieces on the deck.

I stuck close to Walter as he worked. But though the porch seemed to have plenty of room, Walter took up all of it, with hardly enough space for me to get my head into the project. He held a gun-like object in his hand that whined and growled occasionally, and I thrust my head over his shoulder while he laid out a frame and connected the pieces together. I snapped at the whining gun only once and otherwise barked encouragingly, nudging Walter's arms when I saw him pause. Eventually I grew bored and drifted away to a favorite hole that I'd dug beneath a birch tree. I curled up and kept an eye out on the squirrels until eventually I closed my eyes and napped.

I awoke to the clang of tools hitting the beast's metal back. I stretched as I emerged from my hole, dragging my feet behind me and yawning. I shook my head then trotted to the porch where Walter held the fuzzy push stick and brushed sawdust off the deck.

"What do you think?" He watched me, and I wagged my tail.

I loved everything Walter did, and this box had to be one of his best. A rectangular box, taller than me, with a flat roof and a small entry, it in many ways looked like the house I'd had at Lana's. But bigger. I sniffed the entrance then stepped into it tentatively. Rather than the rot and mildew of my previous box, it smelled of freshly cut wood. I had limited knowledge of this type of project – I preferred digging holes to building – but when I stepped inside, it fit me like a glove. The seams fit together tightly, the entrance had ample room for me to go in and out, and, once inside, I could fully stand as well as turn around and lie down. It fit me perfectly. I scratched at the bottom of the flat, hard box, but Walter called me out of it then carefully laid down my porch blankets.

I went back in and sniffed the blankets quietly. They felt soft under my pads. With the exception of the box in the barn with Mama and the first few weeks at Lana's, I'd been out in the open all of my life. My bed had always been the hard, cold ground.

I'd never had anything like this. A soft, sheltered home. New. Mine.

Overwhelmed by happiness, my heart swelled in gratitude, and I whined. Suddenly I felt a wild urge to scratch at the blankets, so I pushed them to and fro inside the house then turned around quickly to adjust them one way then the other. Walter laughed as I worked furiously to get the blankets into the right position, and then, finally, I lay down, placed my head on the threshold of the entrance and looked out at the yard. With a clear view of the driveway and most of the property, I relaxed. I'd been given a home. Walter was my pack, and I had property to protect. I'd be comfortable here. Until I found Rose.

CHAPTER 29
STAY

When I'd lived at the 'man camp, life had been slow-paced with little variation: little movement until mid-day. Activities were limited to searching for food, begging for money, or searching for Trouble.

Walter, however, got up at sunrise. We'd patrol the property first thing, waiting for first light before starting. This, of course, began later and later as summer progressed into fall, and by winter, I awoke long before Walter and our sunrise patrols.

Free to wander, I did. I roamed the area much more quickly with no chicken around my neck, taking in the sights and scents of neighboring properties. Some were filled with livestock and the pleasing scents of manure and grains. Others had dead beasts in their yards and smelled like motor oil and diesel fuel. One property had a dominant and very fresh scent of Sour Smoke Sticks, a property with chain link fencing all around and three dogs who arrived, barking and warning me away from their property. We had a good noisy chase along the fence before I left.

Always, as if I'd buried and lost a favorite bone, I searched for Rose. I had no idea where she'd be, or with whom. If she'd found another 'man to live with, I might never find her. 'Man properties are scattered far and wide, and their beasts travel much farther than my pads. But if she hadn't found a 'man, she might be roaming the countryside and leaving her scent somewhere for me to find. So I searched.

In the earliest days with Walter, I'd head towards the 'man camp in the city. I rarely made it all the way. On several occasions I got picked up, rather roughly and with little warning, by the police 'mans with the long stick. I hated the stick, and I fought and thrashed each time they captured and dragged me into the box on the back of their metal beast. I always ended up at the shelter where I'd stayed in the months before Walter.

I searched the shelter for Rose but never found her scent. Dr. Weathers, the tiny vet, didn't appreciate my visits. She scolded Walter when he picked me up.

"You're not protecting this dog, Walter." They'd just approached my cage, and I leapt in happiness to see him. She had to shout over my barking and the din of the other dogs. "Maybe it's okay to wander the mountains, but what about the highway crossings? What about the coyote traps that your neighbors have put out? How about those crazed pot growers and their penchant for guns?"

"Crazed pot growers? C'mon, Laura, they've got fences, not guns. I'd worry more about the religious nuts living in the woods."

"You know what I mean, Walter. You can't leave a dog to run loose. You're not doing him any favors, letting him run wild. He can get hurt or injured or worse, and you won't know when it happens."

"I can't keep this dog locked up. He refuses to sleep in the house, and I'm not going to chain him at night. I've had no issues with coyotes or raccoons since he's been here, either. If I restrained him, he'd be useless as a guard dog."

Walter ran a hand through his hair and studied me. I wagged my tail and glanced at his treat pocket. *Give me a treat, and let's go!*

"It's as if he's hunting for something, like an internal drive. He just won't stay home. None of my other dogs ran like he does."

"No one wants to chain a dog, Walter. But is his freedom worth his life? I know you've got your reasons, but you're the man here. How good a guard dog is King if he's hit by a car or caught in a snare? You'll be waiting and wondering why he doesn't come back. You'll have directly contributed to his death."

Walter lifted his arms and splayed his hand out. "Okay, I get it. I'll see what I can do. Maybe I'll chain him for a week or so, just to get him out of the habit of his running at night." He reached down to my collar and clipped a leash to it.

"Let's go, King. We've got work to do."

EVENINGS WITH WALTER WERE QUIET. We'd eat dinner then head to the outbuildings to close up the chicken coop and the barn. The chickens went into their roost by dusk, and we shut their coop and locked it tight. Walter always headed into the barn with a handful of oats (tastes like sawdust) to say goodnight to Big Gray and Duchess. Dilly and Dally would rush the barn door to greet him, and he'd toss peanuts (a bit chewy) into their pen before shutting them inside.

With the barn closed up, we'd head back to the porch where Walter would sit on the porch and fill a hollow pipe with a heavily scented (and incredibly bitter tasting) brown leaf. He'd tamp it and light it, puff a few times and sit in the darkness listening to the night sounds of the mountains: the howl of a coyote, crickets, the wind in the trees, far off 'man beasts. He'd sit until he finished the bowl. Unlike Lana's smoke sticks or the sour smoke sticks pervasive throughout the 'man camp, the scent of this smoke varied – sometimes floral with a hint of cedar, other times sweet with a tinge of spice, even fruity. It didn't sting my nose as much as the other types of smoke I'd been around, and I learned to relax as the scent floated over me in the evening breeze.

The night we arrived home from the shelter, Walter and I ate dinner on the porch. He sat at the table to eat, and I lay down at his feet after I'd cleaned and double-cleaned my food dish.

"It'd be nice if you'd stick around the property, King."

I wagged my tail and gazed at him. He looked sober, his face serious. I stilled myself. I could be serious, too. I lowered my head and watched him, chin resting on the wood of the deck.

"I'm just not sure the best way to get you to stop running." Walter didn't normally speak during mealtime. I listened to every word with intent, if not comprehension. When he talked, I listened. No matter what he said, I agreed.

"If I chain you, you'll stay home, but will you actually learn?" I cocked my head sideways in response. Walter stood and carried his dishes into the cabin. I watched him set them next to the sink then retrieve his smoke kit from its box on the bookshelf. He returned to the porch and sat with an unusual heaviness.

Contrary to our normal routine, we didn't go close up the barn. Instead, Walter loaded his pipe and lit it. He sat, puffing and lighting, puffing and lighting, while I lay at his feet and wondered about the open barn. Why hadn't we gone to close it up? I watched three shadowy figures (with the musky scent of deer) cross the driveway and leap over the pasture fence.

"We've got to do something about your night rambling."

I thumped my tail on the porch deck. Walter's voice sounded rich and flavourful, a liquid velvet that blanketed me in goodness.

"I hate to chain you, King. In my experience, that just postpones the running." He puffed quietly. The shadows had disappeared into the pasture, and the yard was still. From the barn, I heard the bleat of a goat, perhaps Dilly waiting for nighttime treats.

"How to teach you to stay without force or restraint... that's the goal right there."

Suddenly he leaned forward and peered at the length of the porch. He stood and pushed the table back under the cabin's front window. My house occupied half of the porch, but with the table pushed back, a long, narrow space opened up. He stared at the space then looked at me over his shoulder. "Damn dog," he muttered.

He set his pipe down on the table and started down the porch steps. I leapt up and beat him down, then dashed to the barn, barking, to alert the goats and horses that Walter was coming. I ran a loop around the barn but cut off the second one as he approached the door. We closed off Dilly and Dally's gate, and I barely coveted the peanuts he threw to them, curling my lip at the head bangers but otherwise ignoring their manic bleating. Walter gave Big Gray and Duchess a handful of oats and a head scratch, and they neighed and nodded their heads. I beat him to the chicken coop and marked all four corners while he latched it.

Instead of heading back to the cabin, however, Walter went into one of the sheds. I joined him, though we barely fit in there together. Tools and machinery filled every corner, and a shelving unit overflowed with foreign objects. I tried to squeeze past him, but Walter's legs buckled and he fell on me with a curse.

I yelped in surprise. Walter may have been the most coordinated and athletic 'man I'd lived with, but there were times when he completely fell off his game.

As he picked himself up, I stood tall on my hind legs, placing my front paws on the middle row of the shelf and craning my head into the boxes. A mouse carcass! Just as my tongue reached for the hard, leathery body, Walter grabbed my collar and pulled me down.

"King, out! Out!" I slunk away and waited for him outside. Too small for both of us anyways.

He emerged quickly with two rolled up items tucked under each arm, shut the shed behind him and headed towards the cabin. I sniffed the rolls, hopping alongside Walter, excited about this turn of events. What were we doing now? The rolls reminded me of the 'man camp beds and even had a tinge of 'man camp scent – unwashed bodies and wood smoke.

At the porch Walter unrolled one of the objects, put its corner to his mouth and blew into it. I stopped suddenly and stared at him. What the heck? Was this a game? Where did I fit in?

I began barking, at first for encouragement. *Go, Walter! You blow, man!*

When he didn't stop or acknowledge me, I barked in confusion. *Talk to me, Walter! What are you doing to that roll? What's it all about?*

As I barked, the roll flattened out then inflated into a thin mat. I lunged and snapped at it. Walter held me off. "King, mellow out! No! " He finished and stood, and I recognized, with shock, a tiny bed. I stepped onto it and circled a few times before lying down.

Not bad, not bad. I felt a bit exposed without any walls around me, however.

But Walter ordered me to leave the bed. I watched him unroll a sleeping bag like Tank's onto the mat, which confused me. I already had a layer of blankets on my bed. And despite his hard work, I preferred to sleep in my house rather than outside. I sniffed the bag then stepped onto it gingerly and lay down again.

Walter barked a laugh at me, and I groaned affably. He surprised me constantly, this 'man, with all of his tricks. "Crazy dog," he said before heading into the house. The familiar sounds of his bedtime routine – water running, drawers opening, the clump of his shoes being tossed to the door – echoed inside the cabin as I sleepily pondered this new development. A second bed. Comfy enough, I drifted off until Walter's voice roused me.

"Get up." I looked sleepily at him. He stood above me, holding a pillow. He tossed his head to one side. "Out. Get in your own bed." I shook my head in confusion. Wasn't this my new bed? I got up reluctantly and watched as he unzipped the bag and slipped his legs into it.

Suddenly I was very awake. This was like 'man camp! I remembered the warmth of Tank's body next to mine, and I shuddered with excitement. Was this the first step in Walter setting up a 'man camp? Would there soon be others arriving with their mats and tent shelters? Maybe Rose would find her way here... and Critter, and Tank. We'd have a big happy family.

I barked at Walter and barked again. I was so into this!

He chuckled and lay down in the bag. "It's time for bed, King. No running off tonight."

Walter lay still, and I sniffed the bag, sniffed the pillow, then sniffed Walter's beautiful head.

"Go to bed." Walter ordered.

I stood over his face. He had his eyes closed, so I licked his nose. His eyes flew open, and I retreated to scope out the situation. He hadn't left much room for me on the bag, but I could probably fit in between his feet at the bottom. I glanced at Walter's face. He had one eye closed, but the other stared at me. I barked again and tread to the bottom of his bag. I stepped onto the space between his feet – not a whole lot of room there! — but I turned several times and dug up the fabric a bit to free up some more.

"Jesus," Walter muttered. "This was a bad idea."

I collapsed in a heap at the end of the bag. Walter's feet were somehow under my body – like I said, a tight fit – but with a few adjustments on both of our parts, I eventually had a smooth padded surface without Walter's bony legs to contend with. I curled up into a ball and closed my eyes. Walter sighed and his breathing slowed.

Though Walter seemed to fall asleep immediately, I found it difficult to relax. His presence magnified the night sounds. At the crack of a branch in the forest I charged barking into the night. Walter sighed heavily as I returned. As the shadow of an animal crept near the shed I leapt off the deck, growling and chasing it to into the pasture. Walter's groans greeted me when I came back. Now that Walter was no longer sleeping securely inside the walls of his cabin, I needed to be highly aware of the surroundings. As chief of security it was my responsibility to chase off any threat.

Throughout the night I erupted at every sound with a frenzy of barking. Walter groaned a lot and tossed and turned grumpily every time I came back from a security jaunt, but he didn't move into the house. Just before daybreak, I fell into a deep sleep and roused only when his legs moved beneath me.

"What a night." He sat up and exhaled deeply. His eyes were puffy and red, and his hair had the look of a matted cat. "You just couldn't stop barking, could you?"

A warmth spread through my belly, and I leaned forward to lick his chin once. Walter pushed me aside. He wanted to play! I leapt on his shoulders, and as he collapsed into the bag, I grabbed his sleeve and shook my head, growling.

"Hey!" Walter shoved me again, and I renewed my frenzy, this time grabbing the bag itself, growling and twisting my head back and forth. The fabric held strong until I yanked it backwards and it released with a rip, leaving me with only a scrap in my teeth.

"Argh!" Walter leapt to his feet, pushing me away and gathering the bag in his arms. After our night together, I wanted to help. I snapped at the bag and growled and jumped on Walter as he tried to fold it up.

"Holy cow, dog. Give me a break!" He stiff-armed me, scooped the bedding up and escaped into the cabin.

After a night spent under the stars with Walter, I felt light! I tore down the porch steps and ran around my favorite spruce tree, circled and came back. I did it again. And again, until my heart raced, and my mind went blank. By the time Walter returned to the porch for our morning patrol, I had settled down, ready to work.

Walter slept outside on the porch again that night. And the next night. And the next. It became part of that summer. I resisted his attempts to push me off. We were partners!

With every passing night I slept more deeply than the last. I stopped alerting to every single noise and only roused when I sensed a true threat – a bear trying to climb into the feed shed, a raccoon climbing onto the roof of the chicken coop. Once in a while I even left Walter alone in his bag and climbed into my own bed. The deep chainsaw-like noise he made when he slept made it easy to track him from a distance. Plus, he had a tendency to kick me when I returned after a barking binge, which led to an awkward exchange of growls and groans and curses. Sometimes, I needed a break.

I never left him entirely alone on the porch. My responsibility for Walter superseded my ache for Rose. Sleeping on the porch left Walter vulnerable, so I stopped leaving the property at night. My burning drive to find her morphed into a low, dull ache of loss and remembrance. When the weather eventually turned cold and Walter moved his bed back inside, I slept soundly in my house at night, content to protect the property and visit Rose only in dreams filled with playful games and teardrop ears.

CHAPTER 30
JULES

And then the beast lumbers into the yard. And the new 'man Jules emerges. And I smell *her*.

Jules will lead me to Rose.

By the time they've unloaded the beast, I've made my plan. I can't catch it once the beast leaves the property, so my only chance to find Rose is to leave with it. I will launch myself onto the beast's back when Walter isn't looking and remain hidden until it delivers me to her. I pace nervously as he dusts off his hands then leans onto the beast.

"Up for a cup of coffee before you head into town, Jules?" Walter nods his head in the direction of his cabin and raises his eyebrows. "I know you've got a few deliveries, but it's not often that King and I get visitors."

He strokes my head, and my pulse races. I begin to pant. The idea of leaving Walter makes me nervous. He's a good 'man. The best, actually.

But I've been waiting for this. My chance to find Rose. It's been years, and this is the first time I've caught her scent. My heart aches. She's all I've wanted since I left the 'man camp. She's my pack.

Walter continues to talk. Odd. He's not normally a chatty type.

"I'd like to hear more about the irrigation system you're putting in. I've thought about irrigating a plot down by the pond but haven't known where to start."

I look up at this new 'man suspiciously. Her hair cascades over her head like a thick rope net. It looks alive, dark brown locks twisting in and around her head in no particular order. She wears jeans, like Walter, with a flannel over a loose gray t-shirt. Nothing special in my book, but I will be the first to tell you that I don't understand the 'mans' world. She smiles at him and shakes her head.

"I'll take you up on the coffee, Walter, but I'm not sure about giving you the lowdown on irrigation. I'll lose customers if I share too many of my secrets." She takes off her flannel and throws it into the open beast. A thick lock of curly brown hair falls into her eyes, and she brushes it away. "But then again, I may be out of the market soon enough, and you'll be on your own once more."

Walter looks at her in surprise, and I follow them as they walk towards the porch. "What? You planning on retiring already? Didn't you just get up and running? Are you shy of customers? I can make a few connections for you if you need them."

"Nah, it's not the sales. I've got a growing list of customers, and I'm doing okay." She halts as Walter ascends the steps to the porch, and she eyes the single chair and tiny table with a raised eyebrow.

"Don't worry." Walter chuckles. "I've got another chair. You sit there, and I'll bring another out after I get the coffee brewing."

"Your porch is half dog house, Walter." The 'man sits in the chair and shouts through the open cabin door. "Why'd you put the house on the porch?"

She looks at me, and I tilt my head to stare back. Most visitors don't get to sit on my porch to have coffee. I wonder briefly if it's because Walter can also smell Rose, but then I shake my head. That's crazy thinking. He's not searching for her. He doesn't even know her.

"You're a big dog, King." She looks at me then hollers back into the cabin. "Did you build the house for him, or do you always have massive hounds?"

Walter laughs as he comes out of the cabin carrying a chair and places it on the other side of the table. He sits down, taking up the only free space left on the porch. "He's the biggest, by far. Refuses to sleep inside, just paces and whines all night. My last dog slept inside and traveled into town with me all the time, but this one refuses to get into the truck and doesn't like to be in the house. So I built him a place of his own."

"You mean a palace of his own!" Jules laughs.

Walter smiles. "Everyone should be able to curl up at night in a comfortable bed. Plus, he's an older dog, so I figure he needs something that he can get in and out of easily. But he's a roamer. I lose track of how many times he's run off. If I hadn't chipped him, I don't know that he'd still be here. He's ended up in the most interesting places. Hasn't run off for over a year now." He lifts his head and stands. "Smells like the coffee's ready."

Jules eyes me. I sniff the cuff of her pants then give it a quick lick. A peppery taste of pollen, but it's the scent I'm after. "Where'd you find him?" she shouts into the cabin.

Walter emerges with two mugs which he places on the table before sitting down in the empty chair. I move into the space in front of him and lay down with a groan. Once he sits in his chair, he doesn't get up quickly.

"The vet at the downtown shelter is a childhood friend. She knew I'd been having trouble with raccoons since my last dog died and called me, worried that King wouldn't be adopted. He's not only a large dog with a lot of scars, but he's pretty aloof and takes a while to warm up to people. She thought we might be a good fit."

"Did it work?"

He chuckles. "He's had commitment issues." His hand strokes my head, and I sigh affably. "He's an incredible watch dog, but he ran off a lot, and not just in the neighborhood. He's been captured twice in town near the building site where the homeless camp used to be. Not to mention the times I've had to retrieve him from neighbors who found him sleeping in their barns or tearing through their pastures with other dogs. He's not caused any harm so far, but he didn't like to stay home. I think that's all in the past, though."

Walter sets his cup down on the table and looks at Jules. "Now what's the reason you might be out of the hay market?"

Jules nods and blows the steam rising from her mug. She fixes her eyes on me and smiles tightly then sighs heavily. "Mine's a dog problem too. Well, actually, my neighbor's the problem. He lives upstream on the creek that I use for irrigation, and I never had a problem with him until my dog strayed onto his property. Then she returned from a jaunt with a target painted on her side and a note pinned to her collar that said, "Next time she won't come back."

"Yikes. Did you try to talk to him?"

Jules nods. "I wasn't sure initially where she'd been. Belle's quite the rambler too. I visited several neighbors, all of whom seemed quite nice and had no complaints. And then I reached this guy's property. I've never seen such a mess. A dump, with cans and bottles lying around, abandoned vehicles and just plain garbage everywhere."

I place my chin on Walter's feet and feel my body sink into the deck. I feel nervous, conflicted. What will he do when I leave?

"I wasn't sure what I was getting myself into, but I got out of the truck and hollered. This ratty-looking guy came out of the trailer in his boxers screaming at me and telling me to get off of his property. He looked like someone who's done years of hard labor and drugs – skeletal body, weathered face, crazed eyes. I half-expected him to pull a gun on me, he was so riled up." She shakes her head, and Walter frowns.

"He doesn't sound rational."

"That's an understatement." Jules sets her mug down on the table and crosses one boot over the other. "I tried to ask him about the target on Belle, and he exploded. Told me that I was lucky he

ELIZABETH OLDHAM

hadn't shot her, that dogs weren't welcome on his property. Every time I tried to speak he shouted louder, and I got so angry that I left before I started a fight."

Walter's eyebrows lift, and Jules' mouth twists into a crooked smile. "I have a short fuse."

I get up and trot over to Jules' green truck. I circle it and inspect the open window on the passenger side, away from the cabin and porch. I'm not sure of the best place to hide – the cab or the flatbed of the truck.

I've got my paws on the driver's door, gauging the distance, when a chair leg screeches. Jules is walking down the porch steps, and Walter is stretching his arms over his head. They're not looking at me. The cab it is. I leap up to the open window, claws scratching metal until they find enough purchase at the top to give me leverage. I yank my body up and through the hole then dive into the blanket that smells of Rose. I paw at it and shift it all around me until I'm curled up and perfectly hidden.

Jules' voice is just outside the cab. "Thanks for the coffee, Walter. I appreciate the break, even if just for a few minutes." Her hand pulls the lever, and the door creaks open. "But I've got other deliveries."

A long silence falls after she opens the door. I shrink into the blanket and shut my eyes tightly, certain she can't see me. Then I feel the warmth of Jules's body and smell the sweet scent of hay as she leans over me and pulls the blanket off of my head. I don't look up.

"Walter, your dog is in my truck." Jules' voice is above my head. I keep my eyes screwed tightly shut. "Any idea what he's doing?"

Walter's footsteps near, and I smell him approach the cab. My heart beats wildly.

"I can't figure this dog out." He sounds confused. Disappointed. I can't look at him. I've just tried to abandon him, but Rose is so close. I keep my eyes closed.

"Is this your way of keeping me from leaving?" Jules's voice retreats, and the cab rocks as Walter climbs into it, the scent of spring rain and apples flowing over me.

"I have no idea what he's up to. He hates trucks." His voice is a thin hard line just above my head. "King, get out."

Rose. I bury my nose in the blanket, her scent woven into its threads. I feel an itch and try to ignore it.

"King. Get. Out."

I note his hard voice, and I whine. I open my eyes and sink onto the floor of the cab, ears back, pleading. Walter is not a hands-on kind of guy. He doesn't drag me around as so many others have done before. But his face is tight, his jaw rigid. I can't meet his eyes, and I look away.

"I don't know what you're up to, King, but you need to get out."

He moves closer and I shrink, but he doesn't grab me. He reaches into his pocket then shoves a handful of Porkies Peanut Butter Bacon Biscuits under my nose!

Have I mentioned that Porkies Peanut Butter Bacon Biscuits is unrivaled as my all-time favorite treat? He waves his hand back and forth in front of my nose and speaks softly.

"You're a goddamned stubborn dog." My tail flips on its own accord. I sniff his hand despite myself. A line of drool slips from my mouth, and I give my head a shake. My body is betraying me.

Focus. Hold your ground.

"I have no idea what you're doing, but you can't do it."

I watch his hand intently. I lick my lips.

"King, stay."

What's this? Commands?

I'm confused. I thought I was in control. But now that Walter's issuing commands, I'm not so sure.

He lifts my Porkies away from my nose, and I keep my eyes on them. When he draws his arm back to throw, I sit up in alarm.

He's going to throw them!

"King, stay."

What does he mean, 'Stay'? How can I stay when he's throwing Porkies?

Walter throws the biscuits towards the chicken house

Chickens! They will eat anything! I bark as the treats land in their midst and again as they cluck and surround them.

This is too much. Walter is looking at me, and I glance at him before looking again at the chickens and shifting nervously.

"King, break."

I don't think. I leap off of the beast and straight into the group of chickens huddling over MY PORKIES PEANUT BUTTER BACON TREATS. I growl as they scatter, then I scarf them up with all the crumbs I can find. I'm searching for remnants as Jules' beast begins to rumble, and by the time I've lifted my head to look, she's driving, too far away for even a dog with good hips to catch.

I watch the retreating beast and realize that my brief connection to Rose has been lost. Damn that *Law #1*. I lift my head and howl.

CHAPTER 31
WAITING

I jog along the west side of the pasture, following the scent of coyote at the far end of the pond. A bad sign. Coyotes are evil beings with sharp teeth and quick reflexes. I usually see them from a distance, hanging out on the edges of 'man territory, waiting for their chance to raid a farm or knock over garbage cans. I smell two of them, young males, and I wonder if they're just passing through or conducting a recon mission for a future attack. I make a mental note to stick closer to Walter's for a while, even though that may hinder my search.

Because, while I've been waiting for Jules to return these past few weeks, she hasn't. Nor has the beautiful scent of Rose. I've taken day trips along the road, trying to pick up her scent a number of times, searching for any meaningful trace. Any number of local hounds have charged me, threatening me off or engaging in a game of chase. They're larks, these interactions, distractions from the serious task of finding her, but each interaction is a breath of fresh air compared to the lack of progress at Walter's place.

Don't get me wrong. Walter's the most consistent, gentle 'man I've known. He's an easy companion. He feeds me regularly – morning and night – and gives me more than I need to survive. More than I've had most of my life! Ample fresh water, attention and care when I need it, the freedom to wander the property at my leisure. It would be the perfect place to finish my life, if only I didn't know that Rose is out there. Because life without Rose is like a bone without marrow – beautiful and promising, but in reality empty and tasteless.

So I go through the motions, trapped by a desire for what I cannot find, living like a dog who's never tasted freedom but knowing, in my heart, what I'm missing. If only I knew how to find her.

The coyote scent fades as the morning breeze picks up. I dip into the pond, soak my legs up to my belly, and stand with my nose in the air. The two goats are near a large rock by the pond. Dally stands atop the rock facing down. She bleats and charges head first towards Dilly who lunges forward and smacks heads with Dally. A loud crack echoes throughout the property. My head aches watching them. I don't understand goats. But because they're Walter's, I protect them as my own pack. Which brings me back to the coyote scent.

As I emerge from the pond and shake off the water, I put my nose to the ground and begin to track the scent into the forest. Strong in the pasture, it disperses across the pond, and I struggle to locate it. Coyotes are clever, I'll give them that – must be their close connection to dogs. I find the scent again on the edge of the forest. But just as I head into the trees, Walter whistles. I still myself and listen.

"King!" He whistles again, a sharp, high whistle. I can't ignore it – *Law #2* compels me to respond. I know my name, and I know my 'man. I toss a longing look into the forest then turn back to the pasture, shimmy under the fence and rise into a lope. Dilly and Dally crash together as I pass them, and again I cringe at the smack of their heads. Walter believes they're smart, but in my opinion, taking repeated blows to the head is not a sign of intelligence.

I arrive as Walter moves around his large red beast. He's preparing to leave. Since scenting Rose in Jules' beast, I've joined him on all of his trips away from the property. Beasts still makes me barf. But despite the drooling and heaving, riding with Walter is going to get me closer to Rose. She's out there, and Walter's beast can take me to her.

He shakes his head as I near him, and he slams closed the hard metal gate on the truck bed. I launch into my special full body greeting, a leap with a hip check that I've perfected with Walter. He loves it.

"Oof." He stumbles back as if he's been drinking Trouble and catches himself on the truck bed. He's a riot! I crouch, hips high and shoulders low, and wait for his next move. He never ceases to entertain me.

He bares his teeth and laughs, and I jump past him – psych! – and run a few laps around him and the beast at top speed. Something about Walter's laugh makes me want to run fast. I throw in a growl or two as I pass him, and his laughter makes me speed up. After a few final laps, I stop and eye him, breathing heavy, but not so heavy that I can't start up again, which I do. It's that kind of day.

I finish my last circle of the beast and eye Walter. He stands with his hands on his hips and shakes his head then throws one hand out towards the open beast. "Jump in, boy. You've got a vet appointment. Then I thought we'd take a detour to Jules' place afterwards, check out her irrigation system. You sure seemed to like her. Totally understandable, in my book."

He beckons to me, and my stomach flips over. My heart tugs me forward, but my stomach twists into knots and holds me back.

"Let's go." Walter sweeps his arms towards the beast's gaping mouth and looks at me expectantly.

I duck my head, lay down, and begin to pant. I want to go with him, but the thought of riding in the beast makes my stomach clench. I roll over onto my back hopefully. Maybe he'll give me an encouraging belly rub first.

He leans over, rubs my belly and speaks softly.

"We've got things to do, King. Namely, your vet appointment." He reaches his hand into his pocket and pulls out a Porkies Biscuit.

I flip back to my stomach and watch his hand closely, prepared to launch myself after the treat if he throws it. Instead he leans down and fastens a leash to my collar.

I am slightly affronted but keep my focus on the biscuit which Walter flashes at me before throwing it straight into the truck cab. "Let's go, King," he says as it lands on the far side.

I jump in and gobble up the Porkies Peanut Butter Bacon Biscuit. Porkies has just the right balance of peanut butter and bacon with no downsides at all. Except, perhaps, for the fact that they only last for half a second before they're gone. I sniff for crumbs and, finding none, look to Walter for another. But Walter isn't looking at me. He starts the beast with a roar.

A heaviness lodges in my chest as we start moving, and my stomach begins the all too familiar churn of beast travel. I sway lightheaded on the bench next to Walter and hang my head out of the opening next to me. Damn these beasts and their gut thundering influence.

CHAPTER 32
CHECK-UP

I hold it together during a very long drive, gulping in fresh air as the beast bounces and shakes. Walter sings and drums his fingers on the steering wheel. *How can he be happy?* We pull into a lot with several other beasts and stop next to the vet's office. We've been here several times, and the treats here – salmon squares – are almost as good as Porkies.

"Survive, buddy?" Walter smiles at me and grabs my leash as he slides out of the door. I follow woozily but gratefully, eager to be anywhere other than inside the truck. The jumbled scents of animals leap out at me as we near the building. A small gray dog with pointy ears and the stub of a tail is standing inside the door as we reach it. He's attached to a purple leash with a graying 'man on the other end. As I lower my head to sniff him, he lets go with a frenzy of barking then jumps away. I pull my head back and eye him warily.

"Now, now, Wilson." The 'man chides the dog who continues to bark as we pass by. He lunges towards me, and I snarl once at him, sending him yelping and scurrying in the other direction. He must not get out of the house much. His 'man tightens the leash and frowns as we proceed to a desk where Walter checks in.

I lay down at Walter's feet as he sits on a hard plastic chair.

We're the only 'man dog combo in the place. The smells of bleach and the strong, musky scent of my kind, a scent that never fails to arouse my interest, fill the room. Bags of dog food sit stacked on shelves with an assortment of treats, brushes and other animal implements. I don't see or smell any Porkies.

As Dr. Evans walks into the waiting room, the scent of cedar, sap and earth flows over me.

Rose! I jolt up, alert.

Dr. Evans has short white hair that looks like a mop, and she's wearing a white coat with big pockets. I sniff her pockets – salmon squares – as she moves closer. Rose's scent is not on her jacket but lingers in the hallway from where she just appeared.

"Good morning, Dr. Evans." Walter stands and shakes her hand.

Rose is here. I tug myself towards the hall, but Walter pulls back on the leash.

"Hi Walter. Good to see you again." She smiles at him then looks down at me. "Hi King. How are you doing?"

I ignore her, pulling the leash taut and pointing my head towards a big silver door. Behind the door I hear the clang of metal and the faint sound of animals shifting and shuffling. *Rose is in there.*

Walter pulls me away, and I whine, even though I love Dr. Evans, whose big, beautiful pockets make my mouth drip like a runny faucet. I lick my lips involuntarily. It's difficult to focus. Visits to the vet are very treat friendly.

"We'll go into this room on the left." She motions us to follow her, but if I do, I'll lose Rose.

I drop to the cold floor and refuse to get up. Walter tugs, but I don't budge.

"King!" He pulls the leash, and I flip onto my back.

From behind the steel door, I recognize a soft woof.

Rose!

I yelp and leap up, yanking the leash from Walter's hands and running down the hall towards the gray door. Walter shouts my name. I ignore him and reach the door as a 'man in blue is exiting. I slam into it before it closes, slip my head in and try to wriggle past the 'man. She grabs my collar, but I've got my head inside, and I see Rose's beautiful red and white head and tear drop ears. She's inside a cage turning circles and barking.

Rose!

I cry out, and Rose sees me. She shrieks in recognition. We call to each other, and I battle for purchase as I'm pulled backwards on the slippery tiles. I'm dragged, keening and yelping, away from Rose, down the hallway and into an exam room. The door shuts, and Rose's bark recedes. The 'man in blue hands my leash to Walter, who frowns and shakes his head.

Dr. Evans laughs. "That's a new one. I've never seen a dog try to get into our kennels before."

"I don't know what the hell that was about." He studies me with steely eyes. I don't like his look. I drop my eyes and look around the room instead. It's like every other vet office – a large rectangular table that slides up and down, a wall of cupboards with a sink and counter space below it, and a bench on which Walter sits heavily. A young 'man is already in the room. She stares at me with wide eyes then turns and begins tapping her fingers on a device sitting on the counter.

Dr. Evans cocks her head as she looks at me. I whip back and forth in front of the door then jump on it, scrape my paws down its length. "King, what's up? You're jumpy today." She turns to Walter and then the 'man tapping at the counter. "Walter, this is Amy, she's the new vet tech." The 'man smiles at Walter and holds her hand out to me.

I sniff and am slightly intrigued by the stale scent of a McDonald's quarter-pounder, not a scent I'd forget after once scooping up one of those delicious treats from a park bench. But the faint scent holds no promise this afternoon.

"What's up with you, King?" Walter's voice is barely audible due to the loud whining in my ears. Mine. He folds his arms, the leash tucked around them, and I stick my nose against the door crack.

Dr. Evans tilts her head to study me. "King, you are restless." She reaches her hand into her pocket, and I sit, alert. "How about a treat?"

I am already on it. Her pockets don't smell like Porkies – they smell like fish – and *Law #1* mandates that I keep close to her until I've tasted them. She tosses a treat which I inhale before it begins its descent, then I turn to the door and whine. I can no longer hear Rose, just the faint sounds of metal clanking and 'mans talking. I bark loudly and cock my head to listen. Her reply sounds far away, as if she's underwater. *Rose!* I yelp and lunge at the door.

"King!" Walter tugs on my leash again, harder, and I lean all my weight away from him and into the door.

"Just let him go."

The leash slackens, and I sit in front of the door and look at Dr. Evans beseechingly.

Open the door. Please open the door.

She washes her hands and dries them with a paper towel then tilts her head to study me, a crooked smile on her lips. "Time to settle down, King." She runs her hand along my spine and begins to gently push her fingers into my scarred hip. "How's he been since our last visit? It's been a year, usually a good sign. We may want to start seeing him every six months now that he's moving into his senior years. Any signs of arthritis? Slowing down or limping? His old injuries put him at greater risk for calcification in his hips."

I stick my nose into the door seam and stand still, waiting and listening. Walter sighs. "I haven't seen any signs of him slowing down. He can still jump into the truck – in fact he jumped into someone else's truck a couple of weeks ago. Never seen him do that before. His hip mostly seems to affect him when it's cold, so it's not an issue right now. And he hasn't lost any of his wanderlust. He'll roam far and wide if given the chance, though he's finally staying at home nights."

"How about his appetite? Still strong?"

Walter laughs. "You'd think he's starving, the way he eats. You might lose a finger if you get in the way at meal time."

"Great." Dr. Evans finishes prodding my hip and moves to my head. I shift and turn away. She's too close, and I don't like to look at anyone on eye level, even Walter. She lifts a black rubbery cord from around her neck, attaches two ends to her ears then takes the third end and holds it to my chest, squatting next to me.

I haven't forgotten about her treats. I shove her pocket with my nose as she leans forward with the tool in hand.

"Whoops!" Dr. Evans is suddenly rolling back on the floor.

Games! We must be playing games! Dr. Evans is a real hoot. I crouch low and huff as she gets back up and bares her teeth.

"Are you looking for something in my pocket, King? A salmon square, perhaps?"

I sit at attention as she reaches into her pocket and pulls out a fishy treat. Dr. Evans is the best! She tosses a treat to me, and I snatch it before it hits the ground. I look up again.

"Let's get this visit done before more treats, got it?"

I stare at her then glance at Walter. He looks at me and shrugs. "She's the boss, King."

She leans over me, and I stiffen as she presses the metal disc to my chest.

"That's a good boy. Just listening to your heart." She moves the disc around and applies pressure while I shift restlessly. Then she stands up and removes the clamps from her ears and speaks to the other 'man taking notes. "Heart's good – strong and steady."

"Ready for the teeth, King?" She rubs my head and lifts my jaw, and I back up into Walter who pats my hips.

"Steady there, boy." He massages the tricky spot between my shoulder blades, and I relax as Dr. Evans lifts my lips and prods my gums with her fingers.

I nose her pocket again as soon as she lets go of my head. Once again, she rolls back onto the floor! What an athlete!

I rush in to search for errant treats, but Walter grabs my collar.

203

"Leave it, King," he says with a low growl.

I glance at him then lick my lips as Dr. Evans stands and laughs at me. "You've caught me twice! Looking for more treats?" She reaches into her pocket and tosses me a fishy treat which I barely taste as I ready for a second toss. She moves to the counter and sets her tool down before reaching into her pocket again.

Yes!

She lobs a treat and then another.

"Well, Walter, he looks good. Honestly, for a dog with this many historic injuries, he's aging very well. We want to keep an eye on that hip for arthritis. I'm surprised he's not been limping more. And at this age, things may start to pop up."

"What kind of things?"

"Oh, incontinence, dementia, polyps, tumors... the same type of stuff we get as we age. Just watch him and note any changes. If anything concerns you, contact our office, and we'll let you know if you should come in." She shakes hands with Walter and opens the door.

I leap out and down the hall, lunging towards the gray door. Walter holds a firm grip on my leash, and I don't even get close.

"What's got into you?" His voice is not amused. He shortens the leash and tightens it around his fist then drags me away from Rose. At the front desk I receive a treat and give a quick snarl at an arriving poodle. I try my best to avoid getting into the beast, but after a few quick turns around Walter, my leash is so completely twisted around his legs, that I can't go anywhere. He pushes me into the cab. I pace on the seat until he orders me to lay down, then I rest my head on the window and resign myself to the tortuous trip home.

As he shuts the door, a familiar voice greets us. "Hey Walter, looks like we share a vet."

Jules. I whip my head up and lunge over Walter's lap towards her. He curses. "Holy crap, dog. Calm down." He pushes me off of his lap, and I try to get back on. He blocks me with his elbow. "Hi Jules. Just wrestling with King here."

She laughs as she peers into the truck. "I don't know if that cab is big enough for both of you."

"I just wish he'd curl up on the seat and fall asleep. Like other dogs."

She laughs. "Good luck with that. My dog's been here since this morning. She's probably eager to get home."

I bark and yelp as Walter keeps me at arm's length from Jules and the window. He shouts to be heard. "King! Shut it!" He suddenly grabs my muzzle between his hands. I drop my head to his lap and breathe heavily but can't make a peep. "Good thing I saw you. I wanted to check out your irrigation system and thought maybe this afternoon would work. But maybe today's not good."

"Give me an hour, Walter." Jules nods her head. "I've got one more stop to make after this, and I'd be happy to show you around."

"Sounds good." Walter turns the key and the beast starts with a roar. "See you soon."

My literal window of opportunity is closing. I lunge once more over Walter's lap towards Jules. He fights me off and yanks my collar to the seat. "What is with you?" His right hand keeps my neck pinned to the seat as we back up. He doesn't let go until we pull out of the parking lot. I move to the window and gasp for air, my head filled with a dull, constant pounding. My stomach clenches and unclenches, and I feel a crushing weight within my chest. I've lost Rose, and I hate beasts.

CHAPTER 33
CHURNING

R iding in the beast is perhaps the only time I let Walter take full control of the agenda. It's impossible for me to focus on anything when my stomach is churning and threatening to spew. We stop periodically for Walter to jump out of the beast and attend to business. He leaves me behind, but I don't mind. A beast at rest doesn't bother me so much. It's the driving that turns me into a quivering mess.

After a tortuous drive up and out of the city, Walter slows the beast and turns onto a long driveway I've never seen before. Despite my churning stomach and heavy chest, I raise my head. We're approaching a yellow house surrounded by green fields. Outbuildings are scattered around the house, and fields of hay stretch out in every direction.

As we slow, the door to the house opens. A dog charges out of the house to challenge us, barking, tail waving like a flag. Her bark is familiar, and my breath catches. I poise, alert, paws on the rim of the beast's mouth, until I see the red and white markings, short wiry fur and silky, teardrop ears.

I launch myself out of the beast before it stops.

"Hey!" Walter yells, but I can no longer hear him.

I run towards her. My Rose.

CHAPTER 34
ROSE

She is upon me, snarling and defensive, until my scent hits her. Her eyes widen, her ears lift, and she stops barking. Our noses touch, and suddenly she is yelping, a long, high-pitched keening that blocks out all other noise. I join her, yelping and whining as we circle each other in a frenzy. She leaps onto my back, and I collapse then roll over. She is on top of me, yelping and rolling with me as we tumble and wrestle. I get to my feet, and we chase each other, kicking up dust in the driveway and tearing past the 'mans who are standing together, hands on hips, mouths agape, watching us.

Rose! My Rose!

My heart feels full enough to burst. We run side by side down the driveway towards the road. I stop suddenly, and Rose skids to a stop just past me, breathing heavy, her tongue hanging out of her mouth. She snarls and jumps onto my shoulder. I shrug her off and sprint towards the house again. On my tail, she veers off into the hay field, and I cut back to chase her. We barrel through the long grass, where I broadside her with a flying leap.

The smell of her – moss, cedar, earth – fills me up. I've spent the past few years empty, but now my heart is full. I have my pack. Rose and Walter are all I need.

We are still in the hay field when the whistle comes. Rose stills, and I pop my head above the hay. Walter and Jules are a long way off – how did that happen? – and they are looking our way, hands shading their eyes as they scan the field. Walter sticks his fingers in his mouth and whistles again. Jules whistles, and both of us leap up.

I glance at Rose and bark. She bounces twice then barks, plows into me with a shoulder check, then takes off through the fields towards the house.

CHASE!

At full speed, I close the gap as we near the house. Rose slows as she approaches Jules and Walter, and I catch her by the scruff of her neck and bring her down at Walter's feet. Surprisingly, and despite the very slow pace of it all, Walter loses his feet and ends up at the bottom of the dog pile. It takes a few seconds of tangled limbs and paws, a lot of cursing and a hand up from Jules before he rights himself and all is well.

Rose and I stand, panting heavily as Walter knocks the dust from his jeans and picks up his ballcap.

"Well, what do you think of that?" Jules asks Walter. "These dogs know each other."

"They certainly do. I've never seen him react like this with any other dog. He likes them, sure, and he'll wrestle with them. But this? Never seen it before."

"Hmm, must have been a previous life. Never can tell where these rescues have been. Have you had him long?"

"A few years. You remember the summer of storms? Three years ago? I got him a few months after that summer. How about yours?"

"That was the same summer I found Belle. She just showed up one day, loose, no collar, underweight, a nasty wound on her shoulder and her head, her body riddled with matted fur. She looked abandoned. I put up signs around the neighborhood and called the shelter, but they hadn't heard from anyone with a missing dog that fit her description. They took my info and told me I could keep her until someone came looking. That never happened, so she stayed with me. I always wondered where she came from."

Walter nods. "King came out of the shelter. He'd been there for a while, from what I understand."

I begin licking Rose's face, cleaning the dust and hay pollen away from her mouth. She rolls to her back and flops her head to one side, and I lay down to nibble on her exposed neck. She's filled out a bit since I've last seen her and a long deep scar now runs across her front shoulder, but she's still my Rose. I sigh contentedly and relax with my head on her belly.

"This explains his reaction when you delivered the hay a few weeks back. He must have smelled her scent in your truck."

"You mean it wasn't just my magnetic personality and charming good looks?"

Walter laughs. "I wouldn't rule that out. King doesn't like bad people. I can usually tell a lot about someone by how he reacts to them."

"I meet the criteria, huh?"

Walter's face reddens. "I'd say so."

Jules glances at him sideways and smiles. "Glad I made the cut." She punches Walter on the shoulder lightly, and I raise my head with a growl. Rose rouses herself and rumbles at me lazily.

"Leave it, King."

Jules starts walking towards the house, and Walter follows. Rose jumps up and trots alongside Jules. I follow Rose.

"Have you eaten? I can make us a sandwich if you've got time. I'd planned to mow the east field this afternoon, but I seem to have wasted most of the day in town."

"I don't want to impose. I wanted to swing by but don't mean to interrupt your day." Walter looks around the property and shades his eyes with his hands as he scans it. "How many acres have you got here? This is a lot of property for one person."

Jules stops and looks at Walter. Her lips form a tight thin line on her face. "You think I need help?"

His face reddens, and he stammers before responding. "No, uh, that wasn't what I meant. I just imagine it's a lot of work."

"For a woman, you mean." Jules opens the door to the house and motions Walter inside. "Or do you question your guy friends as well?"

Rose follows the 'mans, and I whine as they disappear inside. The door closes between us. She returns to touch noses with me through the screen before leaving me again on the porch. I sigh and lay down.

I've found her. I've found my Rose, and we are together. But what happens next? Now that I've found her, will she come back to Walter's with me? Or am I to stay here?

A dull ache grows in the back of my head. Walter is the best 'man pack I've had. Leaving him doesn't feel right. Rose will have to come with me.

I shift uneasily. Will she?

THE CLINK of dishes keeps me on the porch, and I stare through the screen door. Walter doesn't share his food with me, but other 'mans do. Best to stick close by when they're eating. Rose knows this too, and I watch her head swing back and forth between both 'mans as they eat. They don't pay her any mind, however, chatting and laughing until they finally stand and slide their chairs back. Rose leaves them and joins me on the porch before she jumps off with a quick glance back at me and streaks along the driveway and into the fields. I leap after her.

Running through Jules' property is like running through long, green tunnels. It's a maze inside the hay stalks, and I chase Rose through the field without knowing exactly which direction we're heading. It doesn't matter. I'd follow her anywhere. We tear through it, stopping for a drink at a creek that meanders through the forest on the edge of Jules' hay fields.

I fill myself with the cold, clear water, and my heart is full. I have found her. I have Rose. I have Walter. I want nothing else.

Rose stops drinking and lifts her head. She sniffs the ground then follows a scent down the creek and left into a copse of trees. I follow, finding a very intriguing scent line – meat. Fairly fresh, and heavy. I don't wonder about it. This is Rose's territory. I follow the scent and Rose.

But secondary scents begin to assail me, and an unease takes hold. I smell Trouble, lots of it. Diesel fuel, too, tinged with smoke sticks and a general scent of decay. I lift my head to study the land around me. It's familiar, but I can't place it. Have I been here before? Perhaps, in my travels with Rose. We used to spend hours roaming the fields, farms and forests. I shouldn't be surprised if something feels familiar.

But why this anxiety? Why this growing sense of unease? I've been waiting for this. For Rose.

Something's not right.

Rose walks through the trees, inspecting rocks and leaves and marking her presence. I trot after her, stopping at each spot to add my mark to hers. The tree stand suddenly leads us to a dense blackberry thicket. Just on the other side, I can smell meat – a smorgasbord of meat. We slowly crawl on our bellies underneath a long thicket of thorns with sharp spikes that threaten to dig into our flesh. But the smell pulls us forward, and we finally emerge into an open meadow.

Rose pads ahead. I halt.

Across the meadow the creek babbles and winds through the rocks and trees. Beyond the creek lies a metal home propped on blocks, a yard littered with garbage, and a fiery black Beast with flames marking its side. I growl. Up the hill and farther into the property I see the cage. It's vacant, and the gate hangs by one hinge. I lift my nose but find no scent of Lana, just stale Trouble, smoke sticks and a general decay.

Rose proceeds across the meadow, and I whine. The only thing to be found across the creek is pain, loneliness and hunger. But Rose crosses the creek and heads towards the fire pit. Reluctant, I follow at a distance. Close enough, however, to see her pick up what looks like a hot dog from inside the dead ashes of the firepit. She gobbles it up, looks at me and barks. I draw closer. She dips her nose into the ashes again and gobbles up a bun, and I watch as she digs deeper and pulls out a piece of something leathery.

She barks again, and the tension in me breaks. *Law #1 – See Food Eat Food!* I join her at the fire pit. Food! Glorious food, burnt to perfection, discarded by the 'mans and waiting for us like bait. This thought strikes me as a door slams and a hauntingly familiar voice shatters the air.

"Gotcha!"

When I look up, Roy is on the porch, pointing a gun at Rose. She wags her tail, but I hurtle myself toward her. I slam into her shoulder and knock her out of his line of sight. The shot misses and blasts the dirt in a spray to our left.

An eerie sense of déjà vu overcomes me. I've been here. We've been here. We've got to get away. A second shot misses as we cross the creek and zig zag our way through the meadow and into the forest. When we reach the safety of the trees, I relax into a trot, but the whine of a beast makes me turn. Roy is riding a small beast with knobby tires and a high-pitched squeal, closing the distance between us quickly.

I push Rose faster and deeper into the forest, hoping that the trees will slow Roy's which beast tears across the rocks and mud in the open meadow.

I dive under the tight thicket of blackberry bushes. With no time to pick my way through them, the dense thorns snag my fur and rip my skin. I hope that the thickness and thorns will deter him. Rose yelps and cries out then abruptly stops. A large thorn has snagged the flesh above her eye. She tries to move forward but shrieks in pain. She can't move her head. I struggle against the thorns and thick branches to reach her.

Roy stops his beast outside the blackberry thicket and peers into the density of branches. Panic rises like bile in my throat. "I'll teach you to come onto my property."

He raises the gun, and Rose thrashes, her cries deafening. Fear flashes across her face. I reach the branch with its thorns firmly embedded into the flesh above her eye, and I bite down hard on it. Its barbs pierce my gums and lips, but I grip it and twist it sideways. The motion yanks Rose's head down, and the shot flies through the thicket. Roy curses. I bite down and twist the branch again, and Rose screams but is free. A sharp pain stabs my gums, and I taste blood.

Heading towards a gap in the brush, I wriggle on my belly through the brambles with no hesitation, only a single-minded focus to escape this damn thicket and the crazed lunatic. Rose pants behind me, every intake of breath a whine. I can't see Roy, but I hear his beast roar and whine. We finally clear the thicket and run through an old pasture with tilted, sunken wooden fenceposts dotting the perimeter.

We stop to catch our breath. Blood runs in circles around Rose's eye and streaks down her jaw. Her chest heaves and she whines nonstop. This has happened before. Another flight from this same 'man. Another eye injury. Another mad dash to freedom.

We run across the old pasture. Roy's beast blares at us from the far end of the clearing. I look back and see him driving straight towards us. I urge Rose to move faster. She knows where she's going, and she leads us, still shrieking, through a tree stand and back towards the creek. Despite the rough terrain, Roy's beast is gaining on us.

The grass between us explodes as a shot rings out. Rose leaps across the creek and I draw myself shoulder-to-shoulder with her as we enter the hay field. I glance back and see Roy's beast cross the creek and follow us into the field.

Jules' yellow house sits peacefully ahead of us. I head for it, but Rose is losing steam. She's slowing as Roy gains from behind. I nip at her shoulder. She leaps forward but staggers. We draw closer to the house, and I see Walter and Jules near the large field beast, hands shading their eyes and looking our direction. Suddenly Jules points, and they break into a run and jump into Walter's red beast which sputters then roars.

Rose stumbles in the field and slides face first into the long stalks with a yelp. She picks herself up and stumbles again. I nip at her and grab her neck with my teeth, but she is too heavy, too slow. Roy's beast approaches us, and Rose whimpers. I turn to face him and stand in front of Rose with my teeth bared. *Law #4: Protect the Pack.*

This 'man hurt me. He hurt Rose. And he hurt Lana.

I hear Walter's beast lumbering towards us, but I can't take my eyes off of Roy. He swings his legs off of the small beast and walks slowly towards us.

His hands are empty and outstretched. No gun. He reeks of Trouble, and his eyes are bloodshot and fuzzy. He stops and stares at me – blankly at first but then his mouth drops open.

"You." His eyes narrow as he massages his left wrist and stretches the fingers open and shut. "Home wrecker."

He staggers in our direction. I snarl and snap. Rose whines and scrambles to her feet shakily. She pants and whimpers. I keep my eyes locked on Roy. I hear the chug-chug-chugging of Walter's beast as it barrels across the hay field towards us. Roy charges us and kicks me with a thick boot that connects with my front shoulder. I stumble to the ground. But my body surges with energy, and I leap towards him and snap at his leg.

Roy kicks out at me again as Walter's beast screeches to a halt. Roy shifts his eyes to the beast, and he blinks. He backs up as Walter leaps out, eyes blazing.

Walter marches towards Roy. "Who are you? What the hell are you doing?"

"You miserable fool!" Jules charges past Walter, lowers her shoulder and crashes into Roy's chest. They fly through the air, and collapse in a heap, Jules lands with a hard thud on top of Roy who cries out and curses.

Walter pulls Jules off of Roy and holds her arms. She kicks out at Roy's torso but misses, and Walter murmurs and pulls her back further as Roy rolls away and scrambles to his feet.

Roy sneers and holds his shoulder. "That's assault!" His voice is rough like sandpaper. He spits at Rose and points at Jules. "Your damn dog came back to my property. I told you to keep her away." He lowers his finger and stares at me. "And that dog. I know him. He destroyed my life."

He wavers on his feet but shakes his head and focuses on me again. I growl, a quiet warning growl in the back of my throat and take a step towards him. Walter places a hand on my back, and I stop.

"You have no right to be here." Walter's voice is smooth but sharp, like a knife. "You're trespassing, and you're threatening our dogs and property."

"They were both on MY property." Roy's voice starts loud but finishes with a whine. He takes a step back and swivels his head between all of us, as if he's just figured that he's outnumbered. He looks around at Jules' hay field, and a look of confusion flashes quickly across his face. He backs up a few more steps, nearing his small beast.

"I'll call the cops if I see you here again." Jules thrusts her finger at Roy but can't reach him due to Walter's arms holding her back. "Get out of here. Don't EVER let me see you again on my property."

Roy shifts his glance from Jules to Walter then back to me. He licks his lips and mumbles his final words. "I can call the cops on you. You assaulted me. Your dogs are running loose and destroying my property. And that one," he points at me and narrows his eyes again. "That one is dangerous."

He stumbles onto his beast, starts it with a rumble, then turns around and drives back through the field.

CHAPTER 35
AFTERMATH

W alter squats beside me and lifts my head in his hands. I don't want to look him in the eye. I've done something wrong. The blood, the pain, Rose's constant crying. It roils in my head. I shouldn't have followed her. My stomach is queasy, and I turn away from him to retch in the long grass. The thorn stings my gums, and I shake my head to retch again and try to spit it out.

"Whoa, King. It's okay. You're okay." Walter runs his hands along my heaving sides.

I finish and feel better. Rose is quaking and crying beside Jules. Her eye is bleeding heavily and swollen almost shut. Jules pulls her t-shirt off and over her head and uses it to tamp down the flesh around Rose's eye. She's bare skinned except for a black collar of sorts strapped around her chest and shoulders. Walter coughs, red-faced, and quickly turns away. Jules glances at him sideways, rolls her eyes and grins.

"I've got the important parts covered, Walter. But give us a lift to the house, and I'll put a new shirt on." She lifts Rose into her arms and heads towards the red beast.

"Oh, yeah, of course." Walter's voice is strangely tight. He rushes to open the beast, his eyes firmly averted from Jules and Rose. She climbs in as he gets into the other side. I sidle away from the beast and head towards the house. As the beast begins to rumble, I run beside them, keeping pace as they lumber slowly over the field.

When the beast reaches the house, Jules swings her legs around and slides out. Rose has quieted in her arms, panting, the shirt tied around her head like a turban. They climb up the stairs to the porch where Jules sets her down.

"I'll get my first aid kit." Jules stops for a second and leans down to look at Rose then marches into the house.

I climb the steps, and Walter follows, squatting next to Rose as I inspect her. Her good eye is glossy, and she breathes in short, shallow pants. But she wags her tail once as our noses touch, and her trembling stops momentarily. Jules' shirt is wrapped over her wounded eye and tied under her chin. I sniff the shirt and inhale the combination of Jules' scent mixed with Rose's – a wonderful blend of my favorite earthy tones and 'man sweat. I lie down next to her and despite the stabbing pain in my mouth begin cleaning her face of blood. I can't reach the wounded eye but instead remove the blood that's streaked down her nose.

Jules comes out of the house wearing a new shirt and carrying a blue bag in her hand. She sits down on a stool that she pulls from behind the screen door, places her feet on either side of Rose and removes the shirt from Rose's head.

"Let's see what we've got here, Belle."

Rose yelps as Jules begins to examine her eye. It's swollen shut completely and when Jules lifts the lid, Rose cries and scrambles to get to her feet. I move in nervously, sliding my head and shoulders into the space between Rose and Jules. I shield Rose from Jules and lick her again.

"A little help here, Walter?" Jules pushes at my shoulder but doesn't try to move me.

"Sure, of course."

Walter grabs my collar and leads me to the red truck. He pulls a metal cable out of the back, clips one end to the bumper and the other to my collar. Frowning, he moves closer to me, reaches down and pulls my lips away from my teeth then runs his finger along my gums. When the finger reaches the thorn, I yelp and jump away then wriggle on my belly back to him.

"Looks like King's got something wrong with his mouth. I think it's a thorn in his gums. I might need your help to get it, though."

"Well, can you help me with Belle first? She's wriggling like a pile of maggots. I can't even get a good look at what's wrong."

Walter leaves me chained to the beast and climbs the porch steps. I try to follow him, but the chain stops me at the base of the stairs. I lunge at the end of the chain and bark. *Don't cut me out of the action, Walter.* Any action. Especially any action involving Rose.

"King, quiet!"

He squats next to Jules and Rose and begins to stroke Rose's sides which are heaving and shuddering. "Does she need a vet?"

"I can't tell yet. Her eye looks scratched, and I think there's a tear in her eyelid. I can't get her still enough to take a look. I'll probably have to take her in if she can't settle down."

"What do you want me to do?"

"Hold her muzzle."

"You got a rope? I don't want to get bit."

Jules reaches into her blue bag and hands something to Walter. I continue to bark. "Here, use this. It should be long enough to loop around her jaw so that you can close it without risking your fingers."

Walter unfolds a long triangular bandage then loops the centre around Rose's nose. He ties the long ends back over her neck and tightens them. Her good eye is wide and rolls backwards.

What is he doing to her? Rose yelps and thrashes wildly. Walter leans his body over hers and pins her to the ground. I snarl and throw myself against the end of the cable. *Walter, stop it!*

"King, shut it! Quiet!"

Jules lifts Rose's eyelid and pokes her fingers gently around Rose's eye. Rose flinches and I growl. "This is ugly. It's so swollen and there's too much blood to see anything. I'll have to take her to the vet."

Walter ran his hand along Rose's side. "Easy there, pup."

I bark wildly, too far away. I lunge forward but am fastened to the truck's bumper.

Jules releases the knot that holds Rose's mouth shut, loops the bandage back over her head and eye and tightens it so that Rose is wearing her turban again. Rose doesn't move. Jules strokes Rose's head as she stands. "Hardly a pup, though she acts it. I've never had a dog that likes to play as much as she does."

Jules looks at Rose who lies still on the porch and wags her tail slowly. "I hope she doesn't lose her eye. I thought maybe he'd shot her. That was the guy who painted a target on her last month."

I can't stop barking. Rose is free, but I am not! Walter descends the stairs. He unclips me, and I streak up the stairs to sniff Rose. She wags her tail and lifts her nose to mine but otherwise doesn't move. Her pain scent is sharp, and I sniff the wrap around her head intently. I circle around then curl up alongside her and put my head on her back. The thorn in my gums burns and stings. I begin grooming Rose's neck to keep my mind off the ache.

Walter stares at me from the bottom of the porch steps and folds his arms in front of his chest. "I'll take King to the vet to get a look at his mouth. He's reactive and knocking him out's probably the only way. One of my dogs tried to take a bite of a porcupine once, and I couldn't get those quills out myself."

Walter motions towards Rose and I. "King's not going to like leaving her, so let's leave at the same time. It's a good thing we don't live too close, or I have a feeling that he'd be showing up here again solo."

Jules glances at me then at Walter. "You know, she's got a scar over her eye – you can't see it right now – like a crescent moon. It must've been deep, and happened long before I found her. It wouldn't surprise me at all if you told me that they'd gotten their scars together."

"Huh," Walter nods. "It would make sense. They obviously go

back a ways. And they seem to have a penchant for trouble." He walks to the back of the red beast and unclips the cable then rolls it up and puts it in the basket on the beast's back.

"Your neighbor is crazed. He knew King, too. He called him dangerous. Why would he say that?" He opens up the mouth of the beast, reaches in and grabs my leash. I start grooming Rose intently, eyes averted and focused solely on her. If I don't look at him, perhaps he'll leave without me.

"That guy's crazy. Unstable. The problem is, if Belle ends up on his property again, he'll shoot her." Rose flips her tail up and down a few times. "She's obviously used to going over there."

"I've had the same problem. King's a runner. I've got twenty acres, but he couldn't seem to stay within them when I first got him. Took off each night. I didn't want to chain him, so I had to think of another way to convince him to stick to our property."

"Oh yeah? What'd you do? I've got seventy-five acres, and I can't keep her home. You'd think that's enough space to keep her happy, but she can't stay in one place. I don't want to chain her either. How can she be a farm dog if she won't stay on the farm?" She nods at the green beast next to the barn. "Let me get my keys, then we'll leave at the same time. Shouldn't be any issues that way."

I sneak a glance at Walter. He stares at me for a long while, and my stomach flips inside and out. He's the best. I haven't had a better 'man. But when walks to his beast and calls me, I sink next to Rose and lay flat with my ears back. He calls again, and I whine softly. Rose whines ever more softly and presses her back into me.

Rose is my pack. Walter is my pack. Who do I stay with? Who do I protect? The laws don't handle this. But then again, the laws deal with matters of survival. And survival isn't the question here. The question is to which pack do I belong?

CHAPTER 36
KNOW YOUR PACK III

My head droops as Walter approaches. When he reaches for my collar, I roll onto my back and bare my belly.

"C'mon, King. We gotta get you to the vet." Walter talks softly, but I can't look at him. Jules is getting her beast ready. Just as Walter reaches again for my collar I leap up and away from him and into the cab of Jules' green truck. I curl up as tightly as possible on Rose's blanket. I will go with Rose.

But Walter has other ideas. He stomps heavily to the truck, and I feel him studying me, though I can't meet his eyes. When I sneak a peek, he's staring at me. I avert my eyes again and watch Jules carrying Rose towards us.

Walter sighs. Maybe if I scoot over, he'll ride with Jules and Rose too! I whine and shuffle on the bench seat, sure that there's enough room for the three of us. But when Walter clips the leash to my collar and tugs, I don't fight. The pain in my mouth leaves little fight in me. I hang my head, climb into his beast then stand sentry at the window.

As the beast begins rumbling. I sway with my head hanging out of it, gulping fresh air before the queasiness takes hold. Walter talks to me, but I hear a note of uncertainty in his voice.

I don't like it. My 'man Walter is steadfast and strong. He doesn't need to question because he knows all the answers.

"Are you going to start running again? Trying to find Belle?"

As if in response, my mouth fills with saliva, and it leaks from my mouth like a dripping hose. Then my legs begin to shudder, and an invisible coil tightens around my chest. I collapse on the padded bench and whine, panting and drooling for the remaining ride until the beast finally stops.

Walter sighs heavily. "You'll never like these car rides, will you?"

He leads me out of the beast, and I stop to relieve myself on a patch of lawn with a plastic fire hydrant. We are back at the vet office – just hours from our last visit. For the first time ever, I'm not looking for treats. My mouth burns, and my head aches. As we near the door, Jules' green beast pulls alongside Walter's.

Jules smiles at us as she hops out of the beast and walks around to the other side. Rose's nose appears, twitching, at the gap in the window, but her head remains hidden until Jules opens the beast and lifts her out. She still wears the turban and wags her tail without enthusiasm. Her scent is sharp with pain. We touch noses silently and enter together.

Rose curls up on the floor of the empty waiting room, and I lay down beside her. Dr. Evans walks down the hall shaking her head. The smell of salmon squares in her pocket would normally interest me but, contrary to *Law #1*, I have no appetite.

"You were all just here a couple of hours ago! What happened?"

Before anyone can reply, she turns to Jules and studies Rose with her turban. "Her eye? The phone message was not completely clear. I'm surprised she's let that stay on her head though." She puts her hands on her hips and surveys us. "Usually when I've got two dogs in here needing wound treatment it's because they fought. But these guys don't look like they've just fought. What the heck happened?"

Walter and Jules begin talking at once. I lose interest and rest my head on Rose's back. She has sunk into the floor as if her bones have melted. I breath heavily, confused by the afternoon's events.

I've been searching for Rose since the 'mans in black broke up our camp. I found Walter, who introduced me to Porkies treats and ball play. He's given me nothing but kindness. If not for Rose, I would happily settle down with him.

But Rose. My Rose. From that first day when she appeared behind the creek, we've been connected. We need each other. At least, we needed each other. Now that I have Walter and she has Jules, is it still true?

I look at Rose with the shirt wrapped around her head. Her good eye is glassy, and her breathing is quick and rapid. She lifts her tail a few times when I nose her neck but is otherwise still.

Is this the price of a life with Rose? Pain and suffering?

I whine. Walter's hand strokes my head. I've always wanted a life with no limits. No chains, no cages, no 'mans to hold me in one place. Life at the 'man camp with Rose was as close to freedom as I could imagine. But we faced hunger. And violence.

Critter or Tank never hurt anyone. But being harmless didn't stop others from attacking them. Even the 'mans in black hurt them. I'd been unable to stop it, unable to protect my pack.

My mouth hurts. My head hurts. My old hip wound aches, and my body is tired. Life with Walter has been painless until now. Until Rose came back. I look up at Walter. Even without looking at me, he smiles and rubs my ear. I lean into him and whine again. He is steady. He is kind. He meets me where I'm at.

Rose shudders, and I lick her shoulder. She is a part of me. Deep down in my core, my love for Rose blazes like a beacon on the darkest night. It sustains me. Through injury, through loss, through hunger, and fear.

We love each other. But at what price?

She whines softly, and I nuzzle her neck. Jules reaches down to caress her nose. She quiets.

Jules is Rose's pack. Walter is mine. Maybe finding Rose is all I need. Maybe it's not freedom that I need but a pack that won't quit me. Rose has never quit me. Walter has never quit me.

Suddenly I realize that I can't quit Walter just like I can't quit Rose. He's my pack as much as she is. I trust him. I follow him. Rose has my heart, but Walter has my body and soul.

The 'mans have stopped talking, and Dr. Evans takes Rose's leash and tugs her up gently before she turns and walks down the hallway. "I'll come back for King in a second. They'll have to stay overnight, and I'll give you a call in the morning."

I watch nervously as Rose departs. Jules runs a hand through her thick, knotted hair. "Well, my evening is completely shot."

Walter grunts. When he speaks, his voice is gruff but stammers. I glance at him then look at Jules suspiciously. Walter smells nervous.

"Uh, well, I, uh. Well, maybe I owe you a dinner for all this trouble we caused?"

Jules eyes him with a smirk. "You sure you're not just excited because you saw me with my top off?"

Walter's eyes widen, and he blushes a deep crimson. "No! I never... that isn't... I just, you know, I just thought...."

Jules laughs and punches Walter in the shoulder. I growl. Walter puts his hand on my head.

"I'm giving you a hard time. Sure, let's go eat dinner. But I warn you, I'm hungry, and you may not like what you see."

Dr. Evans returns, and Walter hands my leash to her. I look back as she leads me away. They are laughing, and Jules punches Walter in the shoulder again. He rubs his shoulder and stares at her with a look that I can't identify.

CHAPTER 37
FIGHT

.

I lie napping in a hole I dug under a tall spruce just for this occasion, ignoring the chattering squirrel in the boughs above me, one eye surveying the property in the heat of the day. An approaching beast rouses me, a low rumbling with a cough. Jules' beast. Sure enough, a green body flashes through the trees, and I leap out of my hole and streak through the pasture, yelling my ears off. The horses whinny as I slide past them under the pasture gate. I snap at the chickens as I run through them, and they scatter loudly. As Jules steps out, I leap towards her in a full body greeting.

"Whoa!" Jules slams her knee into my chest so that I fall back and flip onto the ground before I have even touched her. *Rude.* She stares at me with her hands on her hips, her eyes dancing. "You've got to learn to properly greet people."

I get up and eye Jules. She's strong and doesn't like to be pushed around. Good to know. Before I can try again, Rose is on top of me, and we are rolling and snarling and leaping around the yard together. We haven't seen each other since the vet several weeks ago, even though I've caught Jules' scent on Walter more than once.

Time has passed slowly without sight of Rose. Once the pain in my mouth went away, I left the property every night to search for her, mostly making it back before sunrise and our morning patrol. I thought Walter hadn't noticed my absence, but I heard him this morning on the phone inviting Jules to the property.

"He's dying to see her. Won't stay home again. How about a visit? I can use your expertise in irrigation, and you get to taste my renowned lasagna."

Walter and I have kept busy on the property. I helped him fix holes in the pasture fence, though, due to some early and painful entanglement with the wire, I let him take the lead and simply barked encouragement. Together we dug a trench in the lower field, my paws putting his shovel to shame. In fact, after a mad flurry of dirt removal, Walter stopped digging to observe me. In appreciation of my efforts, he then reached into the beast, grabbed a ball and threw it. Upon my return he placed me on supervisory duty and kept me out of the trench entirely. I barked instructions and motivated him throughout the afternoon until he finally finished.

Now Rose and I are back together. Her scent fills me with happiness. We stop wrestling, and I study her. The swelling in her eye is gone. A thin white film overlays her pupil like pollen on a pond, but the eye seems to be working. I circle her. She turns and bounces to keep facing me. I lunge at her feet, and she counters with a block and grabs the back of my neck.

Walter follows Jules' beast to the shed, and we race to beat them, sliding to a stop just as Jules steps down from the beast. She crumples as we slide into her.

"Goddamned dogs." Jules mutters as she picks herself up from the ground and dusts herself off. I leap to greet her, but she grabs my collar and holds me down and away from her face as she leans over me. "Stay down, King. You're happy this morning. All healed up from your misadventure last month?"

I wriggle and wag, overflowing with pleasure. Walter grins broadly as he approaches. He's been smiling a lot recently.

"He's as good as new. He had a few days of soft food, but we've been back to normal for a couple of weeks. Belle's better?"

Jules releases me, and I run to her beast to sniff and mark the tires. Rose follows me and covers my scent with hers. I turn around to top them off again after she's left.

"She wore the cone of shame for a while, but it kept her out of trouble. Acted like she couldn't lift her head, dragging herself up the porch and banging the cone on every step. I think she thought she'd been punished. Her eye's no longer 100% but still functional."

Jules walks to the back of her beast and climbs up. She loosens a strap on the hay and picks up a bale with gloved hands. "Same place as last time?"

"Yep. Just throw it down. I'll ferry it under the awning."

Rose and I trot under the gate and into the pasture. The horses shy away from Rose who barks at them. Dilly and Dally are in their usual spots next to the pond, and Dally bleats as Rose and I near. Dilly lowers her head and faces us defiantly. We ignore her. I climb a large rock and lay down in the sun. Rose settles next to me.

The heat of her body and the rock below me lulls me into a dream-like contentment. I sleepily survey the series of deep holes that I've dug throughout the pasture. One never knows when they may be needed for a bone or a cool resting spot. I sigh happily. The wind whispers in the grass beside us, and the sound of Jules and Walter working overlays the chattering of squirrels and the birds singing. I roll over lazily onto my back. Beside me, Rose sighs and stretches her legs out.

We nap off and on while the 'mans continue their work. Every so often I lift my head to check for Walter, but I don't need to. Their voices carry loud and clear even from a distance.

"Have you had any luck keeping Belle at home?"

"She didn't wander when she wore the cone, but since then we've been working on it. She sleeps in the house with me, so night wandering isn't an issue. I'm not sure that your method would be as effective for us. I'm kind of glad though, cause I'm not a fan of sleeping outside when I've got a nice comfy bed twenty feet away."

"Ha! Can't say that I was a fan of that either, but he won't sleep inside. Crazy dog."

Beside me, Rose lifts her nose to the air. It twitches, and her ears perk up, high and alert. I listen. I watch without lifting my head. No foreign sounds. Nothing to see. I set my head back down and close my eyes. But faintly, like a murmur, I pick up a new scent, a wild, acrid smell that stings the back of my throat.

I growl and rise to my feet, nose in the air. I've scented this before. The moving shape beneath the beast. A diamond shaped head and malevolent eyes. The hissing and the rattle. Mama collapsing in the dirt.

Rose stands and sniffs the air intently then moves off the rock and pads, head down, towards the sheltered feed stand near the shed. I growl and follow. A prickly sensation rises in my chest. I tamp it down and push ahead of her, narrowing in on the location. The scent intensifies near a twisted pile of roots and branches that Walter cleared from the pasture last week. I see the small moving body under a large, knotted root just as Rose darts past me and leaps towards it. One end begins to rattle, and a small head rises up from the centre.

A snake! A snake that took Mama away. It could take Rose away. I throw myself into her and knock her off her feet with a growl.

Rose yelps and looks at me in surprise. She gets up and tries to go around me. I challenge her, block her, teeth bared, hackles raised. I snap at her forelegs as she tries to dart past me. She looks confused and then hurt. Then angry.

She meets my final lunge with a snarl then bares her teeth. Rose and I have never fought. We've been allies since our first meeting. But she's not responding to me. She's angry.

I'm angry too. *Just stop, Rose. Follow me this time.*

We clash and wrestle, fully engaged, snake forgotten. Rose snaps at my jawline. I keep my paws on her shoulders and try to pin her down. She fights back with a ferocity that I've never before felt from her.

I am fighting to save Rose. Why is Rose fighting? I don't know. I'm the fighter. I've never seen her fight. She's always been more apt to wriggle out of a challenge than to accept one. But here we are. She grabs my ear and I yelp as her teeth pierce through skin. I slide out of her grasp and then leap onto her neck. She shrugs me off, and we circle each other.

Despite the scars we both carry, Rose hasn't learned caution. She rushes into things without thinking, impetuous, curious, blind to danger. Doesn't she see that her rash actions will cost her? She faces me and curls her lips, growling and panting.

Her anger hits me like a wave. She's furious. I've never tried to stop her before. She lunges to knock me sideways but finds a brick wall. I am taller and stronger, a rock, steadfast. I protect her. We explore together, we search for food, we find adventure. A team. But now we're on opposite sides.

She tries to run around me, but I intercept her with a body-check that knocks her sideways. While she's off-balance, I bring her down to the ground. She yelps and twists, and I stand over her, teeth bared, growling. Warning her.

"King!"

"Belle!"

Both 'mans call us, but I don't look up. Rose wriggles below me and snarls. She grabs one of my forelegs in her teeth and bites down. I yelp and growl and grab for her neck. I need to subdue her and stop this madness. She yelps and writhes uncontrollably, but when I finally grab hold of her neck, she stills and quiets. I stand over her with her neck between my jaws and pant, breathing quickly through the fur, finding my breath after the battle.

"What the heck, King?" Walter grabs my collar and yanks me off of Rose. I snarl and yelp as Rose leaps up and backs away from me. She yelps loudly. Her eyes are hurt and defiant. Jules reaches down to Rose's collar and holds her still, inspecting her.

"What the hell is that about?" Jules steps closer to the root pile to look at Rose, and I bark madly, lunging towards them. I can't see the snake, but it's still there. Its scent stings my nose. Walter tightens his grip, and I strain against my collar. I want to block them from the root pile but can't. I bark wildly.

"King, shut it. Stop!" He tightens his grip, and I increase my frenzy, turning my head back and forth to try to twist free. I throw my body sideways, but Walter holds me fast.

"What the hell, dog? You're crazed."

The snake starts to stretch and move. It's heading away from us. Towards the chicken coop. I whine and yelp. Walter struggles to control me as I twist under his grip.

"What's gotten into you?" He lifts me so that my front feet come off the ground and I have to bounce on my back feet or hang from my neck. I hop and lunge and continue to bark a strangled cry.

Jules' face is pinched in confusion. "What's going on?"

Rose is calm but pants heavily. "You okay now?" Jules squats next to Rose and runs her hands along Rose's back. She lets go of Rose's collar, and Rose's ears lift as she spots the snake slithering away from us. She leaps towards it, and without thinking I snap at Walter's hand and slip my head out of the collar. I launch myself towards Rose and knock her off her feet. She yelps and twists to snarl at me in confusion. The 'mans curse and jump towards us.

"Oh shit, Walter. Snake!"

I bark and lunge at Rose as she tries to bolt past me.

"Grab them!"

Rose and I are tangled up in a new battle, but Jules reaches in and yanks Rose away from me. Walter grabs my collar again.

"I'm putting King in the shed. Chain Rose to my bumper."

I fight Walter as he drags me out of the pasture. He grabs a shovel and an ax then locks me in the shed.

Locked in! I'm locked in! I jump onto the door and scratch at it furiously. Walter's taken me away from the danger just when I'm needed most.

I leap at the door. It shudders and shakes but doesn't yield.

Rose yelps just outside the shed. *Good, she's tied up too.* I have no idea where the 'mans are.

I lie down directly behind the door, my attempts to get out useless. Panting heavily, I'm more stressed than I've been in a long time. I snapped at Walter. I disobeyed him. And I attacked Rose.

I put my nose to the thin gap in the door frame and breathe in deeply. I listen. I hear Walter's voice, and I whine. Rose yelps, and I growl. If she hadn't kept pushing, I wouldn't have snapped at Walter. I wouldn't be locked in the shed.

Suddenly I realize that I don't want to lose Walter. These past years with him have been the most peaceful, pain-free years of my life. He's given me a home and a purpose.

Rose has my heart. But following her has brought pain back into my life.

I whine nervously and stare at the crack in the door as Walter and Jules talk in the yard. I snapped at Walter. Will he forgive me?

Rose has stopped whining and yelping, so their conversation reaches me.

"Well, that was crazy," Jules says.

"Ooh boy. I've never seen a rattlesnake out here before. I heard about a snake incident about a decade ago. Crippled a border collie in the south part of the valley. Maybe they're getting more common. I'm surprised that King recognized it."

"What is it about our dogs, eh? They just can't stay out of trouble."

"They certainly have a knack for it even if they didn't bring this on. That fight though, no fun." Walter pauses. Jules speaks softly to Rose, and I hear the snap of the chain release her. *No fair!* I yelp.

Walter's voice comes closer to me. "My brother would get really drunk when we were younger. My older brother by a year. A hockey player, a big fish in a small pond. Thought he was something. When he drank he liked to tell me how to run my life. Sometimes we'd fight. I never wanted to. I'm not a fighter. But even though he was bigger and stronger, I'd fight until he beat me or someone else broke it up."

Walter's footsteps near the shed, and I stare at the crack of the door.

"How do you guys get along now?"

"He drove drunk into a tree, at twenty-four. Killed his girl-friend, too. My parents never recovered. A long time ago, now." He pauses. His feet shift and his voice turns away from the shed. "King was trying to protect her, but I hate to see families hurt each other."

Walter opens the shed door, and I burst out happily. Then I remember how I snapped at him and am suddenly very ashamed. I sink to my belly and grovel at his feet. I writhe and whine and try to tell him. I needed to protect my pack.

He leans over me and eyes me intently. "You're a complicated dog, King."

His words aren't angry. I twist my head to take a closer look. His eyes are sad, but his face is friendly, his mouth a half-smile. I whine. I offer him my belly.

He's upset but I don't think at me. Maybe the snake scared him.

"Have you seen a rattlesnake before?" He reaches down to scratch my belly, and I whine again. The warmth of his hand calms me and quiets my churning mind.

Jules approaches Walter and puts her hand on his shoulder. Rose follows slowly and dips her head down to touch noses with me. She licks my nose once then sits down and leans into Jules' legs. She's forgiven me.

"So if King and Rose are family, Walter, what does that make us?"

Walter's face relaxes. The sadness leaves his eyes, which suddenly shine with mischief. "I guess that makes you the Mama Hound while I'm the Alpha Dog."

Jules' eyes widen in surprise, and she draws her head back then punches him in the shoulder. "Hah! You've got to earn your alpha status, man."

I growl at her lightly but am more surprised when Walter pulls her close and locks his lips onto hers. Her arms go around Walter's waist, and I rise and bark in alarm. Rose joins me. We dance around the two of them, barking madly as they continue to smash faces. They ignore us until they break and stare at each other.

"I've been thinking of doing that for a while." Walter says.

Jules smiles. "I knew you wanted it from the minute I tore my shirt off, you dirty old man." She leans in, and the face smashing starts all over again. Walter moans and runs his hands along her back.

This is too much, and I don't understand it. Can we just get back to the "King's a good boy" discussion? I tug on Walter's pants firmly, but he doesn't budge. Then Rose nips at my feet sharply and dives away from me when I lunge at her. I leave Walter and Jules to their machinations and sniff out this morning's events. Rose joins me. We trace the scent back under the pasture gate and to a pile of dirt that covers a freshly dug hole.

CHAPTER 38
FAMILY

Jules and Rose stay with us the entire day, something that's never happened before. The two 'mans work side by side, talking and laughing, digging deep holes that extend out from the eastern line of the pasture fence. Unlike the soft, yielding turf of the pasture, this ground hasn't been cleared in years. It's full of small birch and spruce trees, taller than Walter but nowhere near the height of a full grown forest. Their digging is stymied by hard, small root systems and sometimes very large rocks. Occasionally they stop for water and discuss their work, pointing to a particular point along an invisible line. Rose and I stick close to them, digging a few holes and barking helpfully.

At one point Rose and I play a game of chase through the pasture. I leap up to my favorite sunning rock, then Rose swims across the pond towards the valley and looks back at me, an invitation to wander. I bark. I watch Walter and Jules then bark at Rose again. I'm not leaving the property. Rose woofs and bounces playfully and eventually comes back to me.

We engage Dilly and Dally in a game of king of the mountain. The goats, though they lack the advantages of canine teeth, are very aggressive with their horns and manage to keep the mountain despite our teamwork. Though they shy away when we snap at

234

them, they aren't cowed by us. Perhaps they know that we won't bite them. Eventually we lose interest and pad across the pasture and back to the 'mans.

We're all on the porch together for a water break when a beast turns off the road and onto the driveway. Rose and I leap off the porch and challenge it. As it approaches and slows, a dust cloud trails in its wake. A low sleek body the color of blood sparkles in the sun. Walter calls me back, but I've already lowered my threat level. The 'man emerges from the beast's mouth, and I recognize the sweet, chemical flowery smell.

I sneeze.

"Hi Cherry." Walter greets the 'man.

I sneeze again.

Her glance falls to me and Rose. She's wearing a tight purple sleeveless sweater that curves down her body and falls into bright blue jeans and black leather heeled boots that smell like a dead cow. "Hi Walter. You get a new dog?"

"Nah, this is Jules' pup." Walter motions to the porch where Jules lifts a hand in greeting. "Cherry, meet Jules. Jules, this is my cousin Cherry."

Cherry's eyes widen as she takes in Jules' presence – her thick, dark snake-like hair, dirty jeans and broad smile. For a brief moment they darken, then they lift as she gives Jules a red-lipped, toothy smile. "Nice to meet you, Jules. You live close by?"

"Somewhat. I grow hay on the other side of the valley, about 50 klicks away."

"Oh, out here delivering, then?" Confusion fills Cherry's face as she looks from the lunch plates on the porch to Jules' green beast near the barn.

"Something like that." Walter picks up a rock from the driveway and tosses it back and forth in his hands. I watch it intently should he decide to chuck it. "What brings you out here today, Cherry?"

Cherry blinks her eyes then looks back at Walter. "Well, I, uh." Her smile falters then broadens. "Those buyers I talked about last time? Well, they've moved on, but I've got some clients now who are looking to rent a working farm. A family, three small kids, moving from the coast. They're trying to get out of the hustle and bustle."

"Can't say that I blame them," Walter nods. "But I told you that I'm not leaving this place. What makes you think I've changed my mind?"

Cherry glances from Walter to Jules again. "I don't assume anything, but I wanted to let you know that there are lots of options if you consider making a change."

"For chrissakes, Cherry. How many times do I have to tell you that I'm not leaving here?"

Cherry holds her hands up in the air. I marvel at the tips of her fingers that sparkle pink in the sun. "I know, I know. And I understand that. Of course. But do you understand what a gold mine you have here? This acreage, a working hobby farm with a woodworking shop and functional outbuildings…. I'm thinking about your future, and you should be, too. You're not getting any younger." She studies the property, examining the barn and pasture and following the line of holes that Walter and Jules had dug that morning. Her eyebrows lift. "Are you expanding, Walter? What are you doing now?"

Walter puts his arm around Cherry's shoulders and turns her away from the cabin and the barn. I follow as he leads her slowly away from the porch. "I appreciate your visits, Cherry. Always nice of you to drop by."

Cherry stammers and stumbles her way back to the beast. She looks to the porch and to Jules then leans in to Walter's ear conspiratorially. "Carol Gordon's been asking about you. So has Ginny Majors at the aid society."

"Well, you can tell everyone that I'm doing real fine." Walter opens the beast's mouth for her, and Cherry leans in to give Walter a peck on the cheek then waves at the porch.

"I'll do that, Walter. Nice to meet you, Jules," she calls as she climbs in. She starts the beast purring, turns it around, and waves

236

a sparkly-fingered good-bye as the beast accelerates and departs in a cloud of dust.

"What was all that about?" Jules gets up and climbs down the porch steps as Walter stares at the receding beast. "You're not getting any younger? Who the hell is she?"

"Cherry's harmless, but she's got this crazy idea that I should sell my property. Thinks I'm living on a goldmine, too old and lonely to stay out here on my own. Hah! She's a realtor, always looking for the next big deal. I'm not going anywhere, which I've told her over and over." Walter turns around, walks up the porch steps and begins to pick up the lunch dishes. "She comes out every few months or so to let me know how much money I'm losing out on.

"Huh. Well, she's got a nice car." Jules leaps up the steps, elbows Walter out of the way and begins stacking the plates. "Uh-uh. I do dishes. I don't cook, so I'm really good at cleaning up. My contribution to social occasions."

Walter steps back. "I won't argue with that." He sits down on the top step of the porch while Jules carries the dishes into the cabin. Rose and I crowd around him. I sniff his face for food remnants. I like it best when he's got a beard – great for catching crumbs and dribbles – but at the moment he's clean shaven and I'm disappointed. I nose his treat pocket instead, and he chuckles and scratches the sweet spot on my chest. Rose licks his face, then, when he pushes her away, licks mine.

"If you don't cook, what do you eat?" Walter raises his voice to reach Jules in the cabin.

"Eggs. Lots of eggs. Mac 'n cheese." The dishes clink, and I hear the spray of water. Rose goes inside, and I sigh, lying down contentedly next to Walter.

She lifts her voice to reach us on the porch. "So... you have many family get-togethers? Somehow I don't picture you and Cherry hanging out at holidays."

"She's the only family I've got left here. Cousin on my mother's side. Has two sisters who left for the coast and never came back.

Married young and stayed in the valley all her life. No kids, a bible-thumping husband. A true gossip. I stay out of her way as much as I can, but that doesn't mean that she won't come chasing after me. Especially not when real estate prices are so high. Sometimes I wonder if she's not coming out here for a monthly report to the ladies at her aid society. They chatter like squirrels."

I lift my head suddenly and look around the yard. *Squirrels*? I spot one on a fallen log just behind the cabin, and I charge it, chasing it up the nearest tree where it sits just out of reach and scolds me loudly. Rose joins me to circle beneath it and growl. Yep, we've got squirrels.

Jules comes out of the cabin drying a plate with a white dish cloth, and Walter starts putting on his boots. I am immediately by his side, ready to go. Rose dances alongside me and jumps at the rag in Jules' hand.

"Get down, Belle." She turns to Walter with a smile. "You very active in the aid society?"

Walter groans. "Only to deliver pumpkins to their harvest fair fundraiser. Honestly, they're a nice group of ladies. But there's a reason I live so far out of town."

"And that is?"

"Distance. It makes good neighbors."

"Well, so do fences. Let's get cracking." Jules goes back into the house with the towel and comes out empty-handed. She sits down and laces her boots as Walter descends the porch steps and stretches his arms and shoulders. Jules joins him. They pick up their shovels and begin digging.

CHAPTER 39
CHANGE

J ules and Rose visit more and more frequently, and Walter and I visit them. Despite my eagerness to see Rose, however, I still hate the beast ride to her place. It's not rational, I know. On those mornings when I realize that Walter wants me to get into the beast, I typically initiate a taunt and chase session where I taunt and Walter chases. But eventually he stops, ignores my taunts and sits on the porch step and talks to himself. This always catches my attention.

"Hmmm, wonder what I've got in these pockets?" He pats his pockets, each one individually, and then searches them as I stare at him in confusion. Didn't he pack his pockets himself? What is he doing? I bark. I can smell Porkies in the most important pocket. From the other pockets I smell loose change, his knife, and a folded leather wallet. I watch him with concern as he continues to talk and look through each pocket. As his hand nears the Porkies pocket, I shift closer to him and my mouth fills up with saliva.

"What's in this pocket?" I inch closer as he sticks his hand into it. His hand pauses halfway down, and I whine. I stretch my tongue out to swipe his cheek, and he looks at me in surprise. "Oh, King! What are you doing here?"

I wag my tail and sit tall, panting just slightly and drooling only a little. He draws his hand out of his pocket, and I smell the hint of Porkies. As my nose falls towards his hand, the leash clicks around my collar. I barely notice because the Porkies in his palm are so close that I can't take my eyes or my mind off of them. He scoops his hand under my nose, and I inhale the treats in half a second.

"Let's go, big dog."

ONE DAY, after the fall leaves have tumbled to the ground, Walter and I visit Jules and Rose. Her property is larger than Walter's but less developed. She has chickens but no livestock, only empty pens and a barn filled with heavy equipment. In the summer, the fields around the house are so high with hay that we drive between walls of it. But today the fields are cleared, with hay lying in flat bunches on the ground. Winter is coming.

Our approach finds Jules inspecting her large beast in the barn and Rose sleeping in the driveway. She awakens quickly and challenges us noisily. Head hanging out of the beast's mouth, I tell her off, loudly.

"Here we go again," Walter stops the beast and locks its collar before opening its mouth. I barrel out past him and leap onto Rose who meets me with teeth bared and lips flashing. We collide, then I slip past her as we streak into the hay field. Rose catches up to me and snaps at my hind leg. I veer right and stop suddenly, and she shoots past me. I take off in the other direction, and she chases me again. I nearly run into Walter as he steps out from behind the beast, and he curses and grabs onto the beast's back. Rose snaps at my hip, and I cross into the other field.

The air is colder now. The hay is gone, and Jules is inside the barn next to one of her large field beasts. Rose runs to her as Walter and I enter.

Walter's energy changes around Jules. He laughs often and moves quicker. His scent becomes thicker, still fresh rain and apples, but more intense with a hint of musk. It makes me more alert, this extra energy, and I can't help but notice that the space between Jules and Walter gets smaller and smaller with every visit. They work shoulder to shoulder, knocking into each other gently, laughing as they string wire or hand each other tools. Occasionally, I wedge myself into the space between them, just to make sure I still fit.

Rose and I are also shoulder to shoulder, as we have always been. Together we cruise the perimeter of both properties, canvassing the land for anything that may be cause for alarm or warrant inspection. It's reminiscent of our life at the 'man camp, but the food is a lot more predictable, the threat of invasion minimal.

Jules greets Rose and smiles at us.

"Morning Walter. Morning King." Jules does not like a full body greeting, and because I end up on my back when I give them, I greet her with a hip check only. She leans down to stroke my back before I circle round to Walter. "Always so physical!" She looks up at Walter. "Ready for a day of baling?"

"It's a good day for it," Walter replies. "Not too cold, not hot, beautiful blue sky, beautiful woman...."

"Oh, knock it, Walter." Jules tries to punch him in the arm, but he moves out of the way.

"I know how you operate," he says, laughing.

I watch intently, now used to Jules' shoulder-punching ways. In some ways, Jules acts like a dog. She's very physical and will snap at anything that irritates her. She also eats quickly, vacuuming up food with a speed that rivals canines. I've seen her wrestle with Rose occasionally, and though Rose is quick, Jules has an agility that makes it challenging to keep her down. She's strong, too, and stands side-by-side with Walter on every task.

"It always looks so desolate with all the hay mown." Walter walks to the open barn doors and stands with his hands on his hips looking out.

"Yeah, it's a different feel when winter comes."

"How come you don't have any livestock? All this property and nothing to fill it now that winter's here."

Jules looks up with a sparkle in her eyes. "Afraid of commitment."

Walter barks a short laugh, but I catch a whiff of fear. "Hah. Too late for that."

His nervousness hits me in waves as he turns from the barn doors. He's hesitant. His stress floats into the barn like a fog. It fills my head and makes me whine. I stick close to him. He leans onto the beast's big black tire, and his movements look smooth though I notice that his hands tremble slightly.

I have no time to wonder about this because two beasts enter the driveway and hurtle towards us. One sparkles blood-red despite the cloudy day. When it stops, Cherry smiles and waves as she gets out of the car. The other is a dark blue beast with a basket, a truck like Walter's, but smaller. Inside sit five bodies, two large and three small. Rose and I greet Cherry promptly, and she backs up to her beast as we mob her.

"Hi pups!" Her flowery scent washes over me, and I sneeze.

The second beast slows and stops, and Rose and I charge it.

"A little help, Walter?"

Walter approaches, grabs my collar and makes me sit next to him as the 'mans slowly exit. Three 'man pups follow two adults who approach Cherry, wide-eyed and gazing around the property.

Jules calls Rose who trots to her and sits lightly. She sets down her wrench, wipes her hands on her jeans and greets the newcomers. Another scent wave of fear hits me, but this time it comes from Jules.

"Hi all. Nice to see you again."

Cherry smiles and lifts her arm towards the house. "Jules, do you want to give us a tour?"

The fear surges towards me, and Rose feels it too. She dances around Jules. "Sure. Walter, do you want to get the baler ready? No sense losing daylight."

Walter jumps at the sound of her voice and rushes over to the field beast. "Sure thing."

I stick by Walter. Jules and Rose walk the new party around the property. After a lengthy tour, the 'mans go into the house while Cherry runs to her beast, returning with a sheaf of papers that she clutches to her chest as she enters the house. The 'man pups stay in the yard with Rose who brings them a ball to throw. I join her, and as Walter starts the field beast and heads into the field, we play a game of chase. It ends when the 'mans exit a while later, shaking hands with both Jules and Cherry. Rose and I greet Jules while the 'man pups gather around their parents.

"We're so excited about your property, Jules." The 'man with long blonde hair smiles and shakes her head as her partner steps off the porch and towards his beast. "We were nervous about buying a chunk of land this big, but you've given us a great opportunity, renting it to us. The kids are going to love it here, and we're so happy to be on a working farm." She leans into Jules conspiratorially, "I think Rod's glad you'll be continuing to manage the hay production, at least for the first year or two. He's enthusiastic and capable, but he doesn't have any experience."

"It doesn't make sense to let it go fallow." Jules watches the 'man pups as they follow their dad to the beast and push and shove each other before getting in the back. She looks out at Walter who drives the beast in a far field. "I've got a lot of myself invested in these fields. And a lot of customers who wouldn't want to lose the feed."

The blonde 'man shakes Jules hand again. "We'll be moving out here on the first of November. I guess we won't see you much until spring. You have no idea how much this means to us."

"Glad the timing was right." Jules drops the hand and whistles. Rose comes running to her. "I'll leave a checklist of winter chores for the property in the kitchen, and you can call me if you have any questions."

Jules turns towards the fields and Walter, and the 'man joins her family at their beast.

Cherry calls out as she gets into her beast. "Thank you, Jules! Tell Walter that I said good-by. And tell him thanks too!"

Jules lifts her hand in a wave then drops it. Her fear scent subsides into a low hum of nervous energy. Rose and I trot alongside her. She reaches Walter who shuts off the beast and leaps down from the seat.

He stretches out his hand as she nears, and she grabs it, moving closer so that their faces are inches apart. I thrust my head between their thighs. I feel a longing between them, desire that explodes around me and erases the fear and nerves. They are breathing heavily, and Jules' normally boisterous voice is a whisper. "No turning back now."

And suddenly they are smashing faces above me. I whine and wriggle out of their embrace, but neither Walter nor Jules notices.

CHAPTER 40
HOME

A gust of wind blasts my house, and I wake to the earthy smell of thawing soil and winter turning into spring. The air is chilly but not frigid, a clear, cool morning with the sultry hint of a brewing spring storm.

Walter is getting his boots on in the cabin, and I'll be ready when he steps out. I stretch on the porch. The cabin door opens, and he emerges. His boots smell of leather and mud, his pants of juniper and motor oil. My heart leaps to see him, and I fight the urge to throw myself at his feet and grovel. No matter how many years I've spent with him, Walter is the perfect way to start any day.

I thrust my head between his legs, wiping the fuzziness of sleep from my eyes. He laughs and steps back, pushing my head down and scratching my ears.

"Morning, King," he says. I give his hand a quick lick. It tastes like soap, flowery with a lingering chemical flavor. I prefer dirt, but I don't get a choice. Anyway, it wouldn't make a difference. Walter's hands are top-rate despite their cleanliness.

"Let's go, big guy," he says and takes the first step. I rush in front to claim lead as we descend. But a sudden kink in the hips causes my back to cramp up, and I fall down the stairs in a mortifying slide. I end up crumpled at the bottom next to Walter's boots.

"Take it easy!" He laughs. "We're in no rush." I growl, and he laughs harder.

That's my 'man. Walter is no coddler.

I fight my shaky hips to stand, take my place in front of him, lower my head, and move forward. I lead down the driveway towards the road. The wind continues to blow, and tall cedars shudder and lean over us. Each odor and its source tells me a story. I cast aside the benign – squirrels and rabbits – and narrow in on possible threats – bears, coyotes, or cougars. I pause to stretch, raising my hips up and shoulders down, then reverse my hips down to the ground and take a few steps forward dragging my legs behind me. Yeah, now my body is waking up.

A cyclone of dust circles around to our left and suddenly washes over me. Sand and fine pebbles needle my face. I lower my head as my nose is filled with dust and sneeze twice, violently, full body tremors rippling down my spine. The old wound in my left flank flares into fire, my hips collapse, and I yelp as I go down again.

Walter bends over me. I curl my lip at him, flashing my teeth. He curls his lips back and laughs. I growl again and avoid his eyes, lifting my shoulders then hips. I stand, willing the dizziness to pass. It's humiliating, getting old. There are no rules for how to age, nothing to help me understand how I'm supposed to keep up as my body starts shutting down. Daily tasks at which I've always excelled, like sounding the visitor alarm and chasing deer out of the garden, more challenging these days. Last week I spotted a bear only after it had already crossed the pasture and entered the woods.

My eyes are filmy, and I am half-deaf. But I keep up my young dog bravado, and I hold my own around the property. People still back away when they see me. *It's just his size*, Walter tells them. *His heart is gold.*

Shuddering, I refocus then lift my nose in the air. Nothing out of the ordinary. We walk along the edge of the pasture. I stop to sniff a small patch of brush where deer bedded down last night. As we reach the road, I lift my leg on a cold rabbit trail heading down the valley to the south. I patrol slowly left along the creek towards the sun that rises over the fir trees, nose to the ground.

"Hello, ladies." My head snaps up at Walter's voice. Three mule deer are staring at us from underneath a stand of birch trees. *Where did they come from?* I growl and bounce forward, barking sharply. The deer take no chances; they turn quickly away and withdraw into the shadow of the mountain. I bark again at their retreating backs and fight the urge to chase them. Walter has made it clear that I'm not to chase on patrol.

We turn left again to walk along the base of the mountain behind the cabin, crossing the rocks where the creek descends towards the road. I keep my nose to the ground. When I first arrived at Walter's, it took me five minutes to trot from the cedars at one end of the property to the stand of cottonwoods on the far side of the pond. Now it takes me twenty. But Walter walks at my pace and takes a break now and then to let me catch my breath.

As we emerge from behind the cabin and reach the small barn and pasture, Walter stops to greet the horses. They stand close to each other and stretch their necks towards him, nodding their heads and snickering over the stall doors. He sticks his right hand into his pocket, and I am at his elbow, instantly alert.

My eyes are fixed on his hand as he begins talking to the horses. I lick my lips and am suddenly drooling. Darn it! Mind over matter is difficult in times like these.

"Good morning, Duchess. Morning, Big Gray." As his hand emerges from the pocket, I lunge instinctively towards it.

"Hey!" Two treats fall from his hand. I inhale the first before it reaches the ground and the second as soon as it hits. Sugar cubes. Damn.

Disappointed, I search the ground for more. Walter scolds me.

"Greedy King. None of that," he commands. "This pocket is not only for you."

247

Walter is looking at me. "King, sit."

I feel an itch below my neck, which I scratch vigorously. Oh, a good hind leg scratch is just the right thing for an old dog's tics.

When I finish, Walter is still staring at me. "King, sit."

I sit.

"Stay." He motions for me to stay still. Then he turns around, reaches again into his right pocket, and gives Big Gray a couple of sugar cubes. Uneasily, I watch him do the same for Duchess. He strokes her dark nose, then her mane, and he speaks to them softly. His hand stays out of the treat pocket, and I lose interest.

I look to the pasture, bound by barbed wire on three sides and the pond on the other. I think about soaking my bones in the pond later this afternoon, a salve for sore limbs. The muddier the better.

Suddenly a door bangs and a shape flashes red and white across the porch before it streaks towards us.

Rose!

She's running so fast that she can't stop. She slams into me. My hip crumples, and we start the day with a full body roll, growling and wrestling as I try to regain my feet. After three years at Walter's, I still don't take her presence for granted. Every morning I greet her as if it's the first.

Rose and Jules never went back to live at their property, moving their beasts and hay operation to Walter's after the second winter. It was an adjustment for all of us. Jules and Rose had to figure out where they fit into our daily routines, and Walter and I had to learn how to include them.

Rose's muzzle is mottled gray now, and her left eye is now completely white. Her attitude is that of a young dog, but her body betrays her daily. As does mine.

Walter whistles softly, and my attention returns to our patrol. Rose trots alongside us. We walk towards the henhouse. As we reach the coop, I mark each corner. Rose follows behind me and does the same.

When Walter opens the door to the coop and lets the birds out, they rush in a group to the feeder, pushing one another and cutting in front of each other to get there first. He collects the eggs in a bucket. I lift my head and curl my lip as they rush around us. I still hate chickens.

We finish the morning patrol near the vegetable garden. Rose and I mark the fence posts then follow Walter to the cabin. While he climbs the stairs, Rose stops to sniff the corners of the porch. I pause for a few seconds to let the wind wash over me and ruffle my fur. In the cedars, a branch cracks and falls. I turn up the steps of the cabin and climb slowly to the porch and lie down.

Jules meets Walter at the door. She takes the eggs from him in exchange for a mug of coffee. As he turns from the door, coffee in hand, I stand. His knee bangs into my shoulder and his heel kicks my head. Coffee sloshes out of his cup, and he stumbles to set the mug on the table. I forget how clumsy he can be.

"Not even a sip yet!" I stare at him as he moves towards the chair and sits down. I shift side to side a few times, then bark. His lack of coordination doesn't interest me. I fill the space in front of him. His legs straddle my body. I wait – not patiently – that's not my nature. I huff once or twice to speed him up then lower my head and lean forward.

"You're not leaving room for me." Walter scoots the chair back to make room for his boots. They are inches from my nose, thick with the deliciousness of this morning's patrol – dung and pollen. He lifts my head and rubs the jagged zig zag scars above my eyebrow. I sit up, eyes closed, and his hands move to the deeper scar on my jaw, the razor thin line that I barely notice anymore. His face is next to mine, and his scent – leather, spring rain and apples - fills me up. He speaks softly as he rubs his fingers over the taut skin.

"Good, isn't it? Everyone needs their scars rubbed once in a while."

He massages my mangled hip – these scars ache the worst on cold days. One hip spasm away from toppling over, I lean further into him. I groan contentedly.

It's a good life, and I'm know I'm nearing the end of it – a life filled with aches and pains and wounds never fully healed. But I've got Rose beside me and Walter. Gentle, steady Walter who talks softly and doesn't react when I flinch if his hands come near my face too quickly. Who doesn't get angry or afraid when I growl and bare my teeth at him after he's woken me up too suddenly. Who doesn't ask me for anything I wouldn't willingly do. For Walter, this list is small.

Jules steps out the cabin door and sits in the empty chair, placing her cup of coffee next to Walter's on the table. Rose rushes her, and Jules smiles and begins to comb through Rose's fur with a wire brush.

We are nearing spring, with fresh beginnings and life anew. Most of my life is in the past now. I don't know if I'll see another year or yet another spring. When scents blow in on the wind, I find it harder and harder to picture the images that accompany the smells I can't forget. Wild rose, peppermint, smoke, fresh rain – all of it takes me somewhere – places good and bad– with 'mans or dogs who have played a role in this life of mine.

When I met Walter, I was looking for a place to call home, searching for what I didn't have. Food. A dry bed. Comfort. Security. Rose.

Walter gave it all to me. Under one roof. All of it, including Jules, a bonus 'man who is almost as good as he is.

Rose barks once then growls and bolts off the porch to chase a squirrel. I watch her but am not ready to end this part of the morning. Squirrels will always be here.

My life is nearing its end, and my stiff limbs and pace embody my slow progression towards it. The final, inevitable conclusion is out there, but the timing and method, like so many other things in my life, is not up to me.

For now, I relish Walter's hands soothing the soreness of age. I rejoice in every minute that Rose and I spend together. I've got my pack, and I will fight to spend the rest of my days with them. As the wind rattles the branches above the cabin, I lean my head on Walter's thigh and sigh, ready to face the day.

ACKNOWLEDGMENTS

The process of writing this novel has been a long one, and I've had many people, and animals, accompanying me along the way. Indeed, it's been such a long one that I hope I don't leave anyone out. If I do, forgive me.

First, thank you to the Selkirk College faculty and students in the creative writing program, especially Renee Jackson-Harper, Almeda Glenn, and Leesa Dean who saw small iterations of this story as it grew into a novel. Your feedback and support made me dream big, and I never would have attempted this had it not been for that first fateful class.

Thanks to the Earl Grey Hares: Allison Alder and Ellie Knight. You know who I am and love me all the same. May we always find time to trek together.

To my beta readers: Sheila Ramsay, Carin Peterson, Margaret Becker, Jenn McAuley, Tami Jimenez, Gwen Higgins, Joan Alexander, Leigh Bailey and Loreen Hodgkinson, thank you! Your comments and questions throughout the various iterations strengthened the story and encouraged me to keep going.

Thank you also to those who helped me choose the final book cover. I don't even know all of you (looking at you, William), but your input was very much valued. So thank you Kelly, Helen, Sheila, Joan, William, Hannah, Noah, Koan, Johnna, Dee, Lisa,

Zachary, Margaret, Loren, Carin, Loreen, Lynn, Mark, Ryan, Gwen, Ellie, Allison, and Tami.

Much thanks to the hounds in my life who've provided inspiration for this novel: Waraba, Shey, Max, Molly and Poppy. Each of you has proven that a rough start doesn't mean there's no love left to give, only that we have to try harder to reveal it.

Finally, my family. Love and gratitude to Loren. Your unflagging support and encouragement allows me to forge full steam ahead, both in writing and in life. And to William and Hannah, without you life would be dull and empty. Follow your dreams and believe in yourself. You matter. Endless love to all of you.

ABOUT THE AUTHOR

Elizabeth Oldham has been writing all her life - stories, grants, newspaper columns, annual reports - you name it. She loves writing fiction because she can create new worlds and characters that transport people out of the here and now. Elizabeth has a BA in English with an emphasis on Creative Writing, and a Master of Social Science in International Rural and Community Development. She has lived and worked all over the world but now resides in British Columbia with her husband, eleven chickens and a crazed rescue dog. She has two grown children.

Tail of Humanity is her first novel. Her second, Shadows of the Heart, will be published in early 2024.

More information about Elizabeth can be found at her website:
    https://elizabetholdham.com/
    Subscribe to her newsletter here:
    https://elizabetholdham.substack.com/

Made in the USA
Las Vegas, NV
22 May 2023